Learning–

Life in the Castle

The

More Than Conquerors Trilogy

Learning—Life in the Castle

Laboring—Life in the Outpost

Leading—Life at the Battlefront

Learning—
Life in the Castle

Jean Nava

Book One of

More Than Conquerors

An Allegory of the Christian Walk

Kingdom Press
Mountain Grove, Missouri 65711

Library of Congress Catalog Card Number: 97- 94200
ISBN 0-9659952-0-8

Printed in the United States of America
on recycled paper.

3212 East Highway 30 • Kearney, NE 68847 • 1-800-650-7888

To three young converts, whose loss finally compelled me to write this book.

Dear Reader,

This book has been written to help you to grow as a Christian. If you are young, either in years or Christian experience, this first volume, *Learning*, is especially for you.

As a Christian you have embarked on a great adventure, but it is fraught with dangers. There is no stopping place this side of Eternity. You must persevere and endure, and to do so, you must grow and learn.

In this book I have given you the story of a young woman and her struggles and triumphs as she undertakes that adventure. It is an allegory, because I have made visible many things which are invisible in this life.

Do not be discouraged if her progress seems much more rapid than your own. There are two important reasons for this. The first is that as a citizen of the Middle Ages she already possesses much self-discipline, patience, fortitude, humility, obedience, and other qualities that are in short supply in our modern world. Today's new Christian must develop these "old-fashioned" virtues at the same time he is trying to learn spiritual lessons.

Second, she develops so rapidly because I have placed her in an idealized environment designed to promote her Christian growth. There is no Castle in our world. But by showing what kind of atmosphere is conducive to growth, I am advising you how to seek out or create the best possible situation for yourself. For more mature Christians, particularly pastors, who may be reading this book, I hope you will gain some insights on how to promote growth in the new Christians whom the King sends to you.

Christine moves further toward Christian maturity in the few months in which our story takes place, than many real people do in a lifetime. Your growth will not match hers, but be encouraged as you realize that there are higher plateaus to ascend, and ascent is possible. You will probably want to read straight through the first time for the sake of the story. But I hope you will come back to this book and study out the truths which are on every page. You can use it as a devotional, looking up the scripture references and asking yourself what this means to you in your life.

Before you begin, you may want to get a little historical background on a period that is often neglected in the study of history. Read Appendix A — The Feudal System. As you meet new characters in the book you may want to look at Appendix B — Meanings of Names. Appendix C is a glossary of words which you probably don't meet every day.

Even though the setting of this book is in a far-off time and another culture, I think you will be able to identify with the human feelings, because although times are always changing, people are the same. I pray that Christine and Godfrey will help you to see your own struggles through to triumph.

I invite you to correspond with me concerning questions, reactions, and comments you have about this book. Its purpose is to help you, and that is my purpose also.

The Author

TABLE OF CONTENTS

List of Illustrations

Notes on Illustrations: I have included these mostly for those who may not be acquainted with the illuminated manuscripts which are one of the most unique and beautiful products of the Middle Ages. The borders are authentic, although they represent a variety of styles which would not have been seen in a single volume.

Chapter 1

The Spring

Mara emerged from the low door of the stone cottage and hesitated on the stoop, her large brown eyes scanning the fields and peering intently toward the grove of trees where her steps must take her. The fields were empty. It was Saturday, the day on which all the serfs were expected to work in the Lord's fields.

"It's not fair," Mara muttered as she descended the one stone step. "They're all together, and I'm here all..." She shuddered. She would not say the word aloud. But as though she had shouted it, she seemed to hear the echoes bouncing back from every direction, "Alone, alone, alone, alone..."

The empty buckets swung crazily at the ends of the yoke, and Mara thought how heavy they would be as she returned. Inside a little voice whispered, "...if you return."

Mara shook herself, tossing the thick, red-gold braid that hung down her back. Twice, sometimes three times a day, she made this trip to the spring, and each time it took all the courage she could muster.

She glanced again across the stubble field. Yesterday she had been busy there with Father and Tristram getting in the last of the wheat.

When they were together she could almost forget her fears. But today the empty furrows mocked her. If she screamed her loudest, no one would hear. But the openness of the fields at least concealed no enemy. It was the shadows under the trees which held her gaze.

Her head was filled with the stories she had heard of the outlaws, and even as her feet carried her steadily on, her mind tried to reason with her timid heart. The outlaws attacked everywhere. She was really no safer in the cottage than at the spring. But the stout, stone walls were a comfort, even if a false one. The outlaws were fearless. Numbers meant nothing. Sometimes they attacked whole crowds.

But Mara couldn't help wishing for the ten thousandth time that there were no grove of trees around the spring. Father had told her the trees helped the water to be clean and cold, so she didn't tell him how she felt. She ought to be grateful for clear, flowing water so near her door. It made their holding one of the most desirable in the whole fief.

She stopped again in the shade of the first oak to let her eyes adjust from the bright sunlight. Still, she could see only a few feet into the thickets, and the spring itself was in a shallow depression hidden from view.

Today when she came in sight of it, her fears all became reality. Kneeling, drinking at the spring was a figure wrapped in a dark cloak. The last thing Mara wanted was to alert the stranger to her presence, but a small sound escaped her throat before she could choke it back. Her feet were already turning to flee, and her hands were preparing to fling off the hampering yoke, but her eyes had not moved. The stranger looked up quickly, and as he did so, exposed the breastplate of a knight.

Mara was so relieved she sank limply to the ground and began to laugh and cry both at once. The knight stepped to her side and extended a gauntleted hand.

"I beg your pardon, child. I had no intention of frightening you." He wore no helmet. She saw he had removed it to drink. The bearded face smiled kindly at her. With fear temporarily gone, Mara was now embarrassed. He had called her child, and certainly she had acted like one. She quickly stood up, even stretching a bit to emphasize her above-average height.

She was more than a little awed as well, for the knights of the King, though noted for their gentleness and courtesy and even humility, were nevertheless noblemen. It was said that every one of them was somehow related to the King himself. Mara had never been alone with one before.

"I mistook you for an outlaw," she explained. "How very foolish of me!"

"Fear makes fools of us all," the knight's face grew serious.

"What have you suffered at the hands of these villains to put such terror in your heart?"

"Well, I..." all the stories raced through Mara's head. "I guess nothing personally."

"It is part of my duties to aid those who have been harmed by the outlaws. Is there anything I can do to help you?"

Mara tried to think. She couldn't ask him to cut the trees down; that was just one of her silly fancies. He couldn't bring back her mother. "I...I guess not."

"If you would come to the Castle and meet the King, you would soon be rid of your fears. You know there is an open invitation to all."

"Yes, I have heard that," but to herself Mara added, but then I've heard so many things. Who knows what to believe?

"Then I must be on my way. I have urgent business for the King. Thank you for the water. You are very blessed to have this wonderful spring." Even as he spoke, the knight suited action to words. He raised a hand in farewell, and long, swift strides carried him quickly out of sight.

Mara wanted to cry out at him to wait. There were so many questions she wanted to ask. What was the Castle like? Could you really see the King? How...? But no words came, and the knight was already gone.

Slowly Mara filled the buckets and trudged back to the cottage. Regret flowed over her. There were so many things she wanted to know, and such an opportunity might never come again. It was easy to think now. As she washed her fresh-churned butter in the cold spring water, things came to mind that she could have said, should have said, would have said.

Then suddenly, one thought overwhelmed her. What if she had dared? What if she had asked the knight to take her to the Castle? What if she had asked him to introduce her to the King? Would he actually have done it? At worst he could only have refused, and she would have lost nothing for having asked.

If ever, she thought, I have such an opportunity again, that's what I shall ask. But at the same time, she knew she would not. She would be too shy, too frightened to ask. In fact she would be more fearful of her request being granted than of its being refused. A wave of despair swept over her as she realized that no matter how many opportunities presented themselves, she would never take them.

"I am a prisoner of my fear!" she cried, and the truth of it was so devastating that Mara sat down and wept bitterly.

When she finally roused herself, the shadows were lengthening. Her men folk would be coming soon, and she hadn't started dinner. Thank goodness for cabbage which cooked quickly. Mara stirred up the fire, and put the pot on to boil. Then she ran to the garden. A few carrots would be welcome. If she sliced them thin they would cook nearly as fast as the cabbage.

As she chopped the vegetables, she thought with a pang of her mother. She had always seemed so calm, never in such a rush as Mara now found herself.

This winter would make five years since her mother had slipped away in the night. For two weeks she had lain ill with a fever, and then one morning when Mara awoke, her mother was gone.

They had taken the body to the churchyard, but Mara knew that was not her mother. The sweetness, the tender love, the patient endurance, those things had already flown from the wretched body. And to where? The minister said that the King had taken her home to himself. Mara wanted to believe that. But from the pulpit she had heard him say that the outlaws came on people unawares and carried them off to the Lake of Fire!

Still more confusing, she had heard one of the wandering preachers say that if the outlaws destroyed his body it did not matter, because he would be safe with the King. Which was right?

Every Sunday at church the minister read from the King's book, and Mara knew that terrible things were written there. Mara had one scripture in particular that she hated. It seemed to her that it was read more often than any other. It began, "But the fearful..." Mara knew that meant her. Then it listed a lot of sinful persons she couldn't remember and ended with "...and all liars shall have their part in the lake which burneth with fire and brimstone: which is the second death."[1] Mara shivered every time she thought of it. If she had been fearful before, that verse made her more so. She was certainly doomed without hope.

There, the vegetables were in the pot. She snatched up her pail and ran to look for the cow. Her search carried her no further than the barnyard gate. Lily mooed a greeting as soon as Mara appeared. Good

---

[1] Revelation 21:8

old Lily! If she had had to go looking for the cow, she would never have been able to finish before the soup boiled over, but Lily was almost always there waiting. Mara scratched the bony back as they walked together to the byre. She poured out a little grain—not the wormy stuff. That was good enough for the chickens, not for Lily. Tucking up her skirt she sat down and leaned her head against the brown flank. The sweet, creamy liquid began to foam into the pail at once.

Mara supposed that next to Father and Tristram she loved Lily best. She was a wise old animal and a perfect mother. She tried to remember how many calves they had had from her, and she had never lost even one. The steer calves became Father's oxen, and the heifer calves were the most valuable trade item on the farm. She supplied milk for them to drink or make puddings, butter, cream, cheese, clabber, and she helped feed the chickens and pig, and cats and dogs. It was as though the whole farm flowed from her. She supplied even the dung for the garden. Mara scratched her around the horns before she went back to the house. "Thank you again, Lily," she whispered in the scooped ear.

The soup was boiling nicely. She poured out milk for their supper and for the cats, then mixed the rest into the old weevilly flour, and went to slop the pig. Using the wormy grain, she lured the chickens into the coop and shut them up for the night.

Mara glanced down the road. Father and Tristram were coming up the lane. She smiled. Mara loved her family. She was glad the King had not yet arranged a marriage for her, though many girls her age were already mothers. Probably the King saw that she was needed where she was—or the minister. Some folks said it wasn't the King who arranged the marriages at all, but just the minister who did it in the King's name.

Mara put bread on the table from the morning's baking. This was barley bread, but Monday they would be going to the mill, and there would be fresh wheat flour.

Tristram stooped through the low doorway, "Smells good, Sis! I'm starved." Mara's eyes feasted on him a moment, then she leaped to embrace him. He was so tall and handsome. Mara never felt so flattered as when neighbors commented on the close resemblance between brother and sister. Only Tristram never seemed to be afraid of anything. Still—when a sound in the night awakened her, and she sat up on her pallet staring into the darkness, their eyes would meet, and she knew that he too was afraid.

Her father was only a step behind, and she gladly kissed his sweaty cheek.

Chapter 11

What is the Prince Really Like?

Supper was a bit hurried. Tomorrow was Sunday and they wanted to thresh out the tithe of their wheat to take to the village church.

"Never mind the dishes, lass. Get the flails."

Mara ran for the threshing instruments. When she returned, Father was scolding Tristram.

"Not those sheaves! That's the very best we have. It's to be saved for seed. Sometimes I wonder if I'll ever make a farmer out of you."

"But if we give our very best to the King, won't he bless our crops next year?"

"Who knows what he'll do? He expects us to use our heads. The better the seed the better the crop. Doesn't he say that 'whatsoever a man soweth, that shall he also reap?' "[1]

Mara chuckled in amusement. Father always had a scripture to back him up. He had sat in church so many years and seemed to never forget a verse that might come in handy later. His favorites were about

---

[1] Galatians 6:7

sloth, and he had sounded them over her head many a morning when she was slow to rise.

As Mara swung her flail she knew her muscles would ache tomorrow. All of them were out of breath when they stopped to winnow the first basket full.

"All right, Mara," her father panted. "Here's your sum. We beat out four sheaves to make one bushel. How many bushels of wheat did we harvest this year?"

"There were two hundred thirty sheaves." Mara stared off into space and bit her tongue. She did not know how to read or write a single numeral, but she was good at the mental arithmetic so necessary to the peasant. "Just over fifty-seven bushels. Oh, Father, that's the best we've done in years!"

Tristram still had his face screwed up. "Yes, she's right. So our tithe is five and seven-tenths bushels."

"Well, you might make a farmer yet," Father was proud of them, "if you get a good farm wife like our Mara.

"Now get to work. We've four more baskets to fill."

When the fifth basket had been filled, Mara started to carefully gather up what remained on the ground. "Father, this won't make seven-tenths. We'd better beat out a couple more sheaves."

"Forget the seven-tenths, you little Pharisee. The King's not interested in partial measures."

"Then we should round it to six bushels, Father," Tristram advised.

"Suppose you let me worry about the amount. I guarantee you, no one else pays a full tithe. If I don't pay more than practically anyone else, then you tell me about it."

Father's angry voice closed the subject. Mara had to admit she was glad. Her arms felt ready to drop off.

At dark the little family unrolled their straw pallets on the floor. Mara did not feel sleepy; she felt excited. Father was already snoring, but that did not bother Mara; she had heard it all her life. Her thoughts returned to the visitor she had had that day. She had forgotten to tell Father and Tristram about him.

Being a girl had not prevented Mara from daydreaming of being a knight and waging war against the King's enemies. In her imagination she had fought many bloody battles to glorious conclusions. But she was only too well aware of the difference between fantasy and reality.

She was not high-born, she was not a man, and most of all, she was not brave.

She pictured this knight in her mind and decided that he was rather handsome with his dark beard and hair. That mattered little to Mara, however. It was his poise and confidence she envied. He had been gentle and courteous, just as a knight should be, but it was a gentleness that came from strength, from the knowledge that he did not have to prove anything to anybody. Would she ever have such self-assurance?

The knight had said that if she went to the Castle and met the King she would lose her fears. Vain comfort! If she did not first lose her fears, how could she ever go the Castle and meet the King? Mara sighed deeply.

To her surprise, Tristram sat up, "Can't you sleep, Sis?"

Mara was glad to share her thoughts. "Tristram, there was a knight here today."

"Really? Here at the cottage?"

"No, at the spring." Mara scooted closer so they could talk without disturbing Father. "He was just getting a drink."

"Did you talk to him?"

"Yes, he frightened me at first."

"I can believe that! What did he say?"

"He asked how he could help me."

"What did you say?"

"I couldn't think of anything. Then he said I should go to the Castle."

"And are you going?"

"What?" Mara's voice was louder than she meant it to be. Father stopped snoring and rubbed his nose, but he didn't wake up.

"You tease!" Mara whispered. "You know I wouldn't dare."

"Why not? Who would hurt you? I'm beginning to wonder why everyone doesn't go to the Castle. I mean, what have you got to lose? The knights and the wandering preachers claim it's wonderful, that we'd be happy there. The others say it's all poppycock. But if you didn't like it, you could just leave, so why not try it?"

"Are you going? If you do, maybe I could try. But I'm afraid Father wouldn't like it."

"Of course he wouldn't. How would you like it for your family to up and leave you? What would there be left for him?"

"Then we can't go, but maybe someday..."

"I didn't say we couldn't. We'd just have to go in spite of Father. Maybe after we were gone, he'd come after us."

"Leave the holding? He couldn't do that! It's against the law!"

"Sure he could. It wouldn't be running away. It would be running to his liege Lord. If the preachers are right, it would be obeying his Lord."

Mara sat thinking for a moment, then repeated her question, "Are you going?"

"I almost went once. I met this fellow who was telling me about it. He said he'd been there often and knew a secret way to get in and out of the Castle. He offered to take me, and said we could watch all the great lords and ladies and see how they lived. He made it seem really exciting and wonderful."

"Why didn't you go?"

"Because the more he talked, the more it sounded wrong. I didn't think the King would much like people sneaking in and out of his Castle.[2]

"If we go up to the door and ask admittance, we'd either be let in or refused. But if we got in by stealth, I hate to think what would happen if we were caught."

"You're right. I'd think anyone would be afraid to do such a thing."

"That's one of the things I don't understand. People say that the King knows everything—even our thoughts.[3] Then they turn around and act as if he's the simplest fool whom they can easily hoodwink."

"But no one ever gets in trouble."

"I know, the King doesn't seem to enforce his laws, so it doesn't seem worth obeying them."

"Father tries to—I mean, he obeys them more than most—and it doesn't seem to do any good. We lost Mother just the same, and the oxen that time. And when bad weather comes to the shire and ruins all the crops, we're hit as hard as anyone."

Tristram nodded sadly. "You're right. Maybe the outlaws are the smart ones. They do as they please, and acknowledge no Lord."

---

2 John 10:1-9

3 Psalm 139:1-4 and others

"Don't say that! That's treason! The outlaws are wicked and cruel. If it weren't for the King's protection they would kill us all!"

"We've been told that, but how do we know it's true? Have you ever seen an outlaw caught and hanged? The knights ride through, but I've never seen one actually fight an outlaw. A lot of people think the King could do a far better job of protecting us."

Mara did not know what to answer. There were so many things she didn't understand, and no one else seemed to have the answers either. "I wish I could talk to someone ordinary, like us, who had actually gone to the Castle."

"Did you ever hear anymore of that girl, Ida?"

"No, I pray for her everytime I think of her."

"She's probably dead. We'd better get to sleep."

Mara lay down, but she did not go to sleep. She was remembering.

That was a Saturday also, a hot day back in early summer. Mara was going to the spring and as usual was making a careful survey first. She saw a strange shape lying in the road and went to investigate.

The closer she approached the more puzzled she was. It was a hideous, dark lump nearly as large as three bushel baskets, but having no discernible form. Moreover she soon detected a stench emanating from it. It filled her with such loathing that she had almost decided to turn back. But then she noticed something light-colored beside it, and curiosity again got the better of her.

When she saw the light-colored object more clearly, she ran forward. A child—at least a girl, younger and smaller than herself—was prostrate beneath that terrible black thing. For a moment she had thought the girl was dead, but she lifted her head and looked at Mara.

"Can you help me?" she appealed.

Mara hesitated to touch the sticky mass, but she could not ignore the girl's plea. Setting her hands firmly into the goo, she threw her weight against it. It was even heavier than it looked. Her first effort rolled it only a few inches, and it simply settled back. The girl groaned piteously. But Mara had been disciplined all her life to tough jobs. She set her jaw and exerting more strength than she really had, she succeeded in moving the tarry lump. No wonder it was so heavy. She had moved the girl with it, so that while formerly it had lain on her, she now lay on it.

For the first time Mara noticed the cords which bound the girl to the ugly monster. Quickly she searched for the knots or buckles or whatever held it, but they were apparently buried in the mass itself. "How can I free you?" she asked.

"Please give me some water."

Mara went flying up the path and came back with a bottle of water. When the girl had drunk, she revived a little.

Mara's tender heart bled for the girl. She was very fair, with blue eyes and platinum hair. But she was so thin and so smeared with the black stuff, that no beauty remained.

Filled with horror, Mara asked again, "Tell me how to get you loose!"

"If only someone would tell me that," the girl replied wistfully. "There is no way, I've tried everything."

"But how did this happen to you?" Mara wanted to know.

With an effort, the girl shifted the burden until she could set up, with it resting on the ground behind her. "Strange as it seems, I did this to myself—not deliberately of course." She took the bottle from Mara and drank again. "Thank you, I needed that so much. You've saved my life—not that it's worth saving."

Mara was in distress. "There must be some way I can help you get free."

The girl looked at her sadly. "My name is Ida. I've come so far already. I have just one hope. I met a man who told me the Prince could release me from this burden. How much further is it to the Castle?"

"Not far! Only about four more hours..." Mara's voice trailed off. Not far to her, but a great distance to one so nearly spent.

"So near? But this load gets heavier with every step. I'll never get there."

Mara tried to think of a way to help. The cords were so tight they dug deeply into the girl's flesh. There would be no way to cut them without cutting her. If only Father and Tristram were home.

"Do you know?" Ida asked, "Can the Prince help me?"

"I don't know," Mara shook her head hopelessly, "but surely if anyone can, he could."

"But will he, do you think? He probably won't be able to stand the sight of me."

Mara wished she could encourage her, but she had no idea what the Prince was like.

"Do help me up, please. I may die before I reach there, but it's the only chance I have."

Mara lifted on the sticky blackness with all her strength, and the girl struggled to her feet.

Ida laughed mirthlessly. "You wouldn't believe how small and harmless this looked when I first picked it up."

Tears started in Mara's eyes. She did not see how the frail-looking girl even stood under the load.

"Can I get you some more water? I can at least do that." Without waiting for a reply Mara raced back to her home. She grabbed her straw hat that she wore when she worked outdoors, and then she filled the bottle and ran back.

The girl had taken scarcely a dozen steps in the meantime. Mara pushed the hat on Ida's head, and the girl reached out and received the water gratefully.

"You're so kind. You've given me hope. I think I can go on now."

Mara watched her stagger along until she turned the bend in the road. Would she reach the Castle? Would the Prince help her? Please, Mara prayed, please.

It had been over a week before she got all the black stuff cleaned off her hands.

Chapter III

The Village Church

Sunday was always a sort of holiday, and today with the wheat tithe to take, it was even more special. It meant they would be taking the ox cart instead of walking. But it had to be confessed that walking was faster, so they must start even earlier than usual. Mara was up before daylight, and had stirred up the fire and set the porridge to simmer even before she went to milk. She was suffering from yesterday's exercise, but there was no use mentioning it.

After breakfast she hurriedly washed the dishes, and then while the men were hitching the oxcart she washed herself and put on her Sunday dress. She brushed her hair more carefully than on weekdays and today she wound the thick braid about her head instead of letting it hang. If Mara was a little vain about her hair, she must be excused, for she had heard often enough how pretty it was.

Even so, she was done in time to help carry out the threshed wheat. The chickens clucked around her feet as though well aware of what the basket contained. "Go away!" she scolded. "This is the King's grain. You can't have it."

"Don't be so stingy," her father laughed, and he took a handful of the wheat and threw it to the noisy fowls.

Then they were ready. The five baskets exactly filled the bottom of the cart. Tristram swung her bodily up to the seat—just to show off. Her father cried, "Gee up!" and the oxen lumbered off.

Riding in an oxcart gave one lots of time to think. Mara saw a little smile on her father's face. He was thinking about the honor that would be shown him for this fine wheat crop. Tristram had a little frown. She couldn't guess what he was thinking.

She watched the plodding animals before her and thought what sturdy, patient beasts they were. She remembered the year they had no oxen and how little there had been to eat. It had been the outlaws. Her father had gone out the first spring day the fields had been dry enough to plow, and that evening he had come home carrying a quarter of charred ox.

Mara remembered how her heart had failed her as she saw her father's dark, angry look. In answer to her unspoken question he had replied merely, "The outlaws!"

He had instructed her to salt the meat, and had turned to go back calling Tristram to help him. Together they had packed in what remained of the ox team. Later Mara had learned the whole story. About mid-morning a band of outlaws had descended on him at his work. They declared they were hungry and demanded the oxen for their dinner. Father had begged and pleaded. He had tried to offer what little food was in the cottage, but all to no avail. He tried to convince them that one ox would surely fill their bellies, but no, they must slay both. So he had waited all day as his poor cattle roasted, until the outlaws had their dinner and went their way. Then he had salvaged what he could. The weather had been too warm to save much of the meat.

Every day after that her father had tried to pull the plow himself as Tristram guided it, but there was little ground broken, and the harvest had been less than what they now carried in the cart. If the church had not helped them from the tithes of others, they would surely have starved.

Poor Father, thought Mara, and put her arm around his shoulders. He did not know her thoughts, and gave her a smile and wink.

"Tristram," he chuckled, "how long are we going to be able to keep this pretty lass? Half the boys in the village make eyes at her when we go to church, and word is liable to come from the Castle any week. How shall we ever get on without her?"

"Perhaps the King will continue to have pity on us," Tristram smiled. "Or maybe he'll first find me a wife so we won't be without a cook!"

All three laughed, but Father grew serious. “Aye, sons are better than daughters, for if you have a son you will soon have a daughter as well. But when you have a daughter you soon have nothing.”

As they neared the village they saw more and more of their fellow peasants on the way to church. Father hailed each by name, and Mara and Tristram waved. But under his breath, Father grumbled, “Didn’t see that one in the fields yesterday, did we? Leave all the King’s harvesting to a few of us.”

The church bells began to ring just as they turned into the little town. Men, women, and children poured from every doorway into the warm sunlight. The air of festivity grew as the incoming congregation merged into a milling throng in front of the church.

Among the villagers Mara saw Barbara. Why she went to church was more than Mara could fathom. She was a known consort of the outlaws, and ought to have been ashamed to show her face. But she spoke boldly of the charms of the bandits and urged other girls and women to follow her example. And if Barbara did it openly, how many other women did it secretly? But then, Mara had heard it said that some of the outlaws themselves masqueraded as pious peasants or villagers and attended service more regularly than many a true serf. The thought gave Mara a chill, and she looked around with suspicion.

Mara saw that Father had been right. The other carts contained less wheat than theirs. Though she noticed too, that others had not been hesitant to bring partial measures, and as all was dumped indiscriminately into a huge bin prepared for it, she could not see what inconvenience it caused.

Many stopped to comment on Father’s fine crop, and though he made deprecating remarks, she saw him swell with pride.

Suddenly she saw something quite different however. “Oh, look, Father!”

Father did look and grunted in disgust. “Old Eldred showing off again. He always does that. I doubt he raised as much as I did, but he wants everyone to think he’s rich.”

Eldred and Abigail were not rich, and Mara doubted that they could make anyone think so, but their cart was loaded with all the wheat it could carry. Mara counted quickly. Five bushels made a layer, they had three layers—“Fifteen bushels, Father.”

“That’s what I count,” he nodded, then turned to a neighbor to change the subject.

Mara was burning with curiosity. She jumped down and pushed her way through the crowd until she reached the old couple.

"Good morning, Uncle Eldred. Good morning, Aunt Abigail." Mara used the terms from respect rather than relationship.

"Good morning, sweet Mara," Abigail answered, and Eldred touched his hat and smiled.

"What a fine crop of wheat! You must work very hard."

"The King blesses our efforts," Eldred replied modestly.

"But surely you didn't raise a hundred fifty bushels this year?"

"No, no," laughed the old man, "perhaps thirty-five."

"But," Mara was flabbergasted, "then your tithe would be three and a half bushels."

"Child," smiled Abigail, "We won't be able to eat the twenty bushels left us. Why shouldn't we bring the church what we don't need?"

"You could sell it or trade it," Mara protested.

"Are you forgetting that all the land is really the King's. It is he who sends the sun and rain. Even our strength to labor comes from his grace and mercy."

"But no one else gives more than they're supposed to," to herself she added—or even as much as they're supposed to.

"What has that do to with us?" Eldred asked mildly. Mara looked at them with new eyes. She had been told before that they were a bit eccentric. Abigail always seemed to be first on hand when a bit of charity was needed. She had heard them called old-fashioned too, because they lived without even the simple ostentation that peasants could afford.

Once she remembered the minister commending them for their sobriety and simplicity of speech, by which Mara supposed he meant that they did not frequent the tavern or use the common profanities. Well, neither did her father. She was sure he was as good as any man in the realm. But suddenly there was a doubt.

"You're different from other people," she acknowledged. "Why do you try to be so good?"

The old couple smiled at one another. Abigail leaned over and whispered, "We've been to the Castle."

A wave of excitement swept over Mara. Here was someone who had really done it. Were they lying? No, their lives were the proof. So you could really be received at the Castle. These people could tell her all about it! "What is it like?" Mara asked eagerly. "Did you really meet the King?"

"Yes, we really did. But if you want to hear all about it, we need a quieter time and place."

"I do. I want to know everything."

The old faces positively glowed. "We'll come to see you at home. Then we can talk all you like."

"Will you come soon? Can my brother hear too?"

"Yes, very soon. Don't worry we'll come."

It was Father's turn to unload, so Mara ran to help. After all, she had worked for it. It was her offering too. Tristram lifted the baskets out of the cart to Father, and he handed them to Mara where she stood on the steps that had been built up to the bin.

"Five bushels!" exclaimed the minister. "It appears you had the best crop in the fief."

Mara smiled with pleasure, but her smile quickly vanished. Her father was saying with a great show of modesty, "Well, perhaps it wasn't quite that good. A little generosity never hurts."[1]

"Indeed not, Friend George, the Lord will bless you for it."

Mara nearly fell off the step. She looked at Tristram, but he just shrugged his shoulders and lifted up the last basket.

As they were entering the church, Mara looked back. Eldred's cart was the last to be unloaded. The minister and most of the crowd had already gone inside. The few stragglers in the street apparently didn't plan to attend service. They had all those heavy baskets to lift out, and there were only the two of them. Scarcely thinking what she did, Mara went running back to help them.

When she slipped into the back of the church, the singing had already begun. Mara loved to listen to the choir. The words sometimes puzzled her, but the only other music she had ever heard was Old Saul when he was drunk and played his lute.

When the minister got up to read, she prayed that it would please not be *that* verse. It was not. The passage was about light and darkness, and Belial and infidels. Mara was sure that meant her. Then suddenly she started really hearing what was being said.

"Wherefore come out from among them, and be ye separate, saith

---

[1] Acts 5

the Lord, and touch not the unclean thing; and I will receive you, and will be a Father unto you, and ye shall be my sons and daughters, saith the Lord Almighty."[2]

Had she ever heard this before? It seemed to her that she never had. But there it was, right in the King's book. "Come, and I will receive you."

Even more astonishing, "...ye shall be my sons and daughters." That part couldn't be true—but it said, "saith the Lord."

Who were the "them" you were supposed to come out from among? What was the "unclean thing" you weren't supposed to touch? If she could find the answers...

Through the minister's long sermon, Mara kept hearing those other words, "I will receive you and will be a Father unto you." Hope sprang higher than ever before. If Eldred and Abigail had done it? Maybe they had gone together. If Tristram would only consent to go with her, she wouldn't be so afraid.

As soon as service ended she pushed through the crowd to find him.

"Where did you disappear to?" was the first thing he wanted to know.

"Never mind. Tristram, did you hear that wonderful verse the minister read?"

Tristram looked off in the distance dreamily, "About the Lord being our Father and we being sons and daughters?"

"Yes, that one! What do you think it means?"

"Probably just wishful thinking, Sis. It couldn't have been talking about us."

"But it said we should be separate, and do certain things...'Come out from among them...and I will receive you.' It sounded as if the Lord was promising."

"It did sound like that. Well, let's find out. We'll ask the minister what it meant."

Tristram started off through the crowd so quickly Mara was left behind. When she caught up, Tristram had already asked the question.

"Certainly it is true," the minister was saying, "if you understand it correctly. The King feels paternally toward all his subjects, in a sense

---

[2] 2 Corinthians 6:14-18

we are all his children."

"I figured it was something like that," Tristram hid his disappointment.

But Mara wasn't quite convinced. "But, begging your pardon sir, it seemed to say we should do something in order for him to receive us. So, I mean, it isn't just automatic. What did it mean to 'come out' and 'be separate' and not touch 'the unclean thing?'"

The minister chuckled kindly. "So, our little maid is a theologian.

"The 'unclean thing' is sin of course. We must keep his commandments, not lie or steal or fornicate. That word 'separate' should really be translated 'holy,' coming to church as you did today, receiving the sacraments, saying your prayers.

"The advice to 'come out' means out of the world. This is what nuns and monks do, but of course that is not for everyone.

"Be content, children, the King receives you."

Tristram made one more try. "We thought it might have to do with going to the Castle."

The minister chuckled again, "You see how dangerous it can be to try to figure these things out for yourselves. You were very wise to bring these questions to me.

"Do not listen to these wandering beggars who call themselves 'couriers of the King' and 'preachers of the Good News.' If you were to go to the Castle, you would have your journey for nothing. You have heard perhaps that you can see the King. That is a plain falsehood, because the King lives in seclusion in the Keep of the Castle and sees no one. Or perhaps you have heard that you can meet the Prince. That is also false. Our Prince has gone on a long journey, so obviously no one can see him until he returns.[3]

"If you wish to be taken on as servants, that may be possible. Otherwise there is no reason to go the Castle.

"But even that is not necessary. You are already servants of the King. I know how hard you both worked in the grain field, and today you have brought with your father an unselfish offering to the Lord. You are as truly his servants as if you worked in the Castle."

"Thank you," Tristram replied. "You've made it very clear."

The crowd was thinning as they left the church. Mara was

---

[3] Mark 13:34

downcast. All her questions had been answered so neatly, but it did not satisfy the longing in her heart.

She was surprised to see a spark in Tristram's eye. "Was it so clear to you?" she asked.

"Very clear! He has never been to the Castle and doesn't want anyone else to go. I don't think he knows any more about it than we do!"

Chapter IV

The Outlaws

The lumbering oxen at last brought the cart in sight of home. Mara sighed with relief. The threat of the outlaws was ever present with her, and though it was midday, and she had the company of Father and Tristram, home still seemed safer than the road. The warmth of the late summer sun had made her drowsy, so these last few hundred yards she closed her eyes and let her head bounce on Tristram's shoulder.

It was a sudden tensing in that shoulder which brought her wide awake. They were in their own dooryard, but from behind the cottage, men were stepping out—armed men with fierce, beastly faces. Mara would have fallen from the cart seat, if Tristram's arms had not gone protectingly around her.

"What is it villains?" her father's voice was angry. "What are you after this time?"

Father is so brave, Mara thought. But he'll only antagonize them.

"What do you have worth taking?" laughed one who seemed to be the leader. "You've a fine lot of wheat there, but you haven't threshed it yet, and that's too much work for rogues like us." The outlaws laughed together.

"We'll have to drop back some fine day when we smell the

bread a-baking. For now we'll just take that cart and oxen and be on our way."

Mara and Tristram leaped gladly from the seat of the cart, relieved to be let off so cheaply. But Father sat where he was.

"I'll give you nothing," he defied them. "I'm an honest man and have sweated for what little I have. Lay aside that bow if you're not too cowardly, and I'll show you who's the better man."

The outlaw leader laughed again. "Nay, nay, you're a stout fellow, and I don't fancy a bruising. Keep your cart then, and we'll just take the beasts.

"Unhitch the oxen, boys, and let the old fellow sit." Several of the men stepped forward to obey their leader, but when the first reached for the yoke pin, he felt a whip across his shoulders.

Tristram cried, "Father, don't!" But the whip continued to lash out with great effect.

"You old fool!" the outlaw leader wasn't laughing now. "Is a yoke of oxen worth your life? We've killed men for far less. Lay down that whip now and we'll take but one of the cattle. Otherwise you are a dead man."

But Mara's father was clearly emboldened by his success. "Don't threaten me, you scum! I am a loyal subject of the King. He will protect me!"

"Oh, the King!" the outlaw had regained his good humor, "You claim the King's protection? Is this the same King whose tithe you shorted just today?"

Mara saw her father's face turn pale. "How...do you...know that?" he stammered.

"Loyal subject!" the face grew even uglier and more beastly. "If boasting made it so, you would be a loyal subject indeed!"

"You're wrong!" the poor farmer seemed to have aged thirty years in as many seconds. The outlaw raised his bow, "Here's an arrow for your lying throat."

The dart flew true and transfixed the old man in the neck. A torrent of blood gushed forth even as he toppled from the cart.

Mara screamed and ran to her father. There was no hope. His lifeblood was racing from his body, and his wild eyes did not even recognize her.

Something inside Mara burst. She scooped up a stone and flung it at the outlaw leader, catching him on the side of the head. She followed it with another missile, and another. Some missed and struck the men behind him, but none was entirely without effect. The outlaws beat an ignominious retreat, leading off the oxen and cart with them.

When she turned, Tristram was spreading the blanket from the cart seat over their father. He was shaking his head, as if to clear it, but Mara's whole body was shaking violently with passion she had never before experienced.

For a long minute the brother and sister stood looking after the departing outlaws. At least, thought Mara, there was no wondering this time. She knew who had killed her father.

Tristram walked into the cottage, but Mara stood a while longer. Was it only a few moments ago they had all been jogging peacefully along in the sunshine? Perhaps this was a nightmare. "Please," Mara prayed, "let me wake up."

In the cottage she found Tristram throwing things into a sack. "Pack what you can carry, Mara. We're not staying here."

Mara had no desire to stay either. The stone walls had played her false. There where she had felt most secure, the worst had befallen.

"Tristram."

"Yes, Mara."

"Are you afraid?"

The youth stood quietly a moment. "Yes, I am afraid."

"Tristram."

"Yes, Mara."

"Don't be afraid."

Tristram laughed a little, "Is this my fearful little sister?"

"Didn't you see, Tristram? Didn't you see what happened to Father?"

"Of course I saw! That's why I'm afraid."

"No, you didn't see!" Mara took his hands to get his complete attention. "As long as Father wasn't afraid, they didn't do anything to him. They had to make him afraid before they could hurt him."

"You're right, Mara!" Tristram's eyes opened wide with revelation. "They are nothing but cowards and bullies. When Father stood up to them, he was winning."[1]

"If only he had paid that extra bushel of wheat!"

---

[1] James 4:7

"No, Mara, that wouldn't have saved him. Being a loyal subject is more than paying tithes or performing duties."[2]

"What then? What would have saved Father?"

"That's what we're going to find out, Mara. We're going to the Castle!"

Packing was a thing quickly accomplished. Mara was wearing her best dress, and she had but one other. She noticed now that her apron and skirt were spattered with blood. Vaguely the thought ran through her mind that she ought to wash the stains before they set. Then she wondered how she could be thinking of washing clothes at such a time as this.

The outlaws had tumbled things about and smashed pottery. What food they had not taken or eaten was spilled, but she managed to gather a little. Her shawl, hairbrush, stockings, and petticoats completed her bundle.

A gleam of light in the dark interior of the cottage made her turn. In Tristram's hands was a bright sword. She had never seen it before.

"It was Father's," he answered her unspoken question. "I don't know where he got it or why he never even looked at it. I suppose he would have said it was a useless tool for a farmer." Tristram turned the blade admiringly, then thrust it into his belt. "Are you ready?"

Mara nodded and stepped toward the door. It was a long walk to the Castle. Night might overtake them on the way. The thought made her shiver, but she knew now—really knew—that the night was no worse than the day, and the cottage no safer than the road. She was glad for Tristram's company, but she knew she would be going even without him.

Leaving the doorway, they were stopped by the bloody sight of the blanket-covered figure still in the yard. Mara felt only a horror of it.

---

[2] Matthew 5:20

It was not her father. He was gone. This bit of flesh and bone should be taken to the sexton and put in the churchyard as was proper, but Mara had no interest in it.

"The neighbors," she heard herself saying, "will think us unnatural children leaving our father's corpse unburied."

"I don't care," Tristram replied shortly, and they walked quickly away.

He set such a swift pace, that Mara's legs began to ache, but she said nothing. Nor did she look around. Only one thing mattered, and that was to reach the Castle without delay.

She was surprised therefore, when Tristram halted abruptly at the bridge. She was several steps beyond him before she could stop.

"We'll not cross the river," he declared. "The Castle is on this side, and we'll stay on this side."

"But the road crosses it again before the Castle. It's the shortest way."

"I can't explain. Something is telling me not to cross this bridge." He turned down the narrow footpath that followed the twists and turns of the river, and Mara hurried after him.

"This path rejoins the road when it comes back to this side of the river. We'll be in sight of the Castle by then."

Yes, thought Mara, and have lost at least an hour's time. The broad, smooth road was much easier walking than this little winding path with its many ups and downs. The only good thing was that they would avoid the village and not have to stop and answer questions. Perhaps it was the best route after all. Anyway the path was shaded a good share of the time, while the road was hot and dusty. The farther they walked, the more Mara was glad they had taken the path.[3]

Even so, Mara was hot and dry. Her legs were numb now, and she just kept moving them as fast as she could. Luckily Tristram had thought to bring a jug of water. Mara was thirsty enough to drink from the brown, turbid river, but the spring water from home tasted so good. Mara thought that at last she was as grateful for it as she ought to be.

When Tristram judged they were about halfway, he called for a rest. In the shade of an old oak, Mara stretched herself on a mossy rock,

---

[3] Matthew 7:13, 14

and let the delicious coolness seep into her body.[4] They made a light meal of the food Mara had salvaged, then hurried on.

The sun was already setting when Tristram cried, "Look!" Ahead Mara saw the rope suspension bridge that ran across to the village. It was a welcome landmark. The Castle was less than three miles beyond.

"Well, what have we here?" a bold voice hailed them from across the river.

The road was visible from here, and camped along it was another troop of the outlaws. How unfair, Mara thought, to meet them twice in the same day. On the heels of that thought came gratitude for the broad, deep river that separated them. An arrow could cover the distance, but not with much force or accuracy.

Tristram said nothing, but dropped his sack and grimly drew his sword.

"Say, there's a hearty lad. He ought to be one of us!"

One of the outlaws gestured in a friendly fashion. "Come, you'd rather use that sword than a pitchfork all your life. A little ale sounds good doesn't it? And money, and women, and feasting with jovial companions—why it's just the sort of life for a young stalwart like you."

The other outlaws joined in cajoling voices. "Bring along the wench!" called one. "We'll show her a good time too." The jolly beckoning was openly sincere. Even Mara could not suspect they meant anything more than what they said.

Yesterday, Tristram might have thrown back a jest or two and gone on his way thinking that the outlaws were not such bad fellows after all.

Today his eyes flashed hatred. "Begone, you foul murderers! My sister and I go to the Castle to seek the Lord!"

These words threw the outlaws into an uproar. "Don't go there!" one and another cried. "You'll be sorry the rest of your life!"

"He'll make slaves of you!" another warned. "You'll never draw a free breath again."

"Better a slave than a thieving cutthroat!" Mara hurled at them.

"Quick!" one of them shouted, "to the bridge! They must be stopped!" As one man, the outlaws began to run toward the swinging

---

[4] 1 Corinthians 10:4

footbridge.

Mara started into the trees, "We can hide in the woods."

But to her horror, Tristram raced off toward the bridge at full speed. Did he think he could fight them all? He would be killed!

The outlaws reached the bridge first and started across. But to balance the swinging walkway, with so many feet on it at once, was no easy matter.

Tristram came to the other end and raised his sword to hack at the rope. It was dull through lack of use, but four strokes severed the one rope, and suddenly the outlaws were swinging in thin air, holding on for dear life.

Three more strokes brought the whole crashing down into the river. Most of the outlaws still clung to the trailing ropes. A few whirled away downstream. Those who had been tardy in reaching the bridge now clambered to help their fellows, stopping only to curse and threaten Tristram, as he stood waiting for Mara to catch up to him.

She saw the new danger at once. "You were wonderful, Tristram! But they will beat us to the next bridge, and what shall we do then?"

"Ask me then!" Tristram laughed. Then taking her hand, he started off running along the path. Mara cast aside her bundle and ran too, though she had not suspected she had that much energy left.

They ran and ran, and Mara thought gratefully that the summer twilight would be long. Another thought occurred to her also and became a prayer as she ran. The first time Tristram slowed to catch his breath she gasped it out to him. "Perhaps the King will send us help."

Tristram panted along for a few more minutes before agreeing, "Perhaps." Then he added, "Perhaps he already has." And Mara remembered Tristram's refusal to cross the river.

They walked swiftly until, too soon for Mara, Tristram decided it was time to run again. Then when she felt ready to collapse, he dropped back to a walk. Mara was in real pain now and thought there was nothing so much to be dreaded as the next time Tristram took it in his head to run.

But it was Mara herself who initiated the next sprint, when she heard the shouts of the outlaws, like a pack of hounds sighting their quarry.

"Hurry, Mara," Tristram encouraged her. "I see the bridge. We're almost there!"

Mara wondered why she should hurry to the bridge. It was there the outlaws would cross and be upon them. This bridge was stone; Tristram could not hack it down. As they came out of the trees Mara could see the Castle. It was still nearly a mile away and uphill. She did not think she could run that much further, and the outlaws would surely overtake them in that distance. She did not have to look back. She could tell by their shouts that they were gaining.

There was someone ahead on the road, a figure approaching from the Castle. He came so rapidly, he must be—he was!—a knight on horseback.

"We're saved!" gasped Tristram, and Mara collapsed on her face.

The knight drew up his steed near them. "Is the lady injured?"

Mara raised her head to assure him she was not hurt. The knight lifted his visor, and she recognized the stranger she had met at the spring. Was that only yesterday?

He recognized her also. "Ah, thank goodness I have found you!"

As he dismounted, Tristram offered Mara the last drops in the bottle.

"When I reported back to the King, he rebuked me and told me I had failed to recognize your hunger. No business is more urgent than a hungry soul. He sent me to find you, and here you have come to meet me!"

"Where are the outlaws?" Mara asked.

"They have run away, but I will pursue them a bit, if you are certain you can go on from here."

Mara looked up at the Castle. It was very near now. "Yes," she smiled, "I can make it the rest of the way."

Chapter V

Through the Small Door

It was almost dark when Mara and Tristram reached the Castle. The high stone walls of the fortress frowned at them forebodingly in the gloom. It did not seem possible there could be a welcome for them here. No open door or gate was immediately visible. Tristram's steps slowed, and Mara sensed disappointment in him. What had he expected, she wondered.

Her eyes traveled upward over the grey stones, and then, above the battlements, she saw a radiance, as though the courtyard were filled with light.

"Look, Tristram!" Hope sprang up anew in the refugees' hearts.

"Hurry, Mara! We must find the way in!"

And again Mara cried, "Look!" For even as he spoke a small door had opened in the grim wall, letting forth a flood of light. They ran to the opening, but stopped just outside.

Within they could see such splendor as they had never imagined. Gold and silver gleamed in the candlelight. The floor was polished marble. Colorful tapestries hung between marble pillars. Mara saw candlesticks of ivory set with jewels, and not only her eyes feasted, but a fruity odor, as of all delicacies one might desire, reached her nostrils. And from somewhere inside came the faint sound of a choir, too distant to distinguish the words, but the music surpassed anything Mara had ever heard.

Brother and sister stood without moving. If the cold, dark walls had seemed to forbid them entrance, this open door was even more prohibitive. Was what they saw real, or only a dream? It could not be a place for people such as they. How could they ever have imagined the King wanted crude, ignorant peasants to come to his Castle? Thirstily they drank in the glory that they might remember it all their lives.

"Come, come, you are more than welcome!"

For the first time they noticed a young man in rich livery standing in the darkness just beside the door. He emphasized his words with a gesture, and they reluctantly obeyed.

Mara stood on that marble floor surrounded by brilliant light and glistening fixtures. She felt so dirty. She glanced behind to see if she had tracked footprints. She knew Tristram felt the same, because when the page offered them a seat, he said, "No!" so fast it made her jump.

Then the page smiled graciously and said, "I suppose you would like to meet the King."

"Oh, no," Tristram quickly replied. "We wouldn't want to disturb His Majesty."

The page frowned a little, "Then why have you come?"

"To escape the outlaws," Mara answered truthfully.

The page laughed, "One reason is as good as another. The important thing is that you're here." He bowed low, "Wait, and I will go for Uncle. He welcomes all newcomers."

As soon as they were alone, Tristram whispered, "We should not have come. We are totally unfit to be in the King's Castle, let alone to stand in his presence."

"Yes," Mara agreed, turning slowly to gaze at all the wonders. "But I'm glad we're here. Perhaps we shall be slaves as the outlaw said, but I will gladly be a slave if I may remain here."

Tristram smiled, "You are always right. I feel that I have been seeking this place all my life, though I never knew it until now."

Bustling footsteps approached down the hall. A plainly dressed man with a brown, beardless face appeared. His beaming countenance was lined with age, but his hair was still thick and dark. There was something comfortably familiar about him, like an old friend. Mara felt she had always known him. Nevertheless she dropped a curtsy, because an air of greatness hung about him as well.

"Children!" He opened his arms and embraced them both in a bear hug. "We are delighted you are here at last!

"Now come along, I have things to show you." He led Mara and Tristram into the hall holding each by an arm. At the first door he stopped, and taking a key from his belt, unlocked it.

The room they now entered was quite unlike the part of the Castle they had already seen. Walls, ceiling, and floor were white and completely featureless. The room contained only one object, a large wooden cross. Mara did not notice lamp or candle, but the room was softly lighted.

"Now, children," Uncle laid a hand on each of their shoulders. "Look at that cross. Look at it very hard."

Mara stared with all her might at the cross, wondering why, but wanting to obey. For several minutes she continued to stare. The first thing she noticed was that the room was growing darker and she felt cold. Then a breeze touched her, and she sensed that she was not in a room at all, but outdoors. Still she stared intently, and suddenly she saw him.

A Man was hanging on the cross. His naked body was stretched tight, and blood dripped from his thorn-crowned brow, his torn face, and mangled back. Nails through his wrists and one through his ankles held him suspended, and his agony appeared so great that Mara's eyes filled with tears, and she heard Tristram cry out, as though he felt the pain.

After a moment the vision faded from her sight, but remained vividly in her mind. When she turned to Uncle she saw tears in his eyes as well.

"Was it..." Tristram whispered, "was it the Prince?"

Uncle nodded. He seemed too filled with emotion to speak, and beckoned them with his hand out of the room.

Across the hall he unlocked another door. In this room was a small cave as though cut in a hillside. Mara watched as a procession of mourners carried a body into the cave and left it there. She wept with them as they sealed the entrance with a great stone. Then one by one they left. A long, dreary time seemed to pass. Soldiers came and stood guard. One watch was relieved by another. Daylight came and went; soldiers came and went.

Suddenly an angel was there and the tomb was open! It was empty! The body was gone!

Mara heard someone shout "Alleluia!" Then she realized it was she who had shouted. Uncle was beaming again. Strangely, it seemed to her, Tristram was crying now.

"Come," Uncle said, "one more room."

Entering the third room Mara found herself knee-deep in a cloud-like mist. Otherwise the room was empty. But as she waited, a Man appeared before them. He was glorious, dressed in shining garments, and glowing with power.

Mara felt, rather than saw, the resemblance between this Man and the one on the cross. Then he spoke and confirmed it. "I am he that liveth and was dead; and behold, I am alive forevermore."[1]

Tristram and Mara fell to their knees. All the stories about the Prince were true! The vision was gone, and for a moment Mara was keenly disappointed. It had been only a vision, and she wanted to meet the Prince.

Stepping back into the passageway, Mara felt as if a spell had been broken. She could not tell how long she had been in the three rooms, whether minutes or days. During that time, however long or short, she had completely forgotten herself. Now she again felt self-conscious of the contrast between herself and her new surroundings.

"I have shown you all I can at this time," Uncle told them solemnly. "Now you must tell me—what do you most desire?" He gazed at them so intently, as though his very life hung on their answers.

Mara thought hard. What did she most desire? And as so often, her mouth got ahead of her mind. "Please, sir, I desire a bath."

The words weren't out before she realized how unsuitable they were. Her ears burned like fire, and she knew her face was red with shame. She had liked Uncle so much. Now he would think her a fool, as well as dirty and ignorant.

But his round face beamed at her. "That is a very good answer. As good an answer as ever I heard. A bath you shall have, my dear."

Tristram had not laughed at her or been ashamed for her either. He was too engrossed in thought to notice what she had said. "I most desire..." he began, but still hesitated. "I don't know how to say it. I desire the Prince."

---

[1] Revelation 1:18

Uncle did not seem to find this request outlandish either. His smile softened, and laying a hand on Tristram's shoulder, he said quietly, "And the Prince desires you, my son."

Mara and Tristram fell into each other's arms, laughing and crying. They had never known such happiness. What had they expected to find at the Castle? The reality was far exceeding expectation.

When they had somewhat recovered themselves, Uncle led them on up the corridor. They came to a comfortable room, really just a widening of the hall, where there were a dozen or so men and women in various attitudes. Several were at prayer. A few were reading; one was just gazing out a window.

"Felicia, Lucius," Uncle called out two, and Mara and Tristram found themselves escorted off in different directions by a girl and boy about their own age.

"Welcome to the Castle!" exclaimed the girl named Felicia. "I'm so thrilled you decided to come. I've been praying that you would."

Mara stopped suddenly. She knew this girl. "But you're... you're Ida!"

"That was my name," she smiled.

"You've changed. You're so lovely—radiant."

"Come along. I can tell you about it while you get ready."

"Ready for what?" Mara protested.

"For the Celebration! It will be in the Great Hall with everyone present. You must be on time!"

Mara allowed herself to be led along much as one in a dream. What luck, she thought, we've come just in time for a feast of some sort.

At a small anteroom, Felicia stopped. Her voice was solemn now. "Here is where you must bathe."

The anteroom at first appeared to have no floor, but as Mara stepped closer she saw it was like a deep well. Steps led down perhaps fifteen feet to the level of the water. The walls of the place were reddish in color and were reflected in the glistening water.

It made the light a little eerie, but at least it gave an illusion of warmth, for Mara, descending the stone stairs, was certain the water would be icy cold.

At the bottom of the stairs was a small platform, and a towel lay there. Mara undressed as far as the waist and taking the towel, was about to kneel at the water's edge.

Felicia stopped her. "You must remove all your clothing."

Mara looked at her blankly, "All my clothing?" Mara had not had that kind of bath since she outgrew her mother's kettle. A bath to Mara meant that she heated water in a pot and washed all over with a wet cloth.

Next moment Mara flushed with embarrassment as she grasped what Felicia meant. Of course, she thought, it is like the famous Roman baths. She had heard that people of wealth traveled to these ancient spas and went bodily into the water.

Quickly Mara pulled off her skirt and stockings, glad it was summer.

"Over here," said Felicia, "the steps continue down." Mara looked, but could not see the steps. The water was completely opaque. Suddenly she realized what she was looking at.

"Felicia!" she cried aghast, "it's blood!" Felicia looked at her quite calmly, "What did you expect? Haven't you heard all your life that it is the blood of the Prince which cleanses us?"[2]

"Yes," Mara quavered, "but I didn't think of it so real. It's almost as if I had made him bleed just so I could have the bath I wanted."

Felicia took Mara's face between her hands and looked straight into her eyes. "That is exactly right. And if you put your clothes back on, and leave here now, you will have made his death of no purpose. Will you reject this gift he gave his life to buy for you?"[3]

Mara shook her head helplessly. "No,...but must I do this often?"

Felicia smiled, "This one bath will cleanse you for as long as you remain in the King's service."

Thus reassured Mara turned to the steps again. "Are you sure there are steps? I can't see them."

"I'm sure. Remember I was in your place not so long ago. The steps are there, though you will find some of them quite steep."

Mara slid her heel down the stone until she found the first step. Then she was in above her ankles. It was warm, but not pleasant. This was not at all the sort of bath she had anticipated.

The next step was longer and took her up to her knees. She nearly lost her balance. She glanced back, and Felicia nodded encouragement.

---

2 1 John 1:7

3 Hebrews 13:12, Titus 2:14

If the next step was to be longer still, she could not slide just one foot down, so Mara hopped with both feet and came to hip depth.

"Oh, well done!" cried Felicia clapping her hands.

Mara bit her tongue and hopped again. She had to spread her arms to remain upright, but she was now up to her shoulders. "I'm done, aren't I?" she pleaded. "Can I climb out now?"

"One more step," Felicia's voice was sympathetic.

"Oh, no. I can't. I'll drown!"

"It will seem like it, but the King won't let you. You must trust him."

Mara knew nothing of swimming. To her it was the same as stepping off a cliff. She did not hop this time, but just closed her eyes and taking a deep breath flung herself forward.

The thick liquid closed over her, and she was drawn down as in quicksand.

It is the end of me, she thought, but her feet had no sooner touched bottom than she felt she was moving upward again. Within her closed eyes, she seemed to see the Man on the cross again, and this time he was looking at her. With a surge of joy she realized that as he had lived again, so would she.[4]

---

[4] John 14:19

Chapter VI

Celebration

When she opened her eyes she was standing on a rug in a strange room. The liquid dripping from her was water, not blood, and Felicia was drying her with the towel. Truly she felt cleaner than ever before.

This place was a bedroom, for a large comfortable bed was in an alcove, and from ceiling to floor it was draped in velvets and tapestries. There was a door at one end and a shuttered window at the other, but they did not seem to be the way she had come. On one side was an empty fireplace and on the other a small tiled fountain. Sparkling water flowed from the mouth of a stone lion's head. As for the bottom, she could not see it, but it appeared very deep indeed.

Felicia was panting as though she had run to reach here, but she was flushed and happy. "That was wonderful!" she was exclaiming, even as she attempted to undo the thick braid.

"Where am I?"

"This is your place, your very own room. I have one just like it—except the colors in my room are different.

"Now I promised to tell you what has happened to me since we last met. I traveled so slowly because of my burden. I stopped to rest a dozen times in a mile, and when I had drunk all the water you gave me, I was in despair and ready to give up. It did not seem possible I would ever reach the Castle."

As Felicia talked she was getting out a beautiful gown of white silk trimmed with lace. "Now, no use shaking your head at me. This is what you're to wear at the feast.

"As I sat by the road feeling quite sorry for myself, an old lady came by. She sat right down beside me and introduced herself. Abigail, she said her name was."

"Oh, I know her."

"Do you? Well, she was so sweet and good. She seemed to know just what my problem was. She told me she had once had a burden like mine, and had lost it at the Castle. She said all I needed was someone to walk with me. So she helped me up and took my arm, and it was easier. We rested only a few times between there and the village.

"Just before the village we met a band of outlaws. They hooted and jeered at us, and tried to discourage me. But Abigail laughed and smiled, and we just kept going. The village was even worse. People stared, and some told Abigail she was an old busybody, and others said she should be ashamed to be seen with a person like me. I wanted to run away and hide, but she just held on to my arm and kept laughing and smiling, and eventually we were past the town.

"You have such beautiful thick hair!" Felicia was brushing as she talked.

"From there I could see the Castle, and that made it easier. Here in the Castle I went through much the same things as you have. They changed my name from Ida which meant labor to Felicia which of course means happiness."

"And your burden?"

"I lost it in the bath. You can't bring anything ugly or unpleasant out of there unless you hang on to it with both hands. Some people actually do that.

"Now you're ready, we must go."

Felicia opened the door and led the way down a stone corridor. They descended a long stairway, and the voices of the choir came floating to them again. Eagerness hurried the girls along.

"What is the Celebration about?"

"Whenever the King has a new son or daughter there's a great Celebration."[1]

"Well, I should think so! Which is it this time?"

---

[1] Luke 15:7

"One of each, so this is an especially great Celebration.

"Hush! We're there." Felicia stopped in a huge archway. Inside the Great Hall a magnificent feast was spread on white linen cloths. Lords and ladies in gorgeous clothing filled the Hall. Shields, paintings, and every manner of decoration covered the stone walls. The light from so many candles set the whole aglitter.

It was quite enough to take one's breath away. On the dais at the head of the hall, Uncle stood between two empty chairs, so elaborately decorated they were almost like thrones.

Now from somewhere, a trumpeter sounded. Everyone turned, and those who were seated stood to their feet.

Uncle lifted his arms and proclaimed in a loud voice, "I give you—the Princess Christine and the Prince Godfrey."

With Felicia nudging her, our poor peasant girl inched further into the Hall, hoping to see the personages thus announced. A knight standing there offered her his arm, and with Felicia's urging she laid a hand gingerly on his.

To her intense dismay, he led her to the dais, and left her standing beside one of the empty chairs. Opposite her stood a splendidly dressed young man. When she had stared at him for a moment she suddenly recognized her brother!

Now Uncle turned his back to the crowd and addressed the new prince and princess.

"I give you first this," he extended a parchment to each of them. It was covered with writing, the first letters of each paragraph colorfully illuminated, and at the bottom was a seal in red wax. This was all they could tell of it, for of course they had never learned to read.

"This," Uncle continued, "is your certificate of adoption, stating that you are a son or daughter of the King, a member of the Royal Family, with all rights and privileges pertaining thereto, and specifically, that with the Prince and this great company you are heir to the Kingdom."[2]

The words Uncle spoke were almost as hard to grasp as those written in the scratchy black marks of the parchment.

"Now be seated," he instructed them, and they obeyed. From a table he lifted two plain golden circlets. "This simple crown denotes your rank. You have much to learn, and other crowns to gain. But I

---

[2] Romans 8:14-17

charge you here and now—do not forget who you are. Do not forget where you have been seated.[3] Most of all do not forget to whom you belong. Live worthy of your parentage."

He placed the circlets on their heads, and turned to the crowd who began to shout, "Long live the Prince! Long live the Princess!"

Christine and Godfrey rose to their feet, and that whole assemblage was smiling and applauding them.

The choir began again, and for the first time Christine could understand the words:

> We are a chosen generation,
> A royal priesthood, an holy nation,
> A peculiar people.
> We praise him who hath called us
> Out of darkness into his marvelous light.[4]

Christine sat down again, and the feasting commenced, but she kept repeating to herself in wonder, "I am the Princess Christine. I am the King's daughter."

The celebrating seemed to last late into the night. There were more foods than Christine had known existed, and her first resolve, to try just a taste of each, soon proved impossible to fulfill. There were minstrels and jesters, acrobats and jugglers, as well as the choir and musicians. Surely there had never been such a wonderful party, Christine thought.

But the most wonderful moment of all came at the end when Uncle stood up and gestured for silence. When the whole Hall was so quiet that no one even breathed, another choir was faintly heard, singing from some remote part of the Castle. And that music so far surpassed the singing of the present choir, that all stood with shining eyes, open-mouthed, holding their breath and listening. It was so unbearably sweet that Christine felt a stinging in her nose and knew that she would presently burst into tears.

When that other music ended, there was a great sigh from the crowd, and everyone began to slowly depart. Godfrey had risen and

---

[3] Ephesians 2:4-7

[4] 1 Peter 2:9

offered his hand to Christine, but they only smiled their goodnight. The spell was too sacred to be broken by speech.

In the halls, Christine wondered if she could find her room again, but Felicia was soon at her side. They climbed the stairs arm in arm, and Felicia lit the candles in her room and showed her a special gown just for sleeping. Then she kissed her and left.

Alone at last, Christine first whirled round and round for sheer joy. She opened the shuttered window and found she was facing the northern constellations. Moonlight was coming from the other side of the Castle, and all below her lay in dark shadow. She was so high it made her dizzy to look down, but in the distance the moonlight shone on fields and forests. It was the most beautiful night of her life.

She whirled again the length of the room and then began to examine her furnishings. The predominant color was an old rose with moss green and ivory for accents. The wood was cherry; you noticed it most in the large wardrobe that stood by the window. Christine opened it and ran her hand over the silk dress she had just worn. There was a velvet gown in the same rose and green as her room. There were many dresses, mostly less elaborate for everyday wear. She pulled out a brown linen with ivory piping and wondered if it were too fine to wear tomorrow. Putting it down, she felt she must whirl again. This time she plopped down on the padded bench near the fireplace, and sat smoothing its satin cover.

How long ago was it she had stood by her father's body in the dooryard of their little cottage, praying she could wake up?

As she thought of this, a tear fell on the bench top, and she suddenly noticed the stains of many tears. Who had lived in this room before? What sorrows had that person known? She looked around her with new awareness. Other girls, women, had occupied this room. She was not the first. How many hands had smoothed that satin cushion, how many weary bodies rested in that bed? Had they whirled with joy as she had? Somehow she knew they had. But there were tears as well as laughter in this place to which she had come.

Suddenly exhausted, Christine went to the fountain for a drink before bed. As she leaned over the little pool, she saw that its smooth surface was not disturbed by the falling water. It gave her back a clearer reflection of herself than she had ever seen. She studied her face for a minute. The new happiness was there. The old fear was gone.[5]

"Thank you, thank you, dear Prince," she whispered as she leaned to drink. As though the draught were a sleeping potion, she had hardly time to climb into bed before her eyes closed in deep, restful slumber.

[5] 2 Corinthians 5:17

Chapter VII

Lily

Chiming bells awoke the Castle very early each day. Christine sat bolt upright in bed. "Lily!" she cried. She had forgotten the cow completely yesterday evening, but it was the first thing in her mind this morning. She leaped from the bed. Grey light made a feeble entrance through the window she had opened the night before.

"Poor Lily! How could I have forgotten her?" In her mind she saw the gentle animal at the barnyard gate, lowing all night for her mistress. The stretched bag, the swollen teats—Christine could see them, and worse, it would be hours yet before she could reach her.

What can I put on? she wondered. The lovely brown linen she had selected last night was hardly a dress to milk a cow in. She hung it back in the wardrobe and searched for something more appropriate. Where were her own clothes? Oh, yes, she had left them by the pool. Were they still there? Well, her other clothes she had dropped near the footbridge. She could pick them up on the way home, and change before she milked. She must get home at once! As she hurriedly brushed and braided her hair, there was a knock at her door.

"Is that you, Felicia?"

"Yes, are you up?"

Christine threw the door open. "Thank goodness you're here. I must get home as quickly as I can!"

Felicia looked at her strangely, "Christine, you *are* home."

The new name brought Christine up short. And this was her home? She really looked around for the first time that morning. All that had happened last night came flooding back. But then she remembered Lily again. How selfish she had been—enjoying herself while the innocent beast suffered.

"Felicia, I have a cow, a lovely, good-natured cow, the best you ever saw. I completely forgot her. She wasn't milked last night, and now it's time to milk her again. I must go milk her!"

"No, Christine, the one thing you must not do is leave. I understand what you're feeling. The next morning after I came here, I wanted to start right back and try to bring my family. I'm thankful they didn't let me go."

"Do you mean I'm a prisoner here?"

"No, nothing of the sort. If you insist on leaving you may, but you mustn't, Christine," and tears started in Felicia's pretty blue eyes.

"I wouldn't leave for good, you ninny. I'd come right back."

"You think so, Christine, but you wouldn't. If you leave now, you might never return. This is something everyone goes through, if not on the first morning, soon after."

Christine considered this strange advice, then laid it aside. "Look, Felicia. I love you. I didn't mean to upset you. But you're wrong. Do you really think I would give up all that the King has done for me?

"This is just something I have to do. If I hurry I can be back by evening, and I'll bring my cow with me."

At this Felicia began to cry in earnest. "What if the cow isn't there? What if you meet the outlaws? You don't know what will happen once you're outside these walls."

Felicia wiped her eyes, "Listen, come with me now to morning prayer. Then you can talk to Uncle. He'll know what's best. Please."

It sounded like a reasonable request. "All right," Christine said slowly.

"Oh, thank you! Thank you! You'll be glad you did." Felicia was immensely relieved. "I'll bet you haven't had a drink this morning."

"No," Christine turned toward the fountain, remembering how good and sweet it had tasted last night.

"I need one too," Felicia bent beside her, and the girls drank deeply.

Christine hoped it wouldn't put her to sleep as it had the first time, but the effect was quite different this morning. She felt greatly invigorated, and her worry seemed to slip into the background.

"Now get dressed. We're going to be late."

Christine splashed some water in her face. How refreshing it felt. Then she donned the brown linen, and let Felicia lead her to the Chapel.

There a crowd was gathered for morning prayers. The first thing that struck Christine was the noise. To her, praying meant kneeling and bowing her head and closing her eyes and silently speaking to the King. She saw many in this attitude. But just as many were standing, arms lifted, eyes turned upward, loudly praising the King. And others were in variations of these positions. A few lay flat on their faces weeping. The greatest wonder was that she seemed to be the only one who was paying any attention to these things.

Felicia was already busy at prayer, on her knees, hands clasped, eyes closed, but her face was turned upward, and though she made no sound, tears were coursing down her cheeks. She's praying for me, Christine thought, and she felt ashamed of the anxiety she had caused her friend. Now I had better get to business, she told herself, but her eyes strayed around the Chapel. It was much like the village church, if anything a bit plainer. Was Tristram here, she wondered, forgetting that like her, he had a new name. What ought I to pray about? All she could think of was Lily, and that did not seem a suitable subject.

At last she realized she could thank the King, and certainly she had plenty to thank him for. For the next five minutes she prayed more fervently than ever in her life, and she experienced a marvelous sense of acceptance. He was her Father! Think of that! And he sat on his throne listening to his daughter's outpouring of thanks, and he was pleased. Christine felt so good, but she had said all she could think of; what now?

The next half hour was as long and dull as she had ever spent. Her knees hurt on the marble pavement. She seemed to itch in first one place then another. She thought about breakfast, though she was still full from the feast last night. Mostly she thought about Lily, and wondered how long before she could get to her.

Uncle had come up behind her without her noticing. He touched her and beckoned with his finger. How glad she was to go.

In a private corner of the vestibule, Uncle turned. "You wanted to speak to me?"

Christine nodded. “Dearest Uncle,” she began, “I really need to go home briefly.” Then seeing the same expression on his face, she had seen on Felicia’s, she stammered, “I don’t mean home. I mean the cottage where I used to live.”

“I seem to remember you were in such a hurry to reach the Castle. Now are you in such a hurry to leave?”

“No,” Christine shook her head miserably, “I don’t want to leave! But I have a cow, and she wasn’t milked last night. It was wrong of me to neglect my duty and leave her uncared for.”

“Dear child, will you let me decide what is right or wrong?”

“But you don’t understand about cows.”

Uncle smiled indulgently. “I think I know as much about cows as you do. Even about Lily.”

“How?” Christine looked at him in wonder. She had not told him Lily’s name.

“Have you not heard that the King knows everything?”

“Yes, but...”

“Now, as a brand new princess you have a great deal to learn, and learning is your duty at this time.

“Here is one thing you need to learn—you do not have a cow. You belong to the King now. And so Lily also belongs to the King. Are you willing to turn Lily over to the King?”[1]

“Certainly, he may have her. I didn’t mean to sound possessive. I only don’t want her to suffer.”

“Do you think the King wants her to suffer?”

“Oh, Uncle, you know I don’t think that!”

“Then that’s all settled.”

Christine didn’t see what was settled. “But who will milk her? The King won’t.”

“No, but he will either see that someone does, or he will let her dry up. That’s his business. If he wants you to milk her, he will provide a way.”

“You mean he doesn’t want me to leave the Castle.”

“No, child, it is much too dangerous until you have some training.” He laid his arm comfortingly on Christine’s shoulders.

“So, I should just forget about Lily?” Christine wondered disconsolately.

---

[1] 1 Corinthians 6:19, 20 and Acts 4:32

"You probably cannot do that," Uncle admitted, "but as far as you are able, we would like you to forget everything outside these walls, until such time as you are ready to be sent forth."

"I'll try, Uncle. At least I promise I won't talk about it anymore."

Uncle beamed at her in the way she had already learned to love. "Don't promise too much, my child, but you are already doing well with your most important lessons, trust and obedience." And he gave her a squeeze.

Just then the bells started ringing, and the chapel began to empty. Felicia was at Christine's side in a moment.

"I see everything is taken care of," she joined the embrace.

Felicia's smile was so contagious, and besides Christine found she was very happy. She had thought she would be happy if Uncle granted her request, but now he had refused her, and she was happier than ever. Strange, very strange.

Two figures separated themselves from the exiting crowd and approached. It was Lucius and—now that she saw him she remembered—Godfrey. Uncle extended his arms to welcome them.

Godfrey greeted Christine first. "Isn't this great, Sis? You look wonderful!" Then he turned to Uncle and bowed respectfully. "Sir, I would like your permission to borrow a cart, or even two carts and return to my former home today."

Felicia whispered to Christine, "What did I tell you?"

"At the cottage," he continued, "there are fifty-two bushels of wheat, which it would be a shame to leave for the mice and rats. It should be transported to the Castle, for the use of the King's people."

At this point Godfrey became aware that they were all inwardly laughing at him. He was telling Uncle what was a shame and what should be done.

He reddened, "What I meant was—there is a quantity of wheat I wish to place at the King's disposal."

"Very good," Uncle assured him. "The King thanks you."

Godfrey asked a deal more humbly, "May I please borrow a cart? Ours was stolen yesterday."

"Two carts," Lucius interrupted. "I can go along, Uncle, and make sure he stays out of trouble."

"And then I must send Felicia to make sure you stay out of trouble." Uncle's eyes twinkled and Lucius and Felicia both blushed.

Christine thought she caught Uncle's hint. She would have to ask Felicia about it.

"Why do you need a cart?" Uncle asked innocently.

Godfrey reddened still more, "To go after the wheat."

"Did the King ask you to fetch the wheat?"

"No."

"Well, if and when he does, you shall have the cart." That seemed to be the end of the matter. Christine giggled remembering her own reaction when Uncle had said it was settled. Godfrey was clearly not satisfied.

Uncle now smiled more kindly, and taking Godfrey's arm, led him away from the others. "Now tell me the real reason you want to go," were the last words Christine heard.

"We'd better go have breakfast," Felicia urged. "We seem to be late for everything this morning."

"I'll wait for Godfrey," Lucius replied loyally, waving as the girls hurried off.

"I need a map of this place," Christine protested as they started down unfamiliar corridors.

"You'll be surprised how soon you get used to it. But don't worry, I'm not going to lose you!" and Felicia gave her an affectionate hug.

The dining hall they entered this morning was next to the kitchen, and not at all grand. They sat down on a simple wooden bench by others who were already finishing. On the table Christine saw a basket of newly baked bread and another of fresh fruit. It was just what one wanted after the feast last night. But when a smiling woman set in front of her a bowl of milk, still warm from the cow, Christine burst into tears.

Chapter VIII

Morning

They were finishing when Lucius and Godfrey came in. The boys just grabbed a hunk of bread in one hand and a pear in the other, and rushed off after the girls.

Through the maze of passages again and up many stairs, Christine found herself in a room where a writing desk was built all around the wall, and a bench in front of it. Several scribes were already at work.

"This is Sister Agatha," Felicia was introducing her to an elderly lady wearing a plain black robe and a black veil on her head. "She teaches us reading."

Sister Agatha greeted Christine warmly, taking both her hands. "We are so delighted to have you, my dear.

"Now, a princess must be educated. The King wants all his children to read his Book.[1] Watch." Sister Agatha sat down at a bench, and dipped the quill into the ink pot.

"Say ayyy," she instructed Christine.

Obediently Christine parroted, "Ayyy."

Then Sister Agatha scratched on the parchment a large figure. "This is how A looks."

---

[1] 2 Timothy 2:15

She showed Christine five letters then broke them down into individual strokes for her to practice.

As Christine chewed on her tongue trying to duplicate the peculiar markings, she was aware that Lucius and Felicia were practicing reading with Sister Agatha. I'll soon be reading, Christine thought excitedly, and it spurred her to greater effort.

When it was time to leave, Godfrey whispered to her, "That was terrible!" And when he showed her his scratchings, she had to agree.

"You'll like the next class better," Lucius assured him. "Brother Michael teaches us about weapons and fighting. A prince has to be able to handle a sword." They went running off down the hall, but the girls' class was right next door.

In this room there were spinning wheels and looms and baskets of wool and flax, and skeins of bright colored threads. Christine's eyes lit up. Here was something she understood. She walked straight to an idle wheel and started to work. For the next two hours, she sat working and chatting with other girls and women. Felicia was trying to spin too, but having a hard time. One of the women, Sister Tabitha, was helping.

"You do lovely work," she complimented Christine.

But Felicia sighed, "Do you suppose I'll ever get it to look right?"

Christine smiled, "I'll help you with spinning if you'll help me with letters."

"I'm afraid, girls," Sister Tabitha warned, "it's mostly a matter of practice with either spinning or writing."

Christine enjoyed the needlework period, but what came next was even better. Felicia led her to the garden. It was even more beautiful than the Great Hall, for here all the flowers were living, and the colors more glowing than paint or thread could ever duplicate. There were more flowers and plants than Christine had imagined existed. She was disappointed that Felicia could not name them to her, but at least she didn't rush her past them. At last they came to a corner of the garden under the shade of the great, protective wall. Several people sat there on the grass.

One of them pointed past the approaching girls, "Here comes Brother Michael."

Christine turned around and saw her brother and Lucius coming down the path. Between them was a great stalwart fellow with black curling hair and beard. All three were laughing.

When they came alongside, Christine slipped an arm through her brother's. "Well," she asked excitedly, "did you learn to fight with a sword?"

"No," Godfrey replied, grinning sheepishly, "I learned to sharpen it!"

"Brother Michael says first things first," laughed Lucius.

"I spent all morning putting an edge on that old sword I brought."

Now they had reached the others, and the four sat down on the grass, and grew quiet.

Brother Michael was serious now. "What I have to teach you," he said, looking at the newcomers, "is both the hardest task, and the most important, you will ever be called upon to perform—you must learn to wait upon the King."[2]

Christine sat up with a thrill—to actually stand in the King's presence!

"This task," Brother Michael continued, "is called prayer."

Christine's face fell. She had prayed all her life, and there was nothing at all exciting about it.

Of course, this morning for just a few minutes, she had felt the King's presence. If prayer could be always like that...

"Today we are going to discuss a form of prayer, which, though it is really the easiest, we neglect to our shame. That is thanksgiving."

Yes, thought Christine, that's what I was doing. And she listened so intently that the next hour seemed no more than a deep breath.

"And today," he was drawing to a close, "we are especially thankful that, by the King's grace, Godfrey and Christine are with us. Let none of you forget that in your prayers this evening."

As the class separated and each went his way, Lucius explained that he had to clean the stables before dinner.

Felicia took Christine and Godfrey to the dining hall and left them there. She was on kitchen duty this hour.

For the first time since they came to the Castle, the brother and sister had a chance to talk, and there was so much to talk about, but where to begin?

"Christine?"

"Godfrey?" Christine giggled. "Do you really feel like Godfrey?"

---

2 Hosea 12:6, Psalm 27:14

"Yes," he replied excitedly, "I really am Godfrey! Do you know what Uncle told me this morning?"

"Of course I don't know. I've been wondering."

"He told me—but I'd better begin at the beginning. Remember when we were starting out for the Castle, you said the neighbors would think it was terrible to leave Father's body like that?"

Christine nodded.

"I said I didn't care, and I don't, but this morning when I woke up that was the first thing I thought of."

"That was *your* cow," Christine giggled again.

"What?" Godfrey looked blank.

"Never mind. Go on."

"Well, I felt so ashamed—not because of the neighbors, but because of the King. What would he think? I knew he wouldn't ever approve of children neglecting their duty to a parent. I couldn't believe we had really walked off and left it like that. I thought, I've got to go back and take care of father's body."

Christine wondered why she hadn't thought of that. Now that Godfrey had mentioned it, she saw they must do something. Dogs might be worrying it this very minute.

"I was so ashamed, I didn't even want to tell Lucius. Then I thought of the wheat, and it seemed like a perfect reason for going back.

"You know—it didn't work. I have a feeling you can't ever be anything but honest around here—at least not with Uncle. He sees right through you."

Christine nodded again, "So then you told Uncle why you really had to go."

"Yes, I told him why I *thought* I had to go. But he said that when we come to the Castle, we must come as a little child,[3] ready to trust our Father with all our cares and problems. He said a little child has no responsibility except to obey—that just as I'd turned the wheat over to the King, so I must turn over this anxiety about father's body."

Christine wasn't sure. "But that doesn't get it buried."

"I know, but since talking with Uncle I remembered hearing something in the King's book about letting the dead bury the dead.[4] Anyway, I just felt that it would be all right. I knew the King wasn't

---

[3] Matthew 18:3

[4] Matthew 8:21, 22

blaming me, and as Uncle said, if the King wanted me to do something about it, he would let me know."

"I guess it's out of our hands," Christine sighed, "just like Lily."

"Lily!" Godfrey laughed, "Why you were worrying about her just like I was about the body."

Christine smiled, "It seems to be some kind of sickness you wake up with here."

"But I almost forgot what I was going to tell you—why I know I'm Godfrey. Uncle said that my other name, Tristram, meant turmoil, but I wasn't going to have that anymore. Do you know what my new name means? Godfrey means God's peace. And that's what I have. Really and truly, I'm not concerned about the body anymore, or the wheat, or anything!

"It's the same thing Brother Michael just told us, about giving thanks in all things because it's the King's will.[5] I know that whatever happens from now on, the King is taking care of me."

"Godfrey," Christine repeated slowly, "what a wonderful name!

"Oh, I'm going to try to trust too. I agreed not to leave this morning, but I've still been worrying just the same. You've helped me. I'm so glad that even though we're in a new family you're still my brother!"

Godfrey patted her hand. "I'm glad too. If I had come without you, it would have been a lot worse than leaving just a dead body behind."

"Felicia said that was her cow—I mean she remembered the family she had left. I suppose Uncle told her to leave them in the King's hands too."

"I suppose so. Lucius was apprenticed to a miller, and he went off and left the sluice gate open."

Christine had to laugh, though she knew it was undoubtedly serious to Lucius.

"I'm so happy, Godfrey, so, so happy."

"I am too, but right now I'm hungry, and I can smell something good from the kitchen."

Dinner was soon on the table, and Christine thought it was as good in a simple way as a feast. There was fresh-baked bread again, and cider to drink—but it tasted better than the cider at home. Even the

---

[5] 1 Thessalonians 5:18

mashed turnips, which had always been a favorite of Christine's, tasted better here. The main dish was broiled trout, and nothing in Christine's memory had ever been more delicious.

Lucius had joined them, moments after the dinner gong. He was dripping wet from having washed up after the stables. Felicia couldn't sit down until everyone had been served, but as soon as she came, Christine realized how she had missed her the last hour, and what a dear friend she had become.

After dinner Felicia pointed Christine toward her room. "Turn right at the top of the stairs and it's the sixth door."

"Oh, I'll know it when I get there. Where is your room?"

"I'm on the south side of the Castle; I'll meet you back here after quiet time."

Lucius and Felicia had instructed them at dinner that the hour afterward was to be spent alone in their rooms. Christine was grateful. She had had a very busy twenty-four hours.

Lucius said that most of the people in the Castle took this time to read or nap. Some prayed.

"I wish I could spend the time reading," commented Felicia. "I always spend a few minutes trying anyway."

As Christine counted the doors in her hallway, she thought anxiously of the fountain in her room. Its waters satisfied her as the spring at the cottage never had. Once inside, she went straight to it and knelt to drink, but now she noticed something that she had not seen before. Under the head of the lion, letters were carved in the stone. They were raised, not incised, and there were seven of them, divided three and four. With excitement Christine recognized the final letter in each group. They were part of the lesson she had learned that morning.

She ran her fingers over the stone shapes, memorizing them, wondering what their names were, and more important, what they spelled. She had already begun to notice that letters were everywhere in the Castle, inscribed in stone, woven into tapestries, embroidered in frames. How long, she wondered, before she would understand their meanings.

If only she had something to write with. She had seen some rags in the floor of the wardrobe. If she had a piece of charcoal, she could write on the stone wall and clean it up afterward, but the fireplace was swept clean. Well, she would get some from the kitchen at supper time.

Christine drank now. It was so good, she felt she had never tasted real water before. Of all the good things in the Castle, this was the best. As the water ran over her tongue, it seemed her tongue just had to respond.

"Thank you, sweet Prince. Sweet, sweet Prince, how I love you." The words came of themselves, almost as if someone else was saying them, but Christine quickly added in her heart, it's true; I do.

Chapter IX

Afternoon

When the chimes signaled the end of quiet time, they woke Christine. She had not realized she was asleep. Had she been dreaming something? A beautiful feeling lingered with her like a forgotten dream.

Hurriedly she descended the stairs and reached the meeting place a moment before Felicia.

"What now?" she called to her approaching friend.

"Riding lessons!"

The afternoon was just as busy as the morning had been. She spent a half hour at the stable getting on and off a comfortable old mare who stood like a post. Lucius and Felicia were riding around a ring with some other students, but Brother Philip kept Christine and Godfrey going up and down, up and down, until they were breathless with exertion.

The next half hour was even more of a surprise to Christine. Felicia led her out in the garden to where the river flowed through, and in a grove of trees, hidden from view, they undressed.

Half a dozen girls were learning to swim. Christine had never even heard of such a thing. She had always been told that if you fell in the river over your head you would drown. These reckless girls were deliberately throwing themselves into deep water.

Felicia coaxed her gently into the river. It was pleasantly cool, and unlike the river after it left the Castle, this was calm and crystal clear. Christine could feel the current, but it wasn't strong. She let herself be led out shoulder deep, but was all the while determining she would go no farther.

But Felicia stopped there. "Now put your face in," she encouraged.

When Christine hesitated, Felicia demonstrated. "You can hold your nose if you want to."

After dipping her face several times, Felicia wanted still more. "Now bend your knees, so your whole head goes under."

This sounded rash to Christine, but again Felicia showed her how.

"This time open your eyes and look at me under water." Soon she had Christine playing and giggling.

Then one of the other swimmers approached, a young woman with two brown pigtails and a beautiful smile. "Welcome, Princess Christine. I see Felicia has already begun your lesson."

"Christine, this is Sister Celeste, our swimming instructor."

Sister Celeste smiled at Christine, but she took Felicia's hand. "Come, Felicia, let's see you float today."

Felicia leaned back until her head was in Sister Celeste's other hand, and then, to Christine's utter horror and amazement, Felicia's feet came floating to the surface. She lay horizontally in the water, supported—as Christine thought—only by the hand under her head. Then Sister Celeste removed her hand and held Felicia only by the fingertips to keep her from drifting downstream.

Was it a miracle or witchcraft? There was nothing in the universe more obvious to Christine than the fact that a body does not float, it sinks. Water is insubstantial and therefore cannot hold up a solid such as a person. If she needed further proof of what she so very well knew, wasn't she herself standing on the bottom this very moment?

"That's impossible!" she yelled, half angry, half frightened. It's a terrible thing to see something which cannot be.

Felicia came back to her feet laughing. "I felt exactly the same my first day."

"Can a log float?" asked Sister Celeste.

"Yes," Christine answered slowly.

"Even a very large, heavy log?"

"Yes."

"Then water must be pretty strong stuff."

Felicia added, "When the river floods it knocks down houses and moves heavy rocks."

Christine saw they had a point, but she still didn't understand. "If you put a piece of wood in the water, it won't stay down; it bobs to the surface. Why don't I bob to the surface right now?"

In answer, Sister Celeste dove into the deeper water, and immediately bobbed to the top.

Christine shook her head in disbelief. "No, I don't understand it. I'm still on the bottom."

Now Sister Celeste took Christine gently by the shoulders, "Yesterday you were still outside the Castle. You didn't know anything about our life here. But you took a chance on something you didn't understand. You let go of the world you knew and trusted the King. Did he let you down?"

"Oh, no! I should have come long ago."

"Yes," Sister Celeste smiled. "Now trust the water. It won't let you down either.

"Felicia showed you how to put your face in. Hold your breath, put your face in the water, and lift your feet off the bottom. Let's see if you go up or down. I'll keep hold of you."

Reluctantly Christine obeyed. She felt quite certain she would sink to the bottom, but hoped Sister Celeste would pull her out. To her utter astonishment she found herself floating in the water, legs dangling well above the sandy bottom.

She ran out of breath, and Sister Celeste pulled her back to her feet. She looked at them both as though the whole world had just turned topsy-turvy.

"It's true!" she gasped incredulously.

"Now watch the others for a while." Sister Celeste returned to the other girls. Christine watched with growing wonder and admiration as they dove, swam, somersaulted, and played in water over their heads. It was like a new world opening up. She was sorry when it was time to go.

"Hurry," Felicia urged, "the next class is my favorite."

Christine wondered how it could keep getting better. Back indoors they joined a large group heading to the Music Room. The first fifteen minutes was all scales, and Christine thought dourly that Felicia had a funny favorite. But after that the group sang songs, and Christine loved it. The one she liked best went like this.

> He gave me beauty for ashes,
> The oil of joy for mourning,
> The garment of praise
> For the spirit of heaviness,
> That I might be a tree of righteousness,
> The planting of the Lord,
> That he might be glorified.[1]

Christine felt that she could have gone on singing for hours. When they walked down the hall to the next class, she was still humming.

The students gathered here were a much smaller group, and Christine recognized faces she had seen in other classes. Godfrey and Lucius sat with the girls as part of a circle, at the head of which sat an elderly couple.

"That's Brother Uriah and Sister Alathea," Lucius whispered.

When everyone was seated, Brother Uriah looked around. His eyes fastened on Lucius.

"Tell me, Lucius, do you ever make mistakes?"

Lucius looked thoughtful, "Yes, I've learned that I am very prone to make mistakes." Everyone smiled at Lucius' admission.

"That is a very important lesson," Brother Uriah nodded. "I won't ask you what the mistakes are. But, Lucius, what do you do after you have made a mistake?"

"I try to think why I made it, and how I can keep from making it again."

"In other words, you learn from your mistake. That is a very good thing to do with mistakes. In this way mistakes can be very useful."

Sister Alathea spoke, "After a mistake, do you never feel discouraged?"

"Oh, yes, Sister. I feel disgusted at myself, and most of all, I wonder how the King can love me."

---

[1] Isaiah 61:3

"I'm glad you said 'how' and not 'if.' You do know then that the King loves you even when you make mistakes."

"Yes, I know."

"As for how, I can answer that. It is the King's nature to love.[2] His love does not depend on us or on our actions. It has nothing to do with our deserving. He loves us not because we are good, but because he is good."

Those words sank into Christine's heart, and she found herself repeating them over and over, so that she even missed the next part of the conversation. He loves me not because I am good, but because he is good.

What a burden this lifted from her heart. She did not have to do anything to keep the King's love. No doubt he would disapprove of her at times, but he would still love her. Oh, joy!

Brother Uriah was speaking to another student. "Sarah, what do you do when you make a mistake?"

"I pray about it, Brother Uriah. I ask the King to forgive me, and help me to avoid it in the future."

Brother Uriah turned back to Lucius. "What do you think of that answer, Lucius?"

Lucius bowed his head. "I guess it's better than mine. One of the mistakes I keep making is to try to work things out myself."

"Do you agree, Felicia? Is it better to pray, or to try to learn a lesson?"

"Isn't it better to do both? I mean—we need to pray for forgiveness and help, but part of the help is seeing why we fell and knowing how to get going again."

Sister Alathea spoke again, "I like the words you used, Felicia. A mistake is like a fall, and children do fall down, don't they? Especially when they are first learning to walk, but later too. Even grown-ups fall sometimes, but going on is the important thing.

"I have known some who were so discouraged after their mistakes that they left the Castle."

The students drew in their breath in dismay. To think of leaving the Castle! How could anyone do that?

"Please, may I?" a soft voice asked.

"Of course, Hannah," Brother Uriah encouraged her.

---

[2] 1 John 4:8, Romans 5:8

"When I make a mistake it shows me how silly and stupid I am, so I don't try to decide what to do. I always go talk to Uncle, and then I do whatever he says."

The group broke into applause. It was so simple and so obviously right, they felt they should all have thought of it.

Brother Uriah startled Christine by calling on Godfrey next. "Young man, you have been in the Castle less than a full day. Have you made a mistake yet?"

"Yes, sir, I have."

"How did you avoid the discouragement of falling so soon?"

"When I had talked with Uncle, he made me drink from the fountain near the chapel, and then I felt forgiven and strengthened."

Christine's mind flashed to the wonderful fountain in her own room. Yes, you seemed to find whatever you had need of there. What was this marvelous water?

"Nathan," Brother Uriah spoke to another student. "What is the worst thing you can do with a mistake?"

The boy's face showed confusion, but he answered readily, "The worst thing you can do is try to hide it."[3]

The class tittered a little, and Christine felt she was missing a joke.

"And why is that the worst thing you can do?"

"Because it doesn't work!" blurted Nathan. And now everyone laughed.

Felicia leaned over and whispered to Christine, "He was working in the bakery and ruined a batch of bread dough, so he dug a hole under a loose stone of the hearth and buried it."

Christine joined in the laughter as she pictured that warm dough rising and bulging and spreading over the hearth.

"Moreover," Sister Alathea added, "you find no forgiveness that way."

"Correct," Brother Uriah agreed. "And that brings us to our verse for today." He began to pass out scraps of parchment with writing on them. Christine looked at hers in dismay. But Brother Uriah smiled sympathetically, "Now read this, or have someone read it to you, and the King would be pleased if you would commit it to memory."

---

3 Proverbs 28:13

Christine turned hopefully to Felicia, but she was shaking her head in puzzlement. "Please read it, Naomi," she asked the woman next to her.

Naomi, a plump lady with a few gray hairs, smiled obligingly, and put her finger under the first word.

"If we confess our sins, he is faithful and just to forgive us our sins, and to cleanse us from all unrighteousness,"[4] she read.

Christine tingled with joy at these words. "Are they from the King's book?"

"Yes," Felicia assured her. "Everyday we have a verse to learn from the King's book."

The two girls practiced it with Naomi's help. Christine could see a correlation between the spoken words and the ones on paper. "If" and "we" were short. "Confess" was longer, and "unrighteousness" was the longest of all.

The students took turns saying the verse they had memorized from last Friday, and then it was time for the last class of the day.

---

[4] 1 John 1:9

Chapter X

Evening

Godfrey and Lucius went to the smithy to learn the art of the forge. Christine it seemed was destined to be a potter. For two hours she worked on a lump of clay, wedging, kneading, removing bits of grit, adding drops of water, readying it for the wheel. It was hard work and unrewarding. But Christine kept stealing glances at a girl nearby who was working at a wheel. The clay was alive in her hands, magically growing, expanding, becoming. Christine was captivated. If she could learn this, no amount of work would seem too great.

Nonetheless she was glad to clean up and join the others for supper. This day had been so different from any in her life, that the very novelty had been exhausting.

There was thick barley soup, flavored with lamb and carrots. Also there were very fresh greens with a bowl of clabber to use as dressing, and of course fresh bread, so common but so important.

Lucius told them that the next bell would be to summon them to evening prayers, and Christine immediately thought of the ordeal of the morning.

"Is it a whole hour again?" she exclaimed. Oh, I shouldn't have said that, she thought, will I never learn?

Felicia smiled sympathetically. "Vespers is for as long as you want to pray. Most people stay about a half hour."

"Though some leave so quickly," Lucius sneered, "that you wonder why they came at all."

"And some," said Felicia pointedly, "stay a great deal longer—even all night."

"Who could possibly pray all night?" Godfrey wondered.

"Sister Agatha and Brother Michael to mention two you would know.

"I don't really know how many do that or how often, but one night I couldn't sleep, so I went down to the Chapel, and there were several people there. I didn't see who they all were. For all I know some of those who leave early may have a good reason and may come back later after we've left."

"All right," Lucius conceded. "I get the message. Brother Uriah would say I was judging without knowing."

Like Godfrey, Christine had been appalled at the thought of all night prayer, but at the mention of Brother Michael's name, she remembered the things he had taught that day, and she found herself eager to try them out. "What happens after evening prayer?" she asked.

"Nothing really," Felicia answered. "You haven't been to my room. Why don't we go there, and we can work on your letters and on our verse?"

The chimes began then, and as they walked together to the Chapel, Christine began to feel happiness bubbling up inside her, so that she could hardly wait.

The Chapel seemed even fuller than in the morning. Now she saw several faces that were no longer strangers. Sister Celeste passed near them, and greeted Christine with a wink. Someone waved to them, and she recognized Nathan. She turned at a tap on her shoulder and saw Sister Tabitha. Naomi spotted them and came over and gave them a hug and a kiss. All the sweet associations of the day flowed back, and Christine began to feel the sense of belonging to a real family.

When she sank to her knees, she remembered Brother Michael's instructions. First she was to thank the King for being her father. That in itself was so overwhelming, that Christine said it over and over, each time sensing it more fully. Unconsciously she had raised her eyes and her hands soon followed.

"Father, my Father!" she cried, forgetting everything else in the ecstasy of this miracle. She wept for sheer joy.

Now the present, she thought, and she began to give thanks for Felicia, already as dear to her as a real sister. And then for all the others who were helping her. That Godfrey was with her, and a child of the King as well as she. Then she remembered the details of the day, and thanked him for each one.

What did Brother Michael say was next? The past—yes, she thanked him for the knight (wonder what his name was) who had saved them from the outlaws. And for Abigail and Eldred, and even for the minister, yes, and the village church. Wasn't it there she had first heard the stories of the Prince?

And thank you for father (poor father) and mother (wonder where she is) who taught me all they knew. Thank you for all the ways you provided for me before I even knew you.

And thank you—Christine was startled at herself—for the attack of the outlaws, for it was that which drove us to seek you.

Now to thank him for the future: what did it hold? Day after day in this wonderful place, learning, growing, enjoying. She had a conviction that it was going to get better and better.

Had she forgotten anything? Oh! Thank you for Uncle, and for stopping me this morning. Help me not to be so willful again, and not to vex Felicia.

So without even noticing, Christine had passed on to petitions.

Felicia was looking at her to see if she was ready to go. Could the half hour be gone already?

Almost like a guest leaving a party, Christine lingered for one more prayer: thank you, Lord, for a wonderful time.

The girls chattered the next hour away. Felicia's room was like Christine's but on the south side of the Castle, and the colors were all shades of blue, from royal to pale sky blue, so gay like Felicia herself. The wood was light-colored oak.

Christine saw the same letters on Felicia's fountain, and she asked Felicia to read them.

"They say, 'THE WORD.' It's one of the names of the Prince, but it also refers to the King's book. I don't know which it means, maybe both."

"Look," said Christine reaching in her pocket, "I have some charcoal. We can practice writing on the stone wall, and clean it up afterward."

Felicia smiled, “It’s hard at first to remember you’re a princess. You can’t really practice with charcoal.” As she spoke she walked toward her wardrobe. She lifted out a flat box and set it on Christine’s lap.

“Our Father, the King, wants you to learn. If you need anything to help you, you just ask for it.”[1]

Inside the box were parchment, quills, and paste for making ink. The box itself was a lap desk. Felicia mixed up a little ink and watched while Christine worked at her letters.

Then they practiced their verse. “If we confess our sins...” Christine was puzzled.

“Brother Uriah was talking about mistakes, and then he gave us this verse about sins. Are sins and mistakes the same?”

Felicia had to think about that one for a while. “Well, you’ve watched archery contests. To sin means to miss the mark. So all sins are mistakes. But I don’t think all mistakes are sins. Sometimes we don’t know a thing is wrong until after we’ve done it. Or...

“Like Nathan! He should have dipped a spoon in the salt box, but instead he picked up the salt box and tried to pour a little into the dough. He did it wrong, so it was a mistake—but not a sin, because he was inexperienced. When he spilled it, then he knew he was wrong, and he should have confessed. But when he tried to hide the dough that was a sin.”

“I guess I see,” said Christine, but she thought she would like to understand better. She would ask Brother Uriah when she got a chance.

On the way back to her room, Christine asked the question which had been on her mind since that morning, “Felicia, what did Uncle mean about you and Lucius?”

Felicia flushed and dropped her head. “Uncle knows everything. I like Lucius, and I think he likes me, but I haven’t said a word, not even to our Father.”

“Do you think Lucius will ask for your hand?”

“I wouldn’t think so. He’s rather young to think of marriage. But he is impulsive, so who knows.”

“But you’re not too young. If he doesn’t speak, someone else may ask for you.”

---

[1] Matthew 7:7-11, Philippians 4:19 and others

"Christine, I am perfectly content that the King choose my husband. Whomever he approves will be the best for me. Even if he chooses that I am not to marry, I am content."

"Oh, Felicia! Never to marry! Never to have a home and family! The King wouldn't do that to you!"

"Christine," Felicia's voice was stern, "What the King would or would not do is more than you or I know. I didn't mean that it was likely, but he is the King, and when I came to the Castle, I agreed to his dominion. He is all-wise, and I know he loves me. Whatever he chooses is best for me, and if I do his will I will be happy."

Christine found that a little difficult to accept. "Do you mean I am allowed to have no desires of my own?"

"You can't help having desires, but you have always made choices based on which things you desired most. That is, you gave up one thing you wanted to get something else you wanted more. Here at the Castle you give up all things you desire that you might have the one thing you desire most."

Christine looked so distressed at this, that Felicia tried to encourage her. "I don't mean that you're going to be sent away or something for resisting the King's will. It takes some time for your desires to start lining up with his.[2]

"It was probably easier for me, because I was thoroughly sick of having my own way. It was yielding to my own selfish desires that put that burden on me in the first place.

"You've probably never wanted anything really bad, so it's harder for you to see that your desires are wrong. But the King's promise is that if you will lay aside your own desires and seek him and do his will, you'll find happiness.[3] Can you do that?"

"I can try," Christine replied a bit grimly.

"That's good enough for now. I'll see you in the morning." Felicia kissed her goodnight, and the two girls embraced a long minute.

---

[2] Psalm 37:4

[3] Psalm 119:2 and others

Chapter XI

Rainy Day

The second day at the castle was rainy, but it began much easier for Christine. She found her own way to the Chapel and although she finished praying long before the hour was ended, she consoled herself by thinking on yesterday's activities and anticipating today's.

At breakfast they sat opposite the girl, Hannah, and Felicia introduced her.

"Hannah was my sponsor when I first came. She is the dearest person in the whole world!"

Christine felt a pang of jealousy, but she knew it was unworthy of her. And how could you help liking Hannah? She reminded Christine of a mouse, a very pretty little mouse. Her shy little smile seemed to beg you, "Please like me."

Sister Agatha gave Christine six new letters to learn today, but one was H which she had learned the night before. As soon as she had opportunity, Christine printed out the letters from the fountain and showed them to Sister Agatha.

Her teacher's praise was lavish, and Christine glowed with the pride of accomplishment.

She spun happily through the next two hours, pausing occasionally to instruct Felicia.

She was not even too disappointed that Brother Michael's class had to be held indoors because of the slight drizzle.

"This is perfect weather," he told his pupils, "to discuss PRAISE.

"Many people do not understand the difference between thanksgiving and praise. But praise is truest worship, exalting our Lord for who he is, not just for what he has done for us."

Christine wasn't sure if it was what Brother Michael said or something about himself, but she drank in every word with eagerness. He made her look forward to prayer time.

"In praise we acknowledge his goodness, his greatness. The Prince has done all things well, and we give him our undivided devotion."

Christine remembered the pleasant glow she had felt that morning when Sister Agatha had praised her. Was it like that for the King?

"But do not think," it was as though Brother Michael read her mind, "that the King commands us to praise him in order to boost his own ego. No, it is for our own sake that he desires our praise. Nothing draws us so near to him as our sincere worship. And the more we admire his goodness, the more we are inspired to become like him.

"Praise lifts us up to his throne, and gladdens our hearts as well as his. It is always of us he is thinking. He desires our love in order that we might know his joy."

Christine felt her heart overflowing with praise, and she was glad when Brother Michael took the last few minutes of the hour to let them practice what they had been learning.

As they dismissed, Godfrey offered to help Lucius in the stables, and Christine gladly volunteered to work with Felicia in the kitchen, but they were told that they would have to wait until next Sunday when they could sign up for chores. They had come too late and missed the sign-up this week.

When Christine went to her room at quiet time, she found the lap desk she had requested from Sister Agatha. She was not tired today, and spent the hour with the quill, and talking to the King. Praise and thanksgiving just seemed to flow from her. She watched the rain as though it were the loveliest sight in all the world. The bells rang just as she was finished copying her memory verse for the third time.

Brother Philip held class inside the stable, drilling them on the nomenclature of the horse. Christine's head buzzed with withers and pasterns and stifles. As Brother Philip moved from stem to stern citing mysterious cannons, barrels, fetlocks, etc., he brought a laugh by announcing with all solemnity that this was the tail.

It was a disappointment to have swimming canceled, but music made up for it. Brother Jude must have been talking to Brother Michael, for today they learned this song.

> Enter into his gates with thanksgiving,
> And into his courts with praise:
> Be thankful unto him,
> And bless his name.
> For the Lord is good;
> His mercy is everlasting;
> And his truth endureth to all generations.[1]

Who would get called on today, Christine wondered as she took her seat in Bible class. Brother Uriah's eyes looked as though he could see right through you.

"Naomi," he began, "aren't you sad it had to rain today?"

"Well, not sad really, but I do enjoy when we can have Brother Michael's class in the garden."

"What about you, Christine?"

"Yes, sir!" she jumped half out of her skin.

"Did this rain spoil any of your plans?"

"No, sir! Oh, I did want to have swimming class, but there's always tomorrow."

"That's a wise attitude, but what if it rains tomorrow?"

Christine looked perplexed, "It will have to stop raining sometime."

Much to Christine's dismay, the other students seemed to find that answer amusing, but it was friendly laughter.

"That's very true!" Brother Uriah conceded, his eyes twinkling, "and meanwhile you are learning patience. I'm glad the rain has proved only a minor irritation. Lucius, where did the rain come from?"

"His Majesty sent it, I suppose."

"You suppose correctly. And did he send it just to annoy all you students who wanted to go swimming and horseback riding?"

"Oh, no!" the group responded at once

"Then why did he send it? ...Felicia?"

---

[1] Psalm 100:4, 5

"He must have known it was best."

Nathan volunteered, "We've had a long spell of hot, dry weather. The gardens and pastures needed it badly." The others nodded agreement.

"Now what is the lesson we draw from this?"

Naomi was ready, "I've said it to my children often: things we don't like are usually good for us."

"Exactly right," said Sister Alathea. "How many of you have thanked the King for sending this rain?"

Nathan had the satisfaction of being the only one to raise his hand.

"Good, Nathan, Brother Michael would be proud of you."

He looked a bit sheepish, "Well, it was because I'm working in the garden this week, and Sister Chloe was praising the Lord for the rain."

"Now," Brother Uriah continued, "let's do some more supposing. Suppose, instead of a nice gentle rain, this had been a hail storm and beat the garden flat."

The class looked rather thunderstruck themselves at this idea.

But Godfrey spoke up, "I'd thank the Lord that the wheat crop is already in."

"Well thought of! Even in calamity there is usually something to be thankful for if we open our eyes.

"So Godfrey, have you seen then what a hailstorm can do to ripe wheat?"

"Yes, sir! I remember four years ago, we had a hailstorm that destroyed the whole wheat crop. There was famine that year."

"I should think we all remember that. Well, Felicia, was that for the best?"

Felicia squirmed uncomfortably, "Maybe when people were hungry, some of them sought the Lord?"

Brother Uriah nodded. "I never saw as many people come to the Castle in good times as in war or famine or pestilence."

But Sister Alathea shook her head, "But I never saw so many turn back when times were good again. When people come for physical reasons, they don't usually stay."

"Too true, my dear, but nevertheless, some do stay."

Christine suddenly thought of something. "Maybe the famine was punishment for our wickedness. Isn't there a story like that in the

King's book?"[2]

"Yes, there are several such stories. In fact, the King promises to punish wickedness. So now we have two theories, anyone else? Yes, Hannah."

"Talking about hail made me think of a story I read in the King's book. I didn't really understand it that well, but in this story the chief of the outlaws sent a storm that killed flocks and servants and the children of a righteous man.[3] Does that have anything to do with what we're talking about?"

"Indeed it does. Now this was not to turn Job to the Lord, because he was already serving the Lord, and it was not to punish Job—that was what his friends thought—so it doesn't fit the two reasons we have suggested. Why did the King let this storm of trouble come on Job?"

"Wait, sir," Lucius interrupted. "Hannah said it was the outlaw chief who sent the storm."

"Oh, does that make a difference?"

"Certainly—doesn't it?"

"Well, this has been a very interesting discussion. I'm afraid we've opened more subjects than we can handle this hour. We'd better pursue them again tomorrow.

"The truth I am wanting us to see today, is that bad things happen to people, even to good people, and when bad things happen to us, what should we do?"

With this he began to hand around the little scraps of parchment.

"Can you read it?" Christine nudged Felicia anxiously.

"Yes, this one's easy. It says, 'In every thing give thanks: for this is the will of God in Christ Jesus...'" Felicia hesitated to sound the word, "'concerning you.' "[4] She finished triumphantly.

As they were leaving Bible class, a page approached, and to her surprise, singled out Christine.

"Princess Christine, you have a visitor. You are to accompany me to the courtyard."

Christine turned to Felicia open-mouthed. "Who?...What?"

Felicia just shrugged, "Let's go find out."

---

[2] 1 Samuel 12:15-18

[3] Job 1:12-22

[4] I Thessalonians 5:18

Christine was happy indeed for Felicia's company. The page led them to the open courtyard where Christine had never yet been. She looked around for the mysterious visitor and saw to her amazement—Lily.

The cow was standing placidly cropping grass, and only when Christine ran up and threw her arms around her neck, did she look up and acknowledge her mistress.

But Felicia had flown past the cow and was embracing someone else. For the first time Christine saw Abigail, and realized that she, not Lily, was the visitor.

Approaching with some embarrassment, she thanked Abigail warmly for bringing the cow, "I had been worried about her."

Felicia laughed, "That's an understatement! I almost had to lock you up to keep you from running home to her."

"It's good that you didn't," Abigail smiled at Christine. "You would have found her missing and been even more worried. You see the King had everything under control.

"Eldred and I went to see you Sunday afternoon. I was never so upset as when we found your father dead and the house ransacked. I feared the outlaws had carried off you and your brother.

"But we started using our heads, the body was covered, your clothes were taken. We decided you had left of your own volition after the outlaws had gone.

"Eldred said that if you had come to the village looking for help, we would have met you. Then I knew you must have come to the Castle!"

At this she stopped to give Christine a big hug. "I am so happy," she told her, and to prove it, began to cry.

"And how is my Ida?" she turned back to Felicia.

The name sounded strange to both the girls, suggesting something far in the past, almost forgotten.

"I'm Felicia now. And I'm just wonderful thanks to you. And I'm Christine's sponsor."

"So...I didn't know your new names. How beautifully they fit you, and how wonderful you both look. My cup's running over !"[5]

Christine hated to change the subject, but she had to know. "Abigail, what about my father's body?"

---

[5] Psalm 23:5

"Don't fret, child. Eldred and I managed to get it into the cart and took it to the church. We buried it yesterday. That's why I didn't get here until today."

"And you've been milking Lily for me. I don't know how to thank you."

"Just stay here and grow and serve the King with your whole heart. That's all I could desire, and far more than I deserve for the little service I've done.

"Oh, and the wheat you left behind, Eldred took the liberty of taking it to the church. We knew you wouldn't be needing it. I'll go back tomorrow for the chickens. Do you want them brought here?"

"Godfrey—that's Tristram—will be so glad to hear this news. Please keep the chickens for your trouble. It's the least we can do for you. And if you can salvage some of the garden by all means do."

"I'm the one who should do something for you," Felicia urged, "If it weren't for you I would never have reached here."

"Sweet girls," Abigail shook her head, "you still have so much to learn. But someday if you persevere you will know just how I feel today. My service is rewarded by His Majesty; there is nothing anyone can add to that. But I will tell Eldred of your gratitude. We both love you and Tris...Godfrey too." She dabbed her eyes again, and composed herself.

"Now—how are you finding life in the Castle? Aren't you glad you came?"

Christine laughed, "It's too good to be true. I'm a princess! Can you imagine? And I'm learning all kinds of things, and everyone here is so good—especially Uncle. Was he here when you were here?"

"Gracious, child! Uncle has always been here. Don't you know who he is?"

"Isn't he sort of the chief steward or high chamberlain or something?"

"Well, he is something like that, but he's a great deal more. We call him Uncle because he is the King's own brother, the great Archduke Paraclete, who conducts all the King's business throughout the world."[6]

Christine's mouth dropped open in awe. She had sensed his greatness, but..."but he's so comfortable to be with!" she exclaimed

---

[6] John 14:16, 17, 26; 15:26; 16:7-15

aloud.

"As long as your heart is toward the King you will find him that way. Should you ever turn aside, you will find him a most uncomfortable companion."

"Oh, I never will!" Christine was sure.

"Amen!" Abigail agreed fervently, "but don't be overconfident. That's when you are most apt to fall."[7]

Christine felt rebuked. She had so much to learn. "I'll be careful," she promised.

"And I'll be praying for you. Now I must start back if I'm to get home tonight."

"Do come to see us again," Felicia begged.

"If I have any errand here I will be sure to ask for you. When you are able to leave the Castle, try to come and see me."

"We will!" they promised.

Abigail went back to the outside world, and Christine wondered why the old couple would live out there when they could have lived in the Castle. Then she remembered Felicia's words, "If it weren't for you..."

"I'm going to have to run," Felicia was saying. "I'm really late for choir practice. Can you find your way to the pottery shop?"

"I'll be all right," Christine wasn't thinking about pottery. She caressed Lily, and examined her. The cow was none the worse for her move. To think I let myself get so upset, Christine marveled. The King had her all taken care of before I even remembered her.[8]

---

[7] I Corinthians 10:12

[8] Isaiah 65:24

Chapter XII

Red Circles

It took Christine some time to locate the byre and get Lily settled in. She had to ask questions of strangers, a thing she had never done before, but it was easy here at the Castle. She had met so many new people in the last few days, and everyone was friendly.

When she was ready to leave, the milkmaids were just coming, so she stayed and watched them. She would have liked to milk herself, but the girls would not surrender their pails.

Christine followed them back to the kitchen. It was nearly supper time now, and she was eager to see Godfrey, so she went to wait in the dining hall.

She had scarcely sat down, when someone shouted at her. "Get away from there!"

She jumped up looking around. An elderly gentleman carrying a basket of greens was shaking a finger at her. "Don't you see that red circle? Hasn't anyone told you to keep away from those?"

Christine felt the blood rising in her face. It was the first cross voice she had heard since she came to the Castle. If she had done something wrong, it was entirely unintentional. She had seen the red circles painted in the dining hall; she had seen others at various places including just now in the courtyard. But there were so many new and strange things that she had not given any thought to them.

The old gentleman had gone on into the kitchen. Christine chose a different spot to wait, but her scalp was still tingling.

Presently the room began to fill, and she noted how everyone avoided the red circles. Then she saw Felicia and Hannah enter, arm in arm, and she hurried to them. "Would you please tell me what I did wrong," her voice was edged with resentment. "I just got yelled at for sitting in one of those red circles."

The two girls turned pale, and Hannah looked inquiringly at Felicia, "Didn't you tell her?"

"I forgot. I..." she seemed to be thinking of an excuse, but she finished honestly, "I just forgot."

Hannah shook her head, "Well, thank the Lord nothing happened."

Godfrey and Lucius walked up at this moment. Christine turned on them. "Godfrey, do you know about the red circles?"

"Of course, Lucius told me the first evening we were here."

Felicia hung her head in shame. She was very near tears. Compassion for her friend forged to the front of Christine's emotions. "Oh, fiddle!" she exclaimed. "What's all this fuss about anyway?"

"Don't you know?" wondered Lucius, and he too looked accusingly at Felicia.

Godfrey shouted angrily, "She could have been killed!"

Poor Felicia began to sob.

Hannah put a comforting arm around her, "Everybody makes mistakes, and nothing happened. The King is gracious. He was watching over her."

"But I knew better," Felicia looked up at Christine, "so it was a sin to forget, just as we talked about last night. Please forgive me."

"Somebody tell me what this is all about," Christine cried in exasperation.

Godfrey took her arm and led her near one of the red ovals. Pointing up he asked, "What do you see?"

"A window." There were seven high, narrow windows to let light in.

"That is the outside wall of the Castle, and we are on the ground floor here. This red oval describes the trajectory of an arrow if shot through that window."

Christine did not see immediately. Yes, the circles did correspond to the windows. "An arrow?"

"The outlaws have some fine archers. They sometimes stand in the fringe of the wood and shoot arrows at the Castle. When an arrow comes through that window, it will land inside this red circle."

Christine was horrified, "Do you mean we're not safe from the outlaws, even in here?"

"We're perfectly safe as long as we're careful. The King ordered these circles painted, and there's no excuse for anyone to be hurt."

"Unless they're not taught." Felicia had followed along and was wiping her eyes.

Christine was still distressed. "Why doesn't the King brick up the windows? Why doesn't he cut down the woods?"

Lucius tried to calm her, "We need the windows for light. The watchmen on the walls shoot back when an outlaw ventures close. There's no danger if we walk circumspectly."

Christine sat to the table with the others, but her joy had flown. Felicia had to remind her to tell Godfrey of Abigail's visit, and even his rejoicing failed to restore her to good spirits. She stirred the cabbage leaves in her soup, ignoring the delicious aroma. To repeated inquiries from the others, she finally answered, "Leave me alone."

Her new friends respected her wish, but Godfrey took her out in the hall for some private counselling.

"How long did you sit in that red circle?" he queried sarcastically. "You seem to have been wounded by an arrow that the rest of us can't see."

"Maybe if you had had such a narrow escape, you wouldn't feel so gay either."

"Or maybe I'd be praising the King and thanking him for his protection."

Christine pulled away from him, "I'm going to my room."

"It's almost time for evening prayers," Godfrey called after her.

"Tell them I'm sick!" Christine threw back.

It was true. Christine felt sick, though she couldn't quite locate the illness. Her head ached a little, but not that much. Her stomach felt a little upset, but that wasn't what ailed her.

She hurried to her room as to a refuge, and flung through the door. Her window stood open, and she looked expectantly for a red circle on the floor. There was none. There never had been. She remembered how she had stood gazing out that window, and now she wondered why she had sensed no danger.

Cautiously she approached it, and glimpsed out at the vista

below. She was far too high for an arrow to reach. She had not been in any danger, nor was she now. Then why did she feel that cold chill of fear?

She closed the shutters and barred them. Immediately her conscience smote her. She should not have done that. It was not reality but fevered fancy against which she had shut the window.

I must open it, she told herself. I must not be afraid. But she turned instead and lay down on her bed. I need a drink from the fountain. That will give me courage. But she did not move. The vespers' bell rang, and still she lay there.

For a long time she lay quite still, and the dim light in her room grew even dimmer. Through her mind raced the old stories, the old fears. Then she saw again her father confronting the outlaws, saw him die. And then she saw herself standing in the cottage with her brother, and her own words came back to her—"Don't be afraid."

She sat up. Had she learned nothing?

Just then there was a knock at her door. It would be Felicia, and she didn't want to see her right now. "Go away!" she shouted. But the petulant sound of her own voice shocked her. Who had ever been better to her than Felicia?

Christine jumped from the bed and ran to the door crying, "Wait! Come back!"

She jerked the door open, but it was not Felicia. It was Uncle. She had never felt so glad to see anyone. She dropped to her knees and threw her arms around his legs. He seemed not the least surprised, and patted her lovingly.

Hot tears rolled down Christine's cheeks, and it was some moments before she could look Uncle in the face.

"I'm so glad you're here. I've been being very bad, haven't I?"

Uncle smiled ever so gently. "Well, I have a report from Sister Amelia that you weren't in pottery class."

"Oh, that," Christine dismissed it. "I was taking care of Lily." Then the color began to rise as she realized that was only a half-truth. And anyway, Uncle would say she hadn't been told to take care of Lily. "I guess I had time to get back to class," she confessed. "I just didn't want to."

"And one thing leads to another," Uncle said sympathetically. "If you had gone to pottery class where you belonged, you wouldn't have been sitting alone in the dining hall, would you?"

"N..No," stammered Christine, seeing the connection for the first time. "You mean if I had been struck by an arrow, it would have been *my* fault,—not Felicia's?"

"Felicia loves you. She would not let you be hurt for all the world. You have made her suffer terribly."

"Oh, Uncle, I'm sorry. I did feel sorry for her at first, but something came over me."

"You know what came over you. You've experienced it often enough."

"Yes, it was fear. I'm so ashamed. What can I do?"

"You know that too."

Without further hesitation, Christine rose and went to the fountain. She drank deeply, and then, flinging her head back, she went to the window and opened it. Off to the left the sun was setting. It peeked under the clouds that had obscured it all day, and the whole countryside was golden in its rays. Christine laughed aloud. She couldn't imagine what had been wrong with her—then she knew. It had started with disobedience. She should have gone to pottery class when Abigail left. It seemed such a small thing, but she knew better now. Except for the King's grace, it could have cost her her life.

Christine ran to the Chapel. She had apologies to make.

Chapter XIII

The Spirit of Intercession

Christine awoke a few minutes before the chimes. She thought, this is Wednesday. I fell down on Monday and on Tuesday. Oh, please, Lord, let me do better today.

The day turned out sunny, though yesterday's gloom had left a subtle change, and you knew now that summer was nearing its end.

Christine was given seven letters to learn this morning, but O and R were already familiar to her. What was puzzling her was that her memory verses contained so few letters she recognized. Sister Agatha laughed at her question.

"I've never had a pupil in such a hurry. Those are lower-case letters. There are two ways to write each letter, and so far you have been learning capitals. I wasn't going to give you lower-case until next week, but here." Sitting down with a large piece of parchment, Sister Agatha carefully printed each of the letters Christine had learned, and behind each she put another.

"This is capital A and small a, capital B and small b, and so on. Bring this back tomorrow, and I'll put the last eight letters down. If you can learn all of these by Monday, I'll start you on reading."

Christine fairly danced for joy. To think these magical symbols would soon have meaning for her.

She had just sat down to spin when Sister Tabitha came to her. "Christine, you are here to learn, and you already know how to spin.

Come with me."

Down many stairs and around many passages they went, to a room in the lower level of the Castle. Here steam arose from vats and a number of men and women were at work. Sister Tabitha gave Christine an apron and led her to where large irregular mats hung drying. "My dear, you are going to learn to make felt."

Christine was disappointed. This was not the cheery, chatty workroom she had just left. But she remembered her resolve. Thank you, Lord, she prayed, for the chance to learn something useful. And then because she did not really feel thankful, she added, and help me to like it.

Almost at once she received a partial answer, because Sister Tabitha left her with a good friend. "Naomi, will you help Christine to get started?"

The next two hours Christine spent scraping hides that had been steamed to loosen the hair. The hides, Naomi told her, would then go to the tanner, but the fur was what was wanted in making felt.

They had to rinse off and dry with a towel before they went on to the garden for prayer class.

The ground was still damp, so the students sat on stones today, near the river bank.

Brother Michael, earnest as always, told them they would be considering prayers of repentance today. Christine thought ruefully that she was a step ahead of him.

He took up a large rock and set it between himself and Godfrey who was nearest to him. "Our sin is like this rock. It comes between us and our Father.[1] When we wish to approach him, we stumble. If we continue in sin..." he added more rocks to the pile, "our communication becomes difficult and at last will become impossible. Repentance clears away the obstacle." And with one heave of his muscular arms Brother Michael swept aside the whole pile. "Repentance is the necessary first step in our prayers, so that we may enter boldly into the King's presence.[2]

"And what is repentance? Just being sorry? No, to repent is to turn. We must turn away from our sin and turn toward the King."

That hour always seemed the briefest of the day to Christine.

---

1 John 14:23; 15:6

2 I John 3:21, 22

Then right afterward she heard some news that made the rest of the day drag.

"A man came to the Castle this morning," Felicia told her. "There'll be a Celebration tonight!"

"How wonderful! Who was he? Do you know his name?"

Felicia laughed, "He'll have a new one tonight. But it's not quite as wonderful as it should be."

"What do you mean?"

"He brought his family with him, but when he got to the door they wouldn't come in. He begged them, but his wife wouldn't come, and the children stayed with her."

"Can't he just order them? The father is the boss isn't he?"

"No, no one can be forced to come in. Uncle even went out and pleaded with them, but it didn't seem to do any good. The wife said she was going to wait for her husband until he came to his senses."

"Is there anything we can do?" Christine wondered.

"Certainly, we can pray."

When Christine went to her room after lunch, that was what she planned to do, but first she looked out her window, to see if there was any sign of them. Sure enough, she saw a small girl running about on the lawn below. Christine's heart went out to her. She waved, but the little girl did not look up.

Going back to her fountain, Christine knelt down and began to pray for the child she had just seen. She felt dry, so she drank a little, and returned to prayer. She prayed for the whole family, but mostly she thought of that little girl. She identified with her, and inside, Christine could feel how much the King loved that little girl and wanted to open his arms to her. Christine found herself praying as never before. She forgot the passage of time; she forgot everything but that child. Words poured from her lips so rapidly, it seemed to her that someone else was doing the praying, and she did not even know what she said.[3] But she heaved great sighs and finally sobs, and felt that she had never wanted anything so badly as she wanted that child to find her way to the door.

When she heard the chimes she could not believe she had prayed an entire hour. To her even greater amazement she found that Uncle was kneeling beside her. She had not realized when he came, but she knew now it was he who had been praying with her.

---

[3] Romans 8:26

"Try again," he suggested. She stepped quickly back to the window but saw no one now. Anxiously she leaned out, trying to get a glimpse. Far to her right, in the shadow of the wall, she saw the whole family seated on the ground. The mother had her head down, and there was a baby in her lap. Some other children were napping, piled together so that Christine was not sure if there were two or three, but one was sitting a little apart from the others, and Christine thought it was the first child she had seen. She waved again, and this time the girl saw her, and jumping up, trotted closer. Christine doubted her voice would carry that far, but she cupped her hands and yelled, "Hello!"

The child must have heard, for she waved her hand. Christine shouted again. "Come in the Castle. You must be hungry. Come have something to eat."

Now there seemed to be some conversation between the girl and her mother. Christine could not hear anything, but she guessed the mother would not respond favorably.

The girl looked up again. "Please," shouted Christine. "The King loves you. He will be good to you."

The child went running back toward her mother, but she ran beyond her, out of Christine's field of vision. Had she entered the door? She would ask Uncle...but he was gone. Christine wished she knew the way to the little door where she had entered the first night, but she had no idea. Anyway it was time for riding class. Inwardly she rebelled. She wanted to find out about the child. She did not want to hop on and off a horse. But she had learned her lesson, so she hurried out to the stables.

Today was even worse. She had to learn to bridle the horse. The placid mare stood with her teeth clenched while Christine tried to arrange the parts of the bridle to hang in the right directions. The bridle was as bad as a puzzle, and how could she get the bit in, when the horse wouldn't cooperate?

Christine normally loved animals, but she was beginning to have some very unfriendly feelings toward this one. The crowning insult was the ease with which Brother Philip slipped the bridle on and off.

Swimming class was a bore also. She spent the whole time hanging onto a branch, letting her body float out behind her, and turning her face in and out of the water.

At music she finally heard the news she had been waiting for. Brother Jude announced that the little girl had entered the Castle. The whole classroom was in a momentary hubbub as the students rejoiced.

Christine and Felicia hugged each other in glee. How they sang today!

"My soul doth magnify the Lord,
And my spirit hath rejoiced
In God my Saviour.
For he that is mighty
Hath done to me great things;
And holy is his name."[4]

It was hard to settle down for Bible class. Christine wondered where Hannah was.

"Yesterday," Brother Uriah began, "we asked the question, why does the King allow bad things to happen? The first answer suggested was that these things may cause persons to come to him.

"Godfrey, do you think a bad happening might influence someone to come to the Castle?"

"Yes, sir, I guess that was what brought my sister and me, and I hope that doesn't mean we would leave as Sister Alathea thought."

"So do you blame the King for what happened then? Did he do this to you in order to save your souls?"

"It was the outlaws who did it. I guess I don't know what the King had to do with it...unless it's that he hasn't destroyed the outlaws, as I've heard some say he should."

"So the outlaws did you harm, but the King didn't stop them, and it turned out to be for your good."

"Oh, I remember!" cried Naomi. "In the story of Joseph, he told his brothers—you meant it for evil, but God meant it for good."[5]

"And," added Sister Alathea, "at another time he told his brothers, 'It was not you that sent me hither, but God.'"[6]

Godfrey shook his head, "I don't understand."

"This is what you asked me," said Lucius, "whether it mattered if the outlaws or the King sent the storm."

"And does it?"

Lucius shrugged his shoulders.

"Maybe it will help us to look at the opposite side. Felicia told us

---

4 Luke 1:46, 47, 49

5 Genesis 50:16-21

6 Genesis 45:4-8

once that certain persons had helped her. Was that the King helping?"

"Oh, yes," Felicia answered quickly. "I thank the King for sending them to help me."

"Then if persons hurt you, should you thank the King for that too?"

The students looked awkwardly at one another. Christine offered doubtfully, "That was the meaning of our verse, wasn't it? 'In every thing give thanks: for this is the will of God in Christ Jesus concerning you.'"

"Wait a minute," protested Nathan. "It sounds as if the outlaws are working for the King!"

Sister Alathea smiled quietly, "What is the worst thing the outlaws ever did?"

Sarah replied quickly, "They crucified the Prince!"

"And what is the most wonderful thing that ever happened?"

The students looked at one another, "The Prince died for our sins."

"Are you beginning to understand?" asked Sister Alathea.

"No," Lucius replied flatly.

"Let's go back a bit," Brother Uriah suggested. "If you joined the outlaws, then who would be to blame for whatever happened to you?"

"It would be your own fault!" Sarah declared firmly.

"Or if you broke the King's laws in some other way?"

Felicia nodded, "Then you would have only yourself to blame."

"Not the King?"

"No, certainly not," they all agreed.

"And not the outlaws?"

"Well," Godfrey hedged a little, "they might have coaxed you, the way they did Eve."

"Then was Eve innocent?"

"No, I guess it's still your decision."

"All right, so we've established that bad things sometimes happen to us because we cause them to happen. These are the mistakes we talked about Monday. But as Lucius taught us, we can turn these to our good by learning from them.

"Now let's get back to things that we don't cause, like storms. We've been omitting a very important distinction. Do the same rules apply for the children of the King as for those outside the Castle?"

This caused some head-scratching. Brother Uriah was already

passing out the Scripture verses. "Think about it for tomorrow. Our time's up."

Christine wished she could read this without help. But wait, there was the word "God" just as in yesterday's verse. And those words "and" and "we," she'd seen them before. Eagerly she picked out "to" three times and "for" and "the." I'm learning to read, she thought excitedly.

It was a bit disappointing that Felicia had to ask Naomi for help again.

"And we know that all things work together for good to them that love God, to them who are the called according to his purpose."[7]

That was a long one, but Christine found the idea so intriguing, that she memorized it easily.

This day was the best so far, Christine thought, but her steps dragged going to the pottery shop. She still had one more apology to make for yesterday.

"Sister Amelia, I'm sorry for missing class yesterday. I didn't realize classes were compulsory, so I let myself be distracted. It won't happen again." She said it all in one breath, and was glad to have it over with.

"Classes are not compulsory, Christine. Everything at the Castle is voluntary, and everything is for your benefit. If you don't want to learn, no one is going to make you."

"I do want to learn. I wouldn't miss prayer or Bible class for anything. I just didn't think one day would make much difference in pottery."

Sister Amelia lifted one eyebrow very high. "Well, it's your decision if you want to miss, but your clay has dried out, and you'll have to start and work it up again."

Christine's mouth opened in protest. All that work, all to be done over?

For the next two hours she poured her fury into pounding the clay. Every time she slammed it onto the board, she muttered, "It's my own fault." She beat it with both fists, and finally had the satisfaction of seeing it become even more workable than on the previous day. When time was up, and she was putting it away, Sister Amelia picked it up and kneaded it.

---

[7] Romans 8:28

"That's very good, Christine. It will be ready to go on the wheel tomorrow."

"Yes, Ma'm. I'll be here."

Chapter XIV

Learning by Error

Christine met Felicia in the hall near the music room.

"We were a little late," she explained. "We have a new song for the Celebration tonight."

"Sing it for me," Christine urged. Felicia didn't need much coaxing.

> "May the Father of Glory give unto you
> The spirit of wisdom
> And revelation in the knowledge of Him:
> That ye may know what is the hope of his calling,
> And what the riches of the glory
> Of his inheritance in the saints,
> And what is the exceeding greatness
> Of his power to usward who believe."[1]

"Oh, I like it. Teach it to me."

"Later. We have to get ready. Leave your hair down the way I did it the first night you were here. You have the prettiest hair."

"Silly, yours is just as pretty. It's like silver."

"Well, then yours is gold, and it's much longer and thicker than mine."

---

[1] Ephesians 1:17-19

Christine laughed. "Can I wear that white silk again?"

"Sure, wear whatever you like. Can you find your way to the Great Hall?"

"I suppose all the traffic will be flowing that way."

"Right, see you there then."

Christine had never had much opportunity before for primping. She brushed out her hair, and it fell in soft ripples from having been braided. There were several dresses fine enough for the occasion, and she decided to wear a light-weight, soft green one, and keep the white silk for Sunday. When she had put it on, she went to the fountain to look at her reflection, and she liked what she saw, but she suddenly realized she hadn't had a drink since quiet time. She drank thirstily.

Her reflection changed subtly. Christine decided she was no prettier than Felicia or even Hannah. Then she thought of Sister Celeste. She didn't have beautiful hair, but she was the prettiest girl Christine had ever seen. It was poise again she was admiring. Sister Celeste was so sure of herself—or maybe of her Lord.

Christine splashed her hand in the water to erase her image. The water felt so refreshing that she decided to wash up again, although she had done so after pottery class.

When she finished, all her vanity had disappeared, and she had remembered what the Celebration was about. She could hardly wait to see the newcomers, to hear the choir, and would there be that other singing again? Christine went flying down the halls.

The boys were waiting at the door of the Great Hall, but even when Godfrey turned to Lucius and said, "Isn't she the prettiest girl in the whole Castle?" it didn't puff her up.

"You're sweet," she replied.

And Lucius only commented, "It's a fierce competition, I'd say."

Felicia was coming, and she was pretty enough to satisfy anyone. Her dress matched her blue eyes, and Lucius had forgotten Christine existed.

As they went into the Hall, Godfrey pressed something into Christine's hand. When she had sat down, she looked at it.

"A pothook?" she was puzzled. What did she want with a pothook? She didn't even have a pot.

"Do you like it?" he asked. For a minute she wondered if he was teasing, then she remembered he was working in the smithy.

"Did you make it?" she exclaimed.

Godfrey glowed as he nodded, “This afternoon.”

“It’s wonderful,” she enthused. “May I keep it?” She turned it over and examined it with admiration. It was a very ordinary pothook, but Christine sensed how special it was to her brother.

“Here comes Uncle,” Felicia whispered.

Christine thought how different it was to be a part of the family, than to look on in bewilderment as she had just three nights ago.

The trumpet sounded, and Uncle announced, “I give you the Princess Amanda and the Prince Hugh!”

Christine joined in the applause so vigorously her hands hurt. It did not matter that the new prince looked a bit awkward in his fine clothes or that the new princess was rather thin and underfed. Those things would soon change.

Then Uncle was reciting the formula she had heard at her own coronation. The adoption certificates were placed in nervous hands. He was telling them, “Do not forget...” and Christine was surprised to find she *had* forgotten. She had been so excited that first night, but now she listened carefully and promised herself she would remember.

With the whole crowd she leaped to her feet and cheered the new members of her family. And she had helped a little to bring this new princess to them.

She hadn’t noticed Felicia slip away, but now the choir began, and Christine saw her friend singing.

The food and entertainment were splendid, but tonight she realized that the best part of the Celebration was the feeling that they were all brothers and sisters and the King was their father.

Her eyes kept going back to the pair on the dais. “Did I look that scared?” she asked Felicia.

“You looked a little shy and amazed,” she answered. “Everyone does. But Prince Hugh looks distressed. I’m afraid he’s still thinking about his wife and children outside.”

“Do you suppose they’re still sitting there?”

“They were the last I heard, and that was at dusk, so they must be.”

Christine watched with sympathy. No wonder the poor man had no appetite for the feast when his family was going hungry. But, she noted happily, little Amanda seemed to be enjoying herself.

“Felicia,” she suddenly had an idea, “what if we took a plate of food out to them? Maybe we could even persuade them to come in.”

Felicia frowned. "It *sounds* like a good idea," she said slowly. "But I don't know. I guess we can ask Uncle."

Christine approached Uncle eagerly, remembering how he had encouraged her that afternoon. He listened quietly to her request and then just looked at her a long time.

At last he put an arm around her shoulders. "My daughter, the King is pleased at your concern for those outside the Castle. You did very well this afternoon. This plan of yours shows a good heart, but it cannot work. I could forbid it, and I know you would obey me, but you would still think you should have gone. Sometimes it is better to find things out for yourself. You will not be exposed to any great danger as long as you are within a few feet of the Castle. You may go if you wish."

Christine's enthusiasm suffered a severe set-back at this answer, and Felicia quickly replied, "Oh, no, sir! Not as we wish, but as you wish."

Uncle rewarded Felicia with a warm smile, but told her, "It is my wish that you accompany your friend, so that no harm may come to her."

The girls walked slowly toward the kitchen to pick up plates of food. Christine was thinking of her resolve not to do anything wrong today, and she was so nearly through the day, she didn't want to ruin it now. "I don't understand!" she blurted. "Was he telling us to go or not to go?"

"It was a little ambiguous," Felicia agreed, "but I think it's what Lucius said the other day."

"What?"

"That we're making a mistake, but we're going to learn from it."

Christine sighed. "Well, they keep telling me that's what I'm here for. My father—my physical father, I mean—used to say that the only people who never make mistakes are the ones who never do anything."

With something like resignation, Christine entered the kitchen. It was so busy, the girls had to step lively to keep from being run over. They filled two plates with an assortment of the nicest things, carefully arranging them to look attractive.

From there Felicia had to lead the way. They came to the chamber where she had been waiting the day Christine came, and found a number of men and women there. It surprised Christine to learn that certain duties of the Castle went on even during a Celebration.

Felicia seemed reluctant to go on. "I haven't been down this way since the day I came."

"Here! Where do you think you're going?" a knight accosted them.

"We have Uncle's permission," Felicia answered unsteadily.

"Do you?" He was skeptical. "I think you'd better wait here while I go ask."

Christine and Felicia waited, shifting nervously from one foot to the other. The plates seemed to have become very heavy. At last the man returned, and though he still looked disapproving, he apologized for delaying them and waved them on.

"It must be all right then," Felicia whispered. "I mean, we *do* have permission."

Christine remembered coming up this hallway with her brother and Uncle. Suddenly she stopped. "I think I know what's wrong."

"What is it?"

"Uncle's not with us. We should have asked him to come along. Today I invited the little girl to come into the Castle, and she did, but Uncle was with me. That's why it won't work."

"Oh, Christine, how clever of you! We've learned the lesson, and we didn't even have to go all the way."

"Well, as long as we've come this far, we may as well give them the food anyway."

"I suppose it can't hurt..." but Felicia's steps dragged.

They came to the little reception room which had been their first glimpse of the Castle. The page who was tending the door sat cross-legged beside it, and the girls suspected he had been nodding.

He jumped up in surprise. "Is that for me?" he asked eagerly.

Christine gave him a little cake, sorry that he had to miss the Celebration, but shook her head. "We're taking this to that poor family outside. They haven't eaten all day."

"That's thoughtful of you," he said, but he looked as though he didn't think much of the idea.

Outside the door was an oblong of bright light. Everything else was inky blackness.

"We should have brought a lantern," Felicia was still hanging back.

"Can we take a candle?" Christine asked the page.

"I don't know. I guess so," he reached up for one and gave it to her, but his expression was still dubious.

Christine stepped outside, but she could see only the little circle of light from the candle.

"They're just off there to the left," the page helped again.

"Hello" she called, but there was no answer. She nearly stepped on them before she saw them.

The baby was asleep in the mother's lap. The boys were huddled fearfully against her.

"Look," Christine offered, "I've brought you something to eat."

The two children's faces lit up at the mention of food, but the mother growled, "Be off with you! I've had enough tricks this day."

Christine felt Felicia's presence close by. "It's no trick. Here. Help yourselves." The two plates shone in the candlelight laden with good things.

"How do I know it's not drugged? Likely I'll keel over, and you'll drag us all into that dungeon. You've already stolen my husband and my daughter."

Felicia's sweet voice sounded next to her. "It's not drugged, see?" and she popped a grape in her mouth.

The little boys reached their hands toward the delicacies, but their mother was quicker. "No," she slapped their fingers. "Let me try it first and see."

She fingered over the food distastefully. "Looks terrible," she commented, "but I'm mortal hungry." At last she tentatively lifted a piece of cheese and took a bite.

At once she made a horrible face and sprang to her feet, dropping the infant who began to cry. She coughed and sputtered. With alarm Christine realized she was choking.

Felicia had already begun to slap her sharply on the back. In a moment the woman was slapping her in return. Recovering her breath, she began to curse the girls and scream that she was poisoned. She scooped up the food and hurled it at them. Christine retrieved the plates, getting kicked in the process.

She followed Felicia who had run for the open door. When she got there, Felicia had already flung herself down by a bench, sobbing and praying.

Well, I did it again, Christine thought. What a mess I made this time—literally! She looked down at her gown, spattered with food, and was thankful she hadn't worn the white silk. Kneeling by Felicia she begged her forgiveness.

Uncle knew this would happen, she thought in annoyance. Why did he let us go? But it was my idea, and he did warn us. If he hadn't let us go, I would have wondered why, so now I know.

Christine wished the page would stop staring at them. She closed her eyes and began to pray too. What had Brother Michael taught them today about repentance?

A hand patted her comfortingly on the shoulder. She and Felicia looked up at the same moment and found Uncle.

"Now, now, there's no harm done. If you're a little wiser, great good has been done."

"Uncle, dear," Felicia asked through her tears, "why did she choke on the food?"

"All who enter by the Door can come and go and be fed,[2] but what is bread of life to you is the very savor of death to those who will not receive the Prince.[3]

"The food for our feasts is sent over by the King from the other part of the Castle, and it can only be eaten by the King's children.

"If we could, don't you think we would feed all the hungry out there?"

"But will she never come in?" Christine wondered.

"I can't tell you that."

"Please, can you tell me how to get Felicia's gown clean? It's my fault it's ruined."

"You will find the water in the Castle is very good for removing stains. Now I must get back to the Celebration. It's nearly over."

"Oh, no, we'll miss the singing!"

"I think you can get there in time if you hurry."

Felicia and Christine went running down the hall.

---

[2] John 10:9

[3] I Corinthians 2:14; John 6:26-65

Chapter XV

Amanda

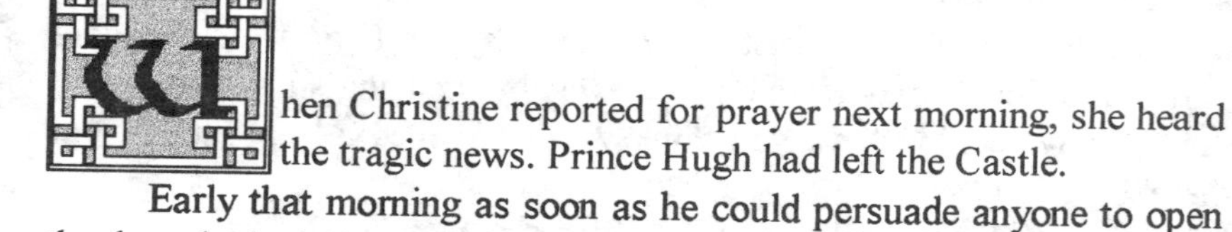

When Christine reported for prayer next morning, she heard the tragic news. Prince Hugh had left the Castle.

Early that morning as soon as he could persuade anyone to open the door, he had gone out to his wife. They had had a joyful reunion and gone off down the road.

There was much weeping in the Chapel that morning. "Oh, please," Christine prayed, "don't let Amanda go."

As soon as they were seated for breakfast, Godfrey asked, "Where did you girls go last night?"

Christine had nearly forgotten her escapade, and now she flushed at the memory.

When she didn't answer, Felicia looked at her inquiringly.

"Do I have to tell?" Christine asked.

"No, but we learned from it, and they might be helped too."

"You tell them then." Christine hung her head with shame.

She listened to Felicia's narrative and found it uncomfortably accurate. When she finished, Lucius began to enthusiastically point out the lessons to be gained. And when he finished, Godfrey spoke.

"The part I don't understand, Christine, is why you didn't see the parallel between this and Lily."

Christine was surprised, "What parallel?"

"Why just that if the King wants you to do a certain work, he will let you know. Did you think you had more compassion for that family than the King has? Or did you think you had an idea he couldn't think of?"

"I guess I'm not learning very well," she admitted.

"Don't worry," Lucius comforted. "I haven't learned that lesson yet."

Just then Hannah approached, bringing a very unhappy Amanda.

"Oh," cried Felicia, "you're Amanda's sponsor. I had been wondering where you were."

"Amanda," Hannah introduced her young charge, "This is Felicia and Christine and Lucius and Godfrey. They want to be your friends."

Amanda's eyes hadn't gotten past Christine. "You!" she exclaimed. "You're the pretty lady who called me from the window."

Christine gathered the child in her arms, and the wan little face lit up in a smile.

"I'm so happy you've come, Amanda. Do you know you are my little sister?"

Amanda nodded slowly, "That's what Hannah says. She says I have a big, new family in place of my old one."

"Well, you can believe Hannah," Felicia assured her. "You couldn't have a better sponsor."

"But I want my mother!" Amanda protested.

Christine debated an instant whether to try to comfort her or distract her, and chose the latter. "Look at the good things to eat. Can I butter a piece of bread for you?"

Amanda accepted the offer, and Hannah looked relieved. "She has to go to reading, and I have a flute lesson. I was afraid to leave her, but it looks as if she's going to get along with Christine."

The young people exerted themselves to be agreeable to the newest princess, and she soon began to brighten. There were so many stairs to climb to the scriptorium that Godfrey insisted on carrying Amanda piggy-back.

Sister Agatha hugged and kissed the new student, and then asked Christine to get her started. "You are doing so well, you can afford a few minutes. Just give her three letters today. I'll check on her later."

Christine got her last letters today, and joyfully viewed the completed chart. Godfrey grumbled that he was only up to L, but she could see he was proud of her.

Just before the hour ended, Hannah came for Amanda. "We're

going to have a sewing lesson. Do you know how to sew?"

"A little," Amanda nodded, "but I want to stay with Christine."

"You'll see her at dinner, and this afternoon you can go with her to horseback riding and swimming. And we'll all be together for music. You're going to have a wonderful time."

Satisfied, Amanda waved good-bye to them. "Mind Hannah!" Christine called.

There was little conversation in the steamy room where the felt was made, so in her mind, Christine kept praying for the child. "Please, let her stay. Let her like it here."

She was ready for Brother Michael's class. "Today," he said, "we will talk about prayers of petition. Some of you thought that was the only kind, but I hope you have learned this week that prayers of petition should be preceded by thanksgiving and praise, which strengthen our faith to expect answers to our prayers, and by repentance whereby we are cleansed and enabled to come boldly to the King's throne with our petitions.[1]

"I find a few people who go to the other extreme and think they should never ask anything of the Lord. They remember the Scripture which tells us to be content with what we have,[2] and that is certainly good as applied to material things. The King does not want his children to be greedy, but he does not want us ever to be content with our spiritual condition. He desires perfection,[3] and until we attain that, we should keep seeking.[4] It is never amiss to ask the Lord to continue his work in us.

"Moreover, if you feel selfish about asking things for yourself, this need not prevent your asking for others. The most important work in the Kingdom is intercessory prayer."

Christine was pleased. Why, that's what I've been doing, praying for Amanda.

At dinner Amanda appeared in better spirits, and seemed to already look a little plumper. She had met the other children of the Castle, but she chose to sit with Christine.

They had almost finished their meal, when a page approached. "Princess Amanda, Prince Hugh is in the courtyard and desires you to

---

[1] Hebrews 4:16, I John 3:21

[2] Hebrews 13:5

[3] Matthew 5:48

[4] Philippians 3:12-14

come to him."

"No!" cried Christine. "He's come to take her away. Hannah, don't let her go!"

Hannah addressed the page, "Has Uncle given permission for this meeting?"

The page was flustered. "I didn't think to ask."

Amanda interrupted, "I want to see my daddy!"

"But, Amanda," Christine was frantic, "he'll want you to go with him."

"I want to see my mother and my brothers!" Amanda insisted. But seeing Christine's distress, she added, "I won't go away. Truly, I won't."

Christine remembered how Felicia had cried at her efforts to go to Lily, and now she found tears running down her own cheeks.

"Come," said Hannah. "We'll go talk to Uncle. He'll know best."

"I'll go with..." Christine began, but she decided she had better wait for an invitation this time.

"Don't worry," comforted Hannah. "Amanda will be at the stables after quiet time."

Christine watched them go, and even smiled when Amanda looked back and waved, but she didn't feel Hannah's confidence. Thank goodness, she could pray. She felt she would have gone crazy just waiting.

True to her word, Hannah delivered Amanda into Christine's care in time for Brother Philip's class. Amanda was allowed to sit on the stolid old mare while Christine led it around the ring.

"Oh, this is fun!" the child bubbled. "I wish I could have told Amos and Mark about this."

"Did you get to see them?"

"Yes, and Mama and baby Seth. Mama was the one who wanted me to come home. I really hated not to, because she needs me to help with the work. But you were wrong about Papa. He told me to stay here and learn all I could and be a princess, and he would be proud of me."

Christine stopped and laid her head against the horse's neck. She had to thank the King, and repent of her worrying before she went on.

At last she continued. "Do you think he will come back?" she asked Amanda.

"Oh, yes, he promised to come again on Sunday, and said he would bring Mark and Amos, but Mama said it was too far, and so he said he would come alone anyway."

"We can pray for him, Amanda, and for your mother and brothers too."

"That's what Hannah said. I already started."

Christine wanted to hug her, but the saddle was too high, so she just said, "Bless you, Amanda."

At swimming Christine began to try floating on her back.

"Relax," Sister Celeste told her over and over. "You're as stiff as a board."

"Well, boards float, don't they?" Christine laughed. Sister Celeste had to laugh too.

"You know the water will hold you. What are you so worried about?"

"Just force of habit." Christine was too happy to mind being scolded.

After music Amanda went off with other children to a different class. Christine suddenly realized she had not studied her memory verse.

"Felicia, you have to help me. I don't know yesterday's verse."

"But we know that all things work together for good to them that love the Lord and are the called according to his purpose."

"Oh, that's right. I guess I do know it."

Brother Uriah gave an extra homework assignment. He instructed them to write down questions they might have and turn them in on Friday so he and Sister Alathea could go over them and select topics for next week's studies. Christine knew just what she wanted to ask.

"For today we will take up the idea of suffering as a penalty for sin. I think we all agreed that the King is obligated to punish wickedness. This is the sacred duty of all rulers.[5] But many have accused the King of being lax.[6] Do we always see the wicked punished?"

The class shook their heads. "Sometimes we do," offered Nathan. "Like Sodom and Gomorrah."[7]

"Sometimes," Brother Uriah agreed, "but not always."

Hannah volunteered, "I think sometimes they suffer in ways we don't see. A bad conscience would be more trouble to me than any

---

[5] Romans 13:1-4

[6] II Peter 3:9

[7] Genesis 18 & 19

outward punishment."

Brother Uriah smiled, "Your conscience is very tender, Hannah. Thank the Lord. Sometimes wrongdoers do suffer that way, but many have a conscience, Paul says, seared with a hot iron,[8] so like the adulterous woman in Proverbs, they wipe their mouth and say I have done no wickedness."[9]

"Well, perhaps," conceded Hannah, "but I feel sorry for them anyway."

"You are right, Hannah," said Sister Alathea, "for the pleasures of sin have a way of growing stale, and the sinner is left miserable, not so much from bad conscience, as from the gnawing of sin at his vitals. Hatred, jealousy, self-pity, spite, wounded pride and vanity are poor bed-fellows."[10]

Sarah felt they were forgetting the point. "But isn't the punishment of sinners chiefly in the next world?"

"Yes, Sarah," Brother Uriah nodded, "by faith we accept that the justice of our King will be meted out when this life is finished. So we do not envy the evil-doer,[11] knowing that death shall surely come to him and after that judgment."[12]

"But," Felicia put in, "he can repent and escape that punishment."

"Right again, the King's justice was completely satisfied at Calvary, so the wicked can turn from his way, and accept the Prince's sacrifice, and avoid the penalty. And then he is accounted righteous, and that brings us to the part which is important for us: Does the King punish his children when they sin?"

"Not if they repent," Godfrey was sure. "If they are forgiven there is no punishment."

"We need to be clear about forgiveness," Brother Uriah nodded. "It means that the sin is completely wiped out, even, though it is hard to believe, from the King's memory.[13] Remember that when you hear an inner voice reminding you of sins of which you have already repented. It is not the King's voice, for he doesn't even recall that sin.

---

[8] I Timothy 4:2

[9] Proverbs 30:20

[10] Proverbs 13:15

[11] Psalm 37:1, 2

[12] Hebrews 9:27

[13] Isaiah 43:25, Jeremiah 31:34

"But suppose you murdered someone—then repented. Would God's forgiveness bring that person to life?"

The class shook their heads.

"Though the King had forgiven you, would man's law excuse you?"

Again the class shook their heads.

"Even if the law did not punish you, would you ever forget? What would it be for you to meet a member of the person's family? Or to pass near the place where the murder was committed? So the consequences of sin follow us in many cases, even if the sin is forgiven. Read about David's sin.[14]

"And what if a child of the King sins and doesn't repent?"

"Brother Michael said he separates himself from the Lord," Christine remembered.

"True, but there is a sin not unto death,[15] that is, that does not bring total separation. Will the King punish his child?"

The students were a bit puzzled. At last Naomi blurted out, "If they were my children, I certainly would!"

The others giggled, but Brother Uriah simply nodded. "We are running out of time. Sister Alathea has a scripture she has been waiting to read."

"For this cause many are weak and sickly among you, and many sleep. For if we would judge ourselves, we should not be judged. But when we are judged, we are chastened of the Lord, that we should not be condemned with the world."[16]

"The sure thing," Brother Uriah commented, "is that no child of the King will be punished in the world to come, for which we ought to be overwhelmingly grateful. But if we do not heed our conscience, or Uncle's warnings, the King will use firmer methods to correct us. Not because he doesn't love us, but because he does, and would not see us eternally lost.

"Here are your verses. Remember when suffering comes into your life to check up and see if you are missing the mark in some way. If you find no unrepented sin, then you will be interested in tomorrow's lesson."

---

14 II Samuel 11 & 12

15 I John 5:16, 17

16 I Corinthians 11:30-32

"What does it say, Felicia," Christine whispered.

Felicia was a little upset at herself. "I don't know. There seem to be so many words I haven't learned yet."

Naomi read it to them. "My son, despise not thou the chastening of the Lord, nor faint when thou art rebuked of him: for whom the Lord loveth he chasteneth."[17]

---

[17] Hebrews 12:5

Chapter XVI

God's Design for the Clay

Christine fairly skipped to the pottery shop. Today she would use the wheel.First she had to wedge the clay a few more times, then Sister Amelia told her to divide it into balls a little larger than her fist, and she had to work those until they were quite round and smooth.

"If clay is not properly prepared for the wheel, it will burst in the kiln and destroy other pieces as well as itself."

Next Christine took one of the balls and made a little pot just with her fingers. "To get the feel of the clay," Sister Amelia said. As though she hadn't been feeling it for four hours already, Christine thought.

At last they went to the wheel. Sister Amelia took one of Christine's balls and sat down. First she showed her how to spin the wheel by kicking with her right foot, and how to control the speed.

"Ours is an ancient craft," she droned. It seemed to Christine her voice had taken on the quality of the whirring wheel. "Perhaps the most ancient of all."

Suddenly she flung the clay onto the wheel. "Adam and Eve probably made vessels of earthenware even in Eden, though we do not know if they burned them."

Christine began to sense the power in Sister Amelia's hands as she pressed her palms into the rotating mass. "At Babel they burned bricks,[1] so the art had been discovered by that time at least. Even the potter's wheel is at least as ancient as any written records, and probably much older."

Her thumbs pushed into the center and suddenly it was a bowl!

"The first potter was our Father himself, for it is recorded that he took clay and made a man."[2] As Christine gasped in wonder, a shimmering tower rose from the whirling board.

"And the prophets tell us that this is still our relationship to the Father: that of clay to a potter."[3] Now the tower was evolving into a graceful urn. "Hundreds of years ago our Father sent the prophet Jeremiah down to the potter's shop to see just what you are seeing.[4] There is much to be learned in the potter's shop."

Then, as if the world had come to an abrupt end, the wheel stopped, and Sister Amelia smashed the lovely vessel back into a shapeless lump and cast it into the clay bin.

Christine was still mourning over the lost beauty, as Sister Amelia put a ball into her hand. "Now you try. Remember that the clay gets tired. Do not work too long with one lump." She walked away and left the wheel to Christine.

During the next half hour Christine found that although she thought she had watched carefully, she had seen nothing at all. At last she realized that she had focused all her attention on the clay, when it was the hands she should have been observing.

Humbly she approached Sister Amelia and begged. "Will you please show me again?"

---

1 Genesis 11:3

2 Job 10:9; 33:6

3 Isaiah 45:9, Romans 9:20, 21

4 Jeremiah 18:1-6

On Friday Christine again spent part of reading class instructing Amanda. Then Sister Agatha came to her desk and said, "Today you will learn to write your name. You will need to be able to on Sunday when you sign the chore roster."

Carefully she lettered the parchment for Christine to copy. "You have a wonderful name, Christine. Have you thought about what it means?"

"Not really. It's just the diminutive form of Christ."

"Yes, it speaks of the unbelievably marvelous plan the King is working out in your life and in each of us."

"What plan is that?"

"Don't you know why he made you?"

"I guess to serve him."

"Do you think he needs your service? Do you think you can really do something for him?"

"Well, why then?"

"Our serving him is just part of his plan to mold us into what he wants us to be."

Excitedly Christine remembered Sister Amelia's words of the previous afternoon. "You mean as a potter molds clay?"

"Exactly," Sister Agatha smiled.

"And what is he molding me into? What am I to become?"

"Just what your name says, a little Christ, a miniature copy of the Prince."[5]

The thought was lovelier than words. Not only had the King taken her to be his daughter, but he was going to make her worthy of that position. To be like the Prince! She had never dreamed she was destined to be anything half so wonderful as that. What more could she ever ask for? Only that the work might progress.

"You see," Sister Agatha continued, "in Eternity before Creation, the Father loved the Son with a perfect love, so the most wonderful plan he could devise was to make many more sons, and all just like the first. That was why he made man."[6]

"But," Christine protested, "there never has been a man just like the Prince."

---

[5] Ephesians 4:13

[6] Romans 8:29

"No, man chose a different path than the one for which he had been created. Instead of starting in infant perfection and growing toward mature perfection, the infant race went astray. But that had been foreseen, and the Prince himself became our Redeemer. Stooping to become a part of his own Creation,[7] he opened the way for men as individuals to be reborn and start again on the path toward perfection. We are hindered in our growth while we remain in this sin-filled world, but our Father promises that when we see the Prince our transformation will be complete, and we shall be like him."

Sister Agatha was no longer speaking to Christine, but her face was turned upward and glowed with the hope of this wonderful future. Tears started in her eyes, and she began to sing.

"We shall be like him, we shall be like him,
For we shall see him just as he is.
When he appears then, we shall be like him.
We shall be pure as he is pure."[8]

Christine, too, had forgotten the present in the prospect of this glorious future. A few days ago Uncle had asked her what she desired most. Until this moment she had not truly known the answer, but now she knew.

The song was a new one to Christine, but as Sister Agatha began again, she sang too. Then she heard Felicia's clear soprano and gradually the voices of the other students joining in. Class was suspended for a season of praise, and it was sometime before they got back to their lessons.

At the end of the hour, Sister Agatha called Lucius to the center of the room.

"Prince Lucius, today you graduate. You are able to read and write well enough to continue your studies without help."

Lucius was pleased but somewhat flustered. He murmured something indistinctly.

"And here," Sister Agatha held out a large leather-bound volume, "is a New Testament of your own. My copyists have spent many hours

---

[7] John 1:10
[8] I John 3:2, 3

of work so that you may have this. See that you spend many more in its study."

Lucius' answer was again inaudible, but everyone saw him nod his head.

The others crowded around to congratulate Lucius and admire the thick book. Christine longed for one like it, then worried that she was committing the sin of envy. I shall have one soon, she told herself. Monday I start learning to read.

"But where will you go on Monday, Lucius?" she asked.

Lucius looked to Sister Agatha for an answer. She just smiled. "Uncle will no doubt have something to say to you about that."

The morning that had started so happily was soon to turn to misery for Felicia.

Brother Michael continued on the subject of intercessory prayer, and told his pupils to ask the King to give them a burden for which they might pray.

Christine saw her friend's face grow increasingly distressed as Brother Michael continued. To Christine the idea was exciting. She had already felt a burden for Amanda, and she had begun to experience the thrill of answered prayer. But Felicia was near tears, and Christine could feel her shaking. At last Brother Michael noticed.

"Felicia, what's the matter? Are you ill?"

Felicia shook her head and replied in real anguish, "Please, Brother Michael, don't ask me to take a burden. I had one once, and it nearly killed me. I'll do anything for the King—even that—but I'd rather die than have another burden."

Brother Michael stood looking at Felicia for several moments. "Dear little sister, you very likely know more of burden-bearing than any of us here. And I tell you all to be warned: carrying a burden is not to be undertaken lightly. It is hard work, and it is sorrow.

"Yet, the Prince bore the cross for our sakes. And I think it was a far heavier load than any other has ever borne. Shall we refuse our cross?[9]

"But let me comfort you, dear children. The burdens which the King gives are of a far different nature than those with which the outlaws would lade you. Those burdens bring despair, but the King gives us hope. Most important, he never asks us to bear our burdens

---

[9] Luke 9:23; 14:27

alone. The Prince has said, 'Take my yoke upon you.'[10] Now a yoke is for two, and it is the Prince himself who shares our burdens. Also he has commanded us, 'Bear one another's burdens.'[11] So we have help from our brothers and sisters.

"As if this were not enough, we have the Comforter, our Paraclete, who is ever alongside us, strengthening us, directing our path.

"Felicia, you will never know true happiness except by bearing the burden which the King gives you. You are in fact bearing a burden right now. Do you not see that sponsoring Christine is a burden?"

Felicia started, "Oh, no! I love her! She is no burden!"

"Praise the Lord! It is love that makes the burden light. But be truthful; hasn't she cost you worry and pain?"

Christine hung her head, "I can answer that. I've been nothing but one problem after another."

She felt Brother Michael's hand under her chin, lifting her face. He was smiling. "If we were to start confessing, I think we would all have to say the same of ourselves."

Then he turned back to the class, "But now you know the secret: if we love enough it will help us forget all the pain. But there is joy too! Every burden has its reward." Christine looked at Felicia. She was smiling.

At dinner when they were all together, Lucius asked Amanda how she liked being a princess.

"Oh, I love it!" she exclaimed eagerly, but then she stopped to reflect. "But it's not like what I thought it would be."

"What did you think it would be like?" Godfrey asked.

"Well, I guess I thought a princess would do nothing all day except sit around in pretty dresses."

Christine was surprised. "You know I think I had a similar idea myself."

"That doesn't seem very interesting," said Hannah. "I'd much rather be busy."

"I would too," agreed Amanda. "Sitting around sounds all right, but it would be terrible if you really had to do it."

"You're a very wise little girl," Felicia nodded.

---

[10] Matthew 11:28-30

[11] Galatians 6:2

"Some parts are hard though," Amanda continued, "Like praying for a whole hour in the morning."

Christine tried to suppress a laugh, but the others laughed so she joined in.

Lucius leaned over and whispered loudly, "Don't tell anybody, Amanda, but it's hard for me too."

"It's hard for everyone at first," Felicia comforted. "And some take longer to get used to it than others," her eyes twinkled at Lucius.

"The hardest things are the ones that do us most good in the end," Hannah counseled.

"Then floating will surely do me a lot of good!" Christine noted skeptically. "I don't think I'll ever learn."

"What could be easier than floating?" Godfrey asked in amazement. "I floated Monday."

"It's true. He did!" Lucius shook his head as though still wondering at it.

Christine was between astonishment and anger. "On Monday! How could you do it so easily?"

"Brother Caleb just told me the King said I could float, so naturally I did."

Lucius shrugged his shoulders, "Naturally. Took to water like a duck."

Christine just stared. So simple, she thought, the King says it, so it has to be true.

That afternoon it was Sister Celeste who was amazed. Christine simply lay back and floated. It was such a lovely feeling, like resting on nothing. I think I could go to sleep like this, Christine mused. She practiced floating the whole period, and found she was doing it better than Felicia. "Just relax," she told her friend.

"Where have I heard that before?" Sister Celeste laughed.

Chapter XVII

His Ways Are Not Our Ways

Bible class began with the collecting of the questions they had prepared. Christine had had to ask Naomi to write the word "What" for her, and even now she didn't realize she needed a question mark at the end. But she turned in her little three-word question, hopeful to soon learn its answer.

Brother Uriah opened the class. "We have been considering the reasons for suffering, and today we will look at the most important. Hannah brought this up on the first day when she mentioned Job. We have seen that we suffer for our mistakes and for our sins, and that the King allows this in order to correct us. But the book of Job emphasizes that sometimes we suffer even though we have not sinned. Why does the King permit this?

"Godfrey, you have been working at the anvil, I understand. When you have an iron bar and wish to make something, what is the first thing you do to it?"

"We put it into the furnace, sir."

"Very interesting. And Christine, you have been working in the pottery shop. What is the last thing you do with a pot you are making?"

"It is fired in the kiln."

"Now Lucius, you have been studying the art of the smith much longer. Will you explain to us all how that iron bar came into being in the first place?"

"Yes, sir. First iron ore must be dug from the earth. Then this must be smelted in the furnace in a very hot fire until it is pure."

"Then what happens to your iron bar after heating in the furnace?"

"You take it out with tongs, and put it on the anvil. Then you hammer it into shape. It goes from anvil to furnace and back many times before the work is finished."

"Nathan, in carpentry class, when you have selected a tree, what do you do to it?"

"First we fell it, of course, then we must cut off all the branches. Depending on what we're making we may split it with wedges or just square it with the axe. Then we smooth it with the adze and finally shape it with chisels and planes. When the shape is right, we bore holes to peg it together."

"Back to Christine, is clay ready to work as it comes from the earth?"

Christine gave an emphatic "No!" Then went on to explain, "Just like the iron, there are impurities to remove, bits of grit or lumps that would ruin your bowl. You have to cut it and knead it and pound it for hours before it's ready."

"You young people sound rather violent to me," Brother Uriah laughed.

"Yes, sir," Christine smiled.

"So a piece of iron goes from fire to anvil many times before it is a well-tempered blade, a log must be sawn and hacked and shaved, and a pot may go through many firings. And what of a man?"

Sister Alathea had been holding her Bible open, and now she read. "The fining pot is for silver, and the furnace for gold: but the Lord trieth the hearts."[1]

She flipped over to another page where she had been holding her finger. "Beloved think it not strange concerning the fiery trial which is to try you, as though some strange thing happened unto you: but rejoice, inasmuch as ye are partakers of Christ's sufferings."[2] And turning back

---

[1] Proverbs 17:3

[2] I Peter 4:12, 13

again, “My brethren, count it all joy when ye fall into divers temptations; knowing this, that the trying of your faith worketh patience.”[3]

Then she looked up, “Isn’t it precious, my little brothers and sisters, that the King has judged us worthy of his time and trouble? It is long since I sat where you do, and many and many a time I have been in the fire, but still I rejoice! I am not cast aside. The Master has not given up on me. He is yet working to change my corrupt nature into the perfect image of his Son.”

Brother Uriah asked, “Lucius, have you never thought how it was for the iron?”

“I guess not.”

“Painful, I should think. Christine, do you feel you are ready for the wheel yet?”

“No, I still need a lot of work.”

“Then remember what we said the first of the week, don’t let it discourage you. Just keep praising our King.”

He handed around the slips with the new verses, and Christine saw it was long with some big words, so she turned immediately to Naomi.

“That the trial of your faith,” Naomi read, “being much more precious than of gold that perisheth, though it be tried with fire, might be found unto praise and honour and glory at the appearing of Jesus Christ.”[4]

Christine sighed, “When he appears, we shall be like him.”

---

[3] James 1:2, 3

[4] I Peter 1:7

Saturday was nearly like a holiday. Right after breakfast they made their way to the courtyard. The great gates of the Castle were open on a bright, sunny landscape. Knights in full armor were mounted on their war-horses, waiting for orders. All the women of the Castle, dressed in gay colors, milled about, ready for a currant-picking expedition. There was laughter and noise everywhere. Barking dogs added to the din. From a cart filled with empty baskets, each of the girls took one.

"Oh, look," cried Felicia. Godfrey and Lucius were approaching dressed in hunting attire with bows and quivers.

Grinning, they explained that Brother Michael was taking out a group of his weapons students to procure meat for the Castle.

"What are you going to shoot?" Christine asked in admiration.

"Whatever we find, I guess."

Lucius added, "If we can hit it."

Peasants were not allowed to hunt, and neither of the boys had ever shot anything before. They had played with bows and arrows since childhood, preparing to be bowmen in the King's army when they came of age. Christine knew that Godfrey was an excellent shot, always among the finalists in village archery tournaments, but could he hit a moving target?

"I bet you bring something back," she encouraged them.

"I'd like some nice venison," Felicia licked her lips.

"I've never tasted venison," Amanda sighed.

"I'll get a deer especially for you," Lucius promised rashly.

"Please don't shoot any squirrels," Hannah begged. "I love to see them playing in the trees. I don't want to eat them."

"That's an easier promise to keep," Godfrey laughed. "We probably couldn't hit one anyway."

"There's Brother Michael. Looks like he's ready to go. We'll see you later."

As the boys hurried off, Christine called, "Good luck!"

Felicia looked at her in mock severity. "There's no such thing as luck."

"Shame on me!" responded Christine. Then she called, "The Lord grant you good hunting!"

"What are you all waiting for?" a voice thundered.

Christine turned to see a large, cheerful, red-faced woman of middle age.

"For you, Sister Hephzibah!" several replied. Then the whole colorful group began to pour out the gate.

Someone struck up a song, and everyone joined in.

"I am the rose of Sharon,
And the lily of the valleys.
As the apple tree among
The trees of the wood,
So is my beloved among the sons.
I sat down in his shadow,
And his fruit was sweet.
He brought me to his banqueting house,
And his banner over me was love."[5]

The currants grew in the borders between the forest and the cleared land and in the hedgerows of the fields. The women and girls swarmed over the bushes pulling the clusters of dried berries off into their baskets. Christine noticed that the knights rode patrol around the group, inconspicuous, yet managing to be everywhere.

Today the peasants were laboring in the Lord's fields. They too, laughed and joked as they worked, but the groups did not mingle. Christine kept an eye out for old Eldred, and when she saw him, went to share news with him.

"Brother Eldred!" she had unconsciously changed her form of address. Less than a week ago he had been only an acquaintance, and though she had not seen him in the meantime, he now seemed an old and close friend. But so many changes had taken place in her life, she did not marvel at this one.

"This is Amanda, our newest princess," Christine introduced her tagalong. Then she gave him a brief account of that adventure.

"Welcome, little maid," old Eldred placed a gnarled hand on the child's head. "From what village do you come?"

"Little Scotsford, Sir."

"Well, Prince Hugh does have a bit of a walk. But he must pass by my holding. I will watch for him Sunday morning, and Abigail and I will especially pray for him."

---

[5] Song of Solomon 2:1-4

"Thank you, sir," Amanda smiled. Christine could see the two had taken an instant liking to one another.

Now Eldred turned to her. "Your holding has been assigned to your cousin, young Kenneth. He was a fourth son, and there would have been little enough for him at home."

"I'm glad. I expect he'll be marrying before long, and he can start out on his own croft."

"Yes, I shouldn't be surprised to hear the banns published any Sunday. Your uncle has a heifer calf, and he hasn't offered it for sale. I rather suspect it will be a wedding gift. And I noticed Dame Penelope bought extra wool last spring and has lately borrowed a blanket loom. I would surmise there's a trousseau in preparation."

"You mean her daughter Mildred?" Christine gasped in surprise. "But Brother Eldred, the King arranges marriages. How would the parents know what was coming?"

"Because we have a beneficent King who sees the hearts of the young people whose marriages he contracts. And old heads like mine, or your uncle's, or Penelope's still have eyes in them. We can't look into hearts and minds as the King does, but we see things written in faces."

Christine laughed, "Brother Eldred, you're as bad as an old woman! Kenneth and Mildred..." she sighed. "Yes, that would be lovely. I must try to find a gift for them."

"You and Godfrey have already given them a home. Are you sure Godfrey won't object? The holding ought to have been his, now your father George is dead."

"Object? No, he gave all that up when he decided to come to the Castle. The holding would have gone to Tristram, not Godfrey. Why would we want to go back to all that?"[6]

"Well spoken, child. Why indeed? But the wish of my heart is that Kenneth, and Mildred too, would follow your example and go to live in the Castle. You know you have been the talk of the village this last week."

"I didn't know, but that's easy to see. Are we much condemned for leaving?"

"Condemned, applauded, excused, wondered at, it all depends on whom you listen to. But it has started some people thinking. The

---

6 Luke 9:62

outlaws have been circulating rumors too. It's said you've been chained in the dungeons for your presumption."

"What!" Christine nearly fell over. "Of all the stupid lies!"

"But some believe it. Those who won't believe in the King's goodness are only too ready to believe anything against him. And others who don't believe it are at least somewhat doubtful."

"Well, let's put a stop to this right now. I'll just go show those workers I'm not in any dungeon!" Suiting action to words, Christine ran lightly toward the nearest group of workmen.

To her dismay they lowered their heads or turned their faces. "Master Titus!" she addressed one of them.

The man did not raise his head, but approached trembling. "Yes, milady."

"What's the matter with all of you? Don't you remember Mara, daughter of George?"

One of them half-lifted his head, "Beggin' your pardon, milady, if I may be egskoozed for askin', we'd be glad to know what's become of the poor child."

"Why, she no longer exists! Now I am Princess Christine!"

At this the men set up a wail and scattered in all directions. "Dead! Dead! Poor child!"

"No, wait!" Christine cried in alarm. "You don't understand!"

Old Eldred had just caught up to her, and she sat down right on the ground in despair. "Oh, what have I done?" she moaned.

"Frightened them right proper, I should say." Eldred stooped down beside her. Amanda put her arms comfortingly around her friend.

"I wanted to dispel the lies, and now I've made it worse!"

Eldred couldn't deny it. He shook his head sadly. "Everyone in the village will know it by nightfall. I doubt Abigail and I can do a thing about it."

Christine began to weep. Between sobs she scolded herself.

"Now, now," Eldred patted her shoulder. "What's done is done. No use looking backward. Next time remember it takes more than just good intentions to accomplish anything for the Kingdom."

"I don't seem to ever learn!"

"Oh, you will, if you're really desiring to learn. The thing to do now is to get busy praying. You can pray: Lord, by your grace overrule my mistakes."

"Will that help?"

"Certainly, I've had to pray that way many and many a time."

"You? Do you still make mistakes?"

"I'm afraid so, but don't be discouraged. I don't make them as often, and I've learned to avoid some of those I used to make."

"Will you help me pray?"

"To be sure, after all this will affect our work here in the village."

"I'm sorry, Brother Eldred. Can you forgive me?"

"Of course, the King forgives you, and it's his work really."

Amanda piped in, "I'll pray too."

Christine hugged the child, "Thank you, Amanda. I know that will help."

The three went on their knees there in the field and earnestly interceded.

Chapter XVIII

Challenge

It was the dinner horn that interrupted their prayers. An appetizing picnic was spread in a grassy spot, but Brother Eldred declined the invitation.

"I'll be accused of putting on airs if I eat with Castle folk. I'd better go eat with the other workers."

Amanda joined the merry group, but Christine excused herself to continue praying. She felt that the King had forgiven her, but she hadn't forgiven herself yet.

By the time dinner was over most of the hunters had returned. It did look as if there would be venison for Sunday dinner. But Godfrey and Lucius hadn't come back yet. Felicia asked Christine if she had seen them.

"Don't worry. I'm sure they'll be fine."

"But you don't realize all the trouble they could get into."

Don't I? Christine thought. If they get into more trouble than I did, it *will* be something to worry about.

Then Brother Michael approached the girls with the same question. No, they assured him, they hadn't seen them since morning.

"Here they come!" cried Amanda. "And they have a deer!"

"They also seem to have company." Brother Michael was puzzled, and he set off to meet them, so the girls followed too.

Yes, there was a stranger with them, a young peasant who looked very fearful indeed. Christine decided she was not the only one who had been terrifying the local populace—if he was local; she didn't recognize him.

"Come now," Lucius was telling him gaily. "You'll have to face the consequences."

When the peasant saw Brother Michael, he stopped in his tracks and his knees knocked together.

"What's going on here?" Brother Michael asked.

Godfrey put on a stern face and answered, "We caught this churl red-handed! He had just shot the King's deer and was preparing to dress it when we came on him."

The poor man flung himself at Brother Michael's feet. "Mercy, mercy, your lordship. I wasn't really hunting; I went out in the woods for some target practice, and when I saw this deer something came over me!"

The boys were nodding and winking at Brother Michael, so he took his cue.

"A likely story! This is undoubtedly not the first time. If you are innocent as you pretend you would have been working in the fields with the King's obedient servants."

At this the man gave himself up for dead, and fell in a swoon. Godfrey had a water bottle and knelt to revive him.

"We convinced him he had to come with us to the Castle to be judged by the King," Lucius explained hurriedly. "Do you think Uncle will be able to do the rest?"

Brother Michael scratched his beard, "It might work. People can be tricked into the Kingdom on occasion, but whether he stays or not will be up to him.

"Here, let me carry him. You fellows bring the deer. We'll see what happens when he gets to the door. We can't take him in against his will."

The girls returned to the currant-picking with reluctance, but it didn't keep them from burning with curiosity, or from praying for the young peasant."

It was dusk when the happy, weary, dusty party came trudging back to the Castle. Christine had almost recovered her spirits. There was a Celebration that night.

Sunday morning. Christine anticipated church service more than ever before, although the day brought some sobering thoughts as well. Was it possible that only a week ago she had been on her way to the village church? It seemed a whole lifetime since then. She remembered her terrible mistake of yesterday too, and knelt to pray as Eldred had instructed her.

"And please," she prayed, "teach me to think before I speak."

Christine was surprised to learn that church would be in the Great Hall, not in the Chapel.

"The Chapel would never hold everyone," Felicia explained.

"But isn't everyone in there during prayers?"

Felicia grimaced unpleasantly. "They're supposed to be."

When they reached the Great Hall, Christine realized the truth of Felicia's words. It was full, and it was at least three times bigger than the Chapel. But where were all these people during prayers? Then she remembered Sister Amelia's words, "Everything in the Castle is voluntary."

Christine sighed. At least some things were the same inside the Castle as outside. It was not a happy revelation. But the service was wonderful!

They sang songs she had learned in music class, and the volume filled that lofty ceiling. Everyone joined in praise, and Christine thought it almost as beautiful as the singing from the other part of the Castle.

The choir sang a song she had heard in the village church, "Glorious Things of Thee are Spoken."[1] She had always wondered if it referred to the earthly Jerusalem or the heavenly one. Now she suddenly understood: the song was about the Church!

Brother Jude, who had led the service so far, now turned to a knight who would be the speaker. Christine was delighted to recognize the same one she had met at the spring and who had rescued them on the road to the Castle. His name was Sir Alexander, and he spoke of the trip from which he had just returned after two years' absence.

---

[1] Psalm 87:3

"I found the King's outposts besieged in every land I visited. In many countries the outlaws actually hold the reins of power and style themselves kings and princes."

As Christine listened she began to appreciate for the first time the privilege she had enjoyed of growing up in the King's own fief. Sir Alexander spoke of whole villages and even cities who did not know anything of the King, but were totally under the outlaws' power.

Sir Alexander was visibly moved as he went on. "I have a list here which I will read. These are the names of princes and princesses who went out from our number to man or establish outposts for the King, and who have within the last two years been martyred."

The names were unfamiliar to Christine, but around her she heard little gasps of recognition and a growing sound of weeping.

"Now I realize some of you are newcomers to the Castle, who have not yet been approved for service in the World, and I know too, that many of you have important duties here in the Castle from which you have not been released. But some of you are sitting here because you lack the courage and the dedication to face life in the Outposts. For shame! Must we admit to the enemy that sons and daughters of the King are afraid? Must we confess that redeemed children of our Lord love comfort and ease more than to do the King's will?

"Our Prince has given us the example that we must go to a lost and dying World with the Good News, even if it costs our lives!"[2]

I will go, thought Christine. I'm not afraid. And the thought was a glorious one. I am not afraid. She read the same thought in Felicia's eyes, and even little Amanda was very earnest.

"See Uncle today!" Sir Alexander urged. "Tell him you are willing to go. Even if you cannot go at this particular time for one of the reasons I mentioned, let him know that you are available whenever the King needs you."

Christine did not see how anyone could resist that plea. She would offer herself at once, although it would likely be many months before she was prepared to leave the Castle.

When the knight sat down, Uncle himself came to the dais.

"He's going to make an announcement," Felicia whispered excitedly.

---

[2] Philippians 2:5-8, Hebrews 12:2

Uncle was smiling broadly, "The King is pleased to announce the creation of a new page. Prince Lucius is herewith promoted to that rank."

The audience burst into happy applause, and Christine craned her neck to see Lucius' face, but he had dropped it into his lap. Felicia was almost beside herself with excitement.

Then everyone grew quite still, for Uncle was apparently not through.

He turned toward Sir Alexander, "Sir Knight, we will not ask you to make such a journey again alone."

A universal intake of breath testified to the suspicion everyone had received.

"He's going to read the banns on Sir Alexander," Felicia whispered unnecessarily.

The knight's face was a study in surprise and anticipation.

"The King is pleased to announce the forthcoming marriage of his son, Prince Alexander, to his daughter, the Princess Celeste."

Christine tore her eyes from Sir Alexander's shining face to try to get a glimpse of her lovely swimming instructor. She surmised that Sister Celeste was in the middle of a group of excited, squealing girls at the far side of the Hall.

Service was over, and what a happy throng spilled from the Hall. Christine noticed however, a number of determined faces seeking out Uncle. I will talk to him later, she thought sadly, it will be so long before I can really go, that there's no hurry.

Just outside, a group was milling around the chore roster waiting their turns to sign up. Christine and her friends joined this crowd and as they approached the roster they found Sister Agatha at their side, ready to help her students on their first sign-up.

"Christine, you can write your own name, but shall I read off the list of chores for you?"

"No, I..."

Lucius interrupted, "Sister Agatha, we four want to sign up for gardening, so we can all be together."

Christine was annoyed. No one had mentioned this to her, and she had been planning to sign up as a milkmaid. Still she remembered that they couldn't sign up for the same chore two weeks in a row, and the King desired them to try many different duties, so when Sister Agatha pointed out the word "Garden" on the roster, Christine wrote her name behind it. Lucius and Felicia signed their names, and Sister Agatha wrote Godfrey's.

"What shall we sign you up for, my dear?" she asked Amanda.

"May I work in the garden too?"

"I'm afraid there are only four spaces. What did you help with at home?"

"Oh, I don't know. I carried water and firewood, and cleaned the cottage, and cooked, and washed dishes, and mended, and milked, and took care of the garden, and did the laundry, and looked after my little brothers, and..."

"Mercy, child!" Sister Agatha was flabbergasted. "What does your mother do?"

"Oh, she takes care of Baby Seth. He's sick a lot. Sometimes she's up all night with him. Then I watch him for a while in the afternoon, so she can get a nap."

Sister Agatha looked a little skeptical. "I'm surprised you can find the time.

"Well, let's just put you down for kitchen help this time. You can do something else next week. I'll put you here for breakfast, if you don't mind missing morning prayer too much."

"No, ma'm," Amanda smiled.

Hannah signed her name next to Amanda's, then turned to Christine. "I want to talk to Uncle. Amanda would rather be with you anyway."

"We'll get along fine, won't we, Amanda?" Christine was sure.

Hannah was hardly out of sight though, when Amanda caught sight of Prince Hugh approaching.

"Daddy!" she cried and ran to hug his neck.

Christine followed as quickly as she could, but it's all right, she thought. He wants her to stay. She gave her hand to the red-faced farmer, "I'm so glad you made it, Prince Hugh. Wasn't it a marvelous service?"

"Yes, yes, it was," he agreed.

But something's wrong, Christine could tell.

"Papa, I am learning to ride a horse. Really and truly, I am. Will you be sure to tell Amos and Mark? If they came to the Castle they could learn to ride too! And Hannah is teaching me to embroider. Can you come to my room and see my embroidery? You are staying for dinner, aren't you? We're going to have venison. Lucius and Godfrey caught a poacher, but now he's a prince, and they brought a deer too. Do you..."

"Sweetheart," he reluctantly interrupted her. "I must start home, for I've a long walk, and I'm afraid..." Christine could see he was struggling with something. "I'm afraid you must come with me. Your mama needs you. Little Seth has been very sick these last few days, and the boys have nearly driven your mama..."

This time it was Christine who interrupted. "If she's having such a hard time, let her come to the Castle, and we'll all be glad to help her. Amanda isn't leaving!"

The farmer looked at her annoyed. "Do you think I like this? I have no choice. My daughter will have to give all this up for a while. Later she can come back."

Christine turned to the child, "Amanda, you don't have to go! Tell him you're staying here."

Amanda looked very uncertain, and there were little pools in her eyes.

"Oh, Christine, I want to stay, of course, but don't you see? They really need me. The King would want me to help my family. It would be selfish to stay."

A wave of panic swept over Christine. Where is Hannah? she wondered. I'm about to make another mess! Oh, dear Lord, what shall I do?

Suddenly she saw Lucius and remembered he had just been made a page. That was her answer. "Lucius," she called, "please get Uncle. We need him at once! Hurry, please!"

Lucius looked puzzled for a moment, but seeing Christine's distress, he started off at a run.

"Young lady, you have no right to interfere between a father and his child. I wouldn't be taking her if there were any other way, but you just don't know what I've been through the last three days."

"I can imagine," Christine assured him, remembering her own encounter with Amanda's mother. Oh, hurry, Lucius, she whispered to herself.

"Will we be able to come here every Sunday?" Amanda asked sadly.

"Yes, I promise, we'll come every Sunday—as long as the weather holds."

At last, Uncle was coming. Christine gave a great sigh of relief.

"Prince Hugh!" Uncle was beaming as usual. "I was so pleased to see you in the congregation this morning. I hope you are staying."

The miserable man shook his head. "No, no, I just came for my daughter. We can't do without her at home."

"Are you speaking of the Princess Amanda? She is the King's daughter."

"I know; that's a pretty game. But real life is that I have a sick baby, and our house is in chaos."

"You are much mistaken, my son, real life is here in the Castle. Your baby's illness and the confusion are the illusions. Bring your family here to us, and all will be well."

"Dear Uncle, you know I tried that. What more can a man do?"

"A man can stick by his decision. It was not the King's wish for you to leave the Castle. You have disobeyed him."

"I am still loyal to the King. Surely it is no sin to live with one's family! Just this morning I met an old fellow on the way here. He claimed to be a son of the King, yet he lives on a holding like any peasant."

"Prince Eldred is indeed a child of the King. He is, in fact, a retired knight. Now he and his wife live like peasants on the King's orders, that he may thereby help someone find their way to the Castle. Their farm may look like an ordinary holding, but it is actually an Outpost of the King."

"But can't I do the same thing? Can't I serve the King wherever I am?"

"No, you can only serve the King wherever he places you. It is not good to live in the World until you have learned to shut out the voice of the World. It is that voice which has drawn you into disobedience. Did you never hear that the Prince said, 'No man, having put his hand to the plough, and looking back, is fit for the kingdom of God'?"[3]

Christine was praying with all her might, and she saw that Hannah, and others had come up and were praying also. What would his answer be?

"I suppose I shall have to wait then. When the children are older perhaps, or when my wife agrees to come with me, then I will return to the Castle and obey the King."

---

3 Luke 9:59-62

"Will you? You are telling me that those things are more important to you than the Lord is. The King doesn't want second place in your life."[4]

"I can't help it. Come, child. We have a long way to go." He held out a hand to Amanda. Amanda looked at Uncle.

Uncle smiled very gently at her, "The King, your Father, wishes you to remain here."

Amanda went to the broken prince, and put her arms around his waist. "I'm sorry, Daddy, I can't come now. I truly love you and Mama very much. And give my love to my brothers too. I will come to you at once when the King says I may."

Christine began to sob with relief. Thank you, dear Lord, thank you.

Still she felt sorry for Prince Hugh. He looked so desolate. He seemed unable to speak for a time. At last he knelt and embraced Amanda.

"You are right, child. You always did have more sense than the rest of us. You stay here. I'll try again to get your mother to come, but whatever happens, you stay here."

Christine had to thank him. And Hannah and all the others were crowding around him too, so Prince Hugh was sent off amid many prayers and expressions of love.

Godfrey hoisted Amanda to his shoulder, and like a triumphal march they went off to dinner.

---

[4] Matthew 14:26.

Chapter XIX

The Second Week Begins

When the others had gone, Christine found herself alone with Uncle and remembered what she had wanted to see him about.

"Thank you, Uncle, for coming so quickly. I was afraid we were going to lose Amanda."

"I couldn't have come if someone hadn't summoned me. You behaved wisely."

"I thought of Hannah and what she would have done."

"Yes, you will do well to follow Hannah. She is an exceptionally wise young lady."

"She just spoke to you about volunteering for an Outpost, didn't she?"

Uncle smiled mildly, "You don't need to know that, do you?"

Christine blushed, "I didn't mean to be inquisitive. I just meant that I want to volunteer too, though I realize I'm far from ready."

"Yes, you have been here only one week, but we are very pleased with your progress so far. Perhaps you will be ready sooner than you think."

He must not know about yesterday, Christine thought. "I tried yesterday to do a little service in the world, and I'm afraid I did a great deal of damage."

Uncle looked down at his bare toes, as though he did not like what he had to say. "That was pretty bad," he agreed at last. "I hope you will wait for me next time."

"Oh, I will! I will!" Christine asked hesitantly, "Did I keep someone from coming to the Castle?"

Uncle hesitated again. "You discouraged some who were thinking about it. But that is not to say they would necessarily have decided to come, or that they will not yet decide to come. Pray fervently, and we will manage to mend things."

That relieved Christine enormously. "But Uncle, why did Lucius and Godfrey succeed in bringing someone to the Castle? Are they so much wiser already than I?"

"Do you remember what you said to them as they left?"

Christine tried to remember.

"You said, 'Good luck!'" Uncle helped her.

"Now I remember, and Felicia said there was no such thing."

"Correct. Then you understood that what came their way would be of the Lord's grace. The encounter with the young peasant was not something they arranged, but something I arranged."

"I see, and I went running off, trying to do it myself."

Uncle nodded, and put an arm around Christine's shoulders. "You learn quickly. We are proud of you."

"I'm not proud of me," she replied with some bitterness.

"Now," Uncle waved his finger at her, "that was Mara talking."

"Sorry," she shook her head ruefully.

"It is not your opinion that matters, but ours."

Christine smiled, "Thank you, Uncle. You've really helped me."

"It's dinner time," he reminded her.

She thought of the venison and the laughter and fellowship at the dinner table, but then she thought again of how the consequences of her sin were still working. "I think I'd rather go to my room and pray."

Uncle smiled, "I'll go with you."

It was evening when Felicia timidly knocked on Christine's door. It opened at once.

"Are you all right? I was beginning to worry about you."

"I guess I fell asleep," Christine yawned. "I'm fine. Thanks for worrying."

"Would you like to go to Naomi's room? She's having a little party. It's her first birthday."

"It's what?" Christine asked in amaze.

"It's one year since she came to the Castle."

Christine had to laugh. It was so ludicrous thinking of Naomi as one year old. "I'd love to come!"

The girls sailed down the hall, and Felicia felt that whatever had been the matter, Christine was all right now.

Naomi had a pleasant room on the floor right above Christine's. The colors were earth tones with bits of bright green to accent. She had invited Sarah and Hannah and the five of them quite filled up the little space.

"Oh, where did you get the cakes?" Christine asked. Naomi had arranged a miniature feast on a small table, and Christine suddenly remembered she hadn't eaten dinner.

"I just asked," Naomi laughed. "You haven't learned to be a princess yet."

The conversation soon turned to all that had happened that morning. Every one of them had volunteered to go to an outpost, but Naomi had the most exciting news.

"Uncle said there will be one more mission leaving before winter," Naomi's eyes glowed, "and I am to be included!"

"How wonderful!" the other girls congratulated her, but Christine suddenly felt a great loss. There would be no friend in the steamy felt room, no one to read the verses in Bible class. It seemed much more than a week that she had known Naomi. Then she remembered the list of names. Her friend might never return.

"Christine, you don't look as though you were glad for Naomi," Sarah observed.

"I'm going to miss her." Christine could not pretend to be glad.

"I'll miss you too," Naomi put her arms around her. "I'll miss all of you. Will you remember to pray for me?"

They all promised. "It's too bad," said Felicia, "you'll miss the wedding."

That set the conversation in a new direction. It was a happier subject for Christine. Hannah showed them a piece of tapestry she had been working on. "If I really try I can have it done in three weeks. I want to give it to Sister Celeste for her wedding."

They all admired it and wondered if they could come up with gifts as nice.

"I'm nearly through weaving a blanket," Sarah commented. It's not as pretty, but it's useful."

"It will be a fine gift, Sarah," Naomi encouraged her. "I was making myself a felt hearth rug, but now I won't be here, I can give it to the newlyweds."

Christine had an idea, "Friday I made my first bowl, and Sister Amelia said it was good enough to fire. Perhaps in three weeks I can make something good enough for a gift."

Four pairs of eyes turned expectantly toward Felicia. She bit her lip, and said nothing.

"You'll think of something before then," Naomi comforted her.

"There is nothing to think of!" Felicia declared miserably. "You are all so clever with your hands, and I can't even learn to spin. I'm worthless!"

"No!" they all reacted at once.

"You are the best friend in the whole world!" Christine was emphatic.

"Ability to work with one's hands is hardly the measure of a person's value," Sarah assured her.

Hannah looked wistfully at her, "I wish I could sing as beautifully as you. I wouldn't care if I couldn't thread a needle."

Felicia was little comforted. It did not solve the problem of a gift.

When the two of them were walking back to Christine's room, Christine tried to reassure her friend again.

"Felicia, don't ever again say you are worthless. You can't know how much you mean to me, and I know Hannah loves you dearly too."

"Thank you, Christine. I know I am loved, but as Sister Alathea says, that doesn't go by deserving."

"No, not with our Father, but for me some people are easier to love than others." That brought up something that had been bothering Christine.

"Felicia, why don't I—I know it sounds awful—but why do I find it hard to love Sarah? I just don't feel about her as I do about you and Hannah and Naomi."

"I know what you mean. Sarah has a sort of self-sufficient air about her, as though she needs no one, so it's hard to get really close to her.

"It's not just imaginary. Uncle has never approved her as a sponsor, even though she knows her Bible better than any of us. I think she has trouble relating to ordinary people."

Christine was puzzled. "Isn't she 'ordinary people'?"

"No, she was a princess before she came to the Castle. Nearly all of us here are from peasant families, but Sarah was born to royal parents. Here, of course, that doesn't help her. I'm afraid it might even be a hindrance."

"You mean it makes her proud."

"I don't know. She never tries to claim special privileges, in fact, she's quick to volunteer for the worst jobs, but it makes her different somehow."

Christine went to bed that night thinking about Sarah, and finally concluded she felt a certain pity for her. I am going to be her friend, she determined. I will pray our Father to give me love for her.

Monday morning Christine awoke quite a while before the bells. It's because I napped so long yesterday, she reasoned. I'll go down early to chapel.

Even before she dressed, she went to her fountain. She had learned to seek it first thing of a morning and last thing at night, and each time she entered her room and each time she left it. Not only that, but she never passed one of the fountains that were scattered through the Castle without stopping to refresh herself. She found it had a wonderful effect on her spirits, and even a few hours without a drink made her terribly thirsty.

How can I ever go to an outpost, she wondered, I would die of thirst before I was a day's journey from the Castle.

The chapel was nearly empty at that early hour. But her attention was immediately drawn to a man lying on his face near the entrance. He did not seem to be praying, just weeping. Uncle was hovering nearby, and she quietly approached.

"Has he done something terrible, Uncle?" She was thinking of the sorrow she still felt for her own error.

"Shh," Uncle put a finger to his lips, "he is Prince Hugh's sponsor."

She understood at once, and was surprised she hadn't thought of him before. She knew everyone was assigned a sponsor, but she had been so worried for Amanda, that she hadn't really considered Prince Hugh.

"Poor man!" she whispered, "Can I help?"

Uncle nodded, and she knelt down nearby and began to intercede for Amanda's family. At first she tried to love them with Amanda's love, but presently she found the Prince's love was greater still. As she let it flow through her, the tears streamed down her cheeks, and she felt a kinship with the unnamed brother who had prayed there through the lonely night watch.

A little light was beginning to come through the stained glass windows when she felt the burden begin to lift. The chapel was full now, and soon the bell rang for breakfast.

They missed Lucius at the breakfast table. He was already on duty as a page. In the midst of the usual chatter and clatter Christine caught a flash in her peripheral vision, and heard a dull thud.

The hall had gone dead silent, and all eyes turned to an arrow that had just landed in one of the benches. Sure enough, the area was marked with a red circle. In the silence they could hear clearly the voices of sentries shouting on the battlements. One young fellow leaned over as if to inspect the missile, but a friend pulled him back.

Thank the Lord! breathed Christine, because another arrow whistled in near the first, narrowly missing the bench and skidding along the stone pavement.

In a few moments the shouting had ended, and everyone turned back to their meal and conversation. Christine was amazed that there seemed to be so little concern over the incident, and most amazed that she herself felt no anxiety. The arrows might have landed on the moon for all the trouble they gave anyone in the dining hall. It occurred to her that the one who shot the arrows had exposed himself to greater danger than what he had caused them.

Today Christine would begin learning to read. The thought so excited her that for the first time she wished she didn't have to help Amanda. But it didn't matter, because Sister Agatha was busy with her newest pupil, Lucius and Godfrey's poacher, Prince Justin.

At last she sat down with Christine and explained how letters had sounds, and the sounds taken together made words. They practiced on some words she already knew from her memory verses. Just before the hour ended, Sister Agatha gave her a little book.

"This is the gospel of Mark. It is the shortest and easiest of the gospels, so I always start my pupils in that. Take good care of it, because when you have read it all the way through, we will exchange it for a gospel of John. When you finish that, you will be ready to graduate, and you will receive a New Testament to keep."

They worked on the first verse until time to leave, and Christine hated to go.

At prayer class, Lucius appeared in his new livery, and the girls made an appropriate fuss over him. They tried to welcome Justin, but he did not seem to care to socialize. Brother Michael taught them about fasting. "There are many instances mentioned in both the Old and New Testaments. The Prince said that when he went away his disciples would fast.[1]

"Why do we fast? Because we need to esteem the words of our Lord more than our necessary food.[2] When we really want to hear from the King, when we are in earnest about an answer to our prayer, we fast to demonstrate our sincerity.

"How do we fast? There are many ways. Just skipping one meal to pray is fasting. Another form is to give up just certain foods, such as meat."

Why, thought Christine, I fasted yesterday and the day before. I didn't think about it as fasting, but please, dear Lord, accept it, and grant my petition.

"The idea of fasting is to discipline the flesh, so if it seems more appropriate, we can give up other comforts besides food.

---

[1] Mark 2:18-20

[2] Job 23:12

"A fast can be of any duration. The longest mentioned in the Bible were for forty days, but there seems to have been supernatural help. I have fasted for three weeks, but I usually find one week is about right. I allow myself milk during a prolonged fast.

"The important thing is to be reasonable in setting your goal, and then stick to it no matter what. Try shorter fasts first.

"But remember this is not a way to bribe the King, or force him. Fasting can be a useful spiritual exercise to bring our flesh into subjection.[3] It must not be an occasion for pride. The Prince has warned us not to show off by fasting.[4] Nor are we to moan and feel sorry for ourselves. Avoid the abuses, but don't avoid fasting."

When prayer class ended they were already in the garden for chore time. They put smocks over their clothes to keep them clean, and Lucius wished he had changed.

The idea of being together didn't quite work out. Sister Chloe assigned the girls to thinning a bed of carrots that were the beginning of the fall garden, and she set the boys to preparing another bed.

"You'll find rotted manure in the bins behind the stables," she told them.

Lucius had to laugh at himself, "Yes, I know where. I spent all last week filling them. I thought I'd have a cleaner job this week.

But Christine and Felicia were able to visit as they tediously pulled at the tiny seedlings.

Felicia decided to skip dinner and pray for her family. Christine was not surprised, but she wasn't quite ready for the boys' announcement that they weren't hungry. In fact when she reached the dining hall, Hannah was the only one she could find from her prayer class, and it soon appeared that Hannah was there only to keep Amanda company, not to eat. It made Christine feel strange to eat, almost guilty, until she noticed Brother Michael at another table enjoying his dinner.

---

[3] 1 Corinthians 9:27

[4] Matthew 6:16-18

Chapter XX

What is Sin?

Christine spent quiet time looking at her new book—though it was not really hers and not really new. She couldn't read it, but she could admire the graceful initial letters and the colorful designs in the margins. On some pages were pictures from which she could guess the story. It was the first book she had ever held, and she thought it the most beautiful object in the world. Christine couldn't bear the thought of returning it. She decided to try to make one just like it. She would ask Sister Agatha for brushes and paints.

Today, a week after she had come, she was finally allowed to ride the old mare around the ring. It didn't seem to Christine any more exciting than riding in an ox cart, and at least then, she went somewhere.

At swimming it was hard to think about the water. Christine gave Sister Celeste a shy kiss on the cheek by way of congratulations. The bride-to-be colored a little at all the well-wishes of her pupils, but she was obviously very happy. Christine briefly told her of the part Sir Alexander had played in bringing her to the Castle. The other girls all expressed admiration of the knight, and their certainty that the union would be a blessed one.

Before the class ended, Sister Celeste took Felicia aside for a private conversation. The result was a radiantly happy Felicia.

"What did she say to you?" Christine wanted to know.

"Oh, Christine! I've never been so surprised. She asked me to sing for her wedding!"

They ran all the way to music. Felicia wanted to talk to Brother Jude about a suitable song. The girls bubbled through the whole hour.

When they were seated in Bible class, Brother Uriah greeted Justin, then looked around on expectant faces. They all hoped their question had been chosen.

"We have a really fascinating subject to talk about today," he whetted their curiosity. "Sin."

Oh, thank you, Father, Christine prayed silently.

"Our question is—what is sin? That might look easy at first glance, but I wonder who can give me a good definition."

"Sin is the transgression of the law,"[1] Sarah asserted.

Sister Alathea chuckled, "Sarah knows if she quotes scripture no one can contradict her."

Brother Uriah nodded, "Yes, we can't say that is incorrect, but does that satisfy everyone? Is that a complete definition?"

Lucius was frowning, "What law is that talking about? I read in the law of Moses 'thou shalt not wear a garment of divers sorts, as of woolen and linen together.'[2] So I asked Sister Chloe why we wear a smock of linsey-woolsey when we work in the garden, and she said we aren't under the law."

"Didn't the Prince sort of change the law?" Felicia asked. "He said, 'Ye have heard that it was said by them of old time...' then he'd say, 'But I say unto you...' and he'd give a new law."[3]

"Ah!" Brother Uriah smiled, "we have more students of the scripture. But it's beginning to complicate our definition."

Hannah offered, "Another verse says, 'To him that knoweth to do good and doeth it not, to him it is sin."[4]

"Very good, Hannah, another scholar! So a sin can be something you do or something you fail to do. But it says 'to him that knoweth,' so if a person doesn't know what is right is he not sinning?"

They chewed on that one for a bit. Finally Nathan shrugged his shoulders, "It says something like that in Romans. That before the law

---

[1] 1 John 3:4

[2] Leviticus 19:19, Deuteronomy 22:11

[3] Matthew 5:21-48

[4] James 4:17

came we were ignorant, so we weren't sinning. I don't remember exactly."

"No, it says we were sinning, but sin was not imputed,[5] that is, we would not be judged according to the law when we did not yet have the law."

Christine felt more confused than ever. "Wouldn't I be better off then if I didn't know the law?"

"Not once the law exists, because you are expected to seek to know it, and not to do that would be a sin."

"But," Lucius protested, "are we under the law?"

"No, Lucius, we here in the Castle are not under Moses' law. Read Galatians[6] before you go back to your readings in Deuteronomy. It's almost as if the King himself had struggled with this question of how to teach his subjects what is sin.

"In the beginning he put our consciences into us to teach us right from wrong, but we dulled and abused our consciences until they were no longer accurate guides.[7] Then he tried writing out a long list of dos and don'ts, but they only made the ones who kept them feel self-righteous. Now in this age he has given us a better guide—the Holy Spirit to convict us of sin and lead us into all truth."[8]

Sister Alathea turned to Naomi, "When did you punish your children? Whenever they failed to please you?"

"No," said Naomi, "Only if I had already given them orders, and they disobeyed."

Brother Uriah nodded, "We're going to miss Naomi from these discussions."

"Our Father is the same way," explained Sister Alathea. "There is really only one sin, and that is disobedience. It seems that there are many paths from which to choose, but really there are only two—his way and our way."

That made Christine remember something Felicia had said about not doing what we want to do, but letting the King make our decisions. It didn't seem as hard now as when she had first heard it.

---

[5] Romans 5:13

[6] Galatians chapters 2, 3, 4, and 5, especially 5:18.

[7] 1 Timothy 4:2.

[8] John 16:7-15.

Godfrey spoke thoughtfully, "When you first asked what sin was, I thought of things like lying and stealing, but I see now that the real sin is not trusting the Lord to direct your life."

"Do you mean," asked Sarah, "that I can't know whether a thing is right or wrong until I ask Uncle?"

"If you're in genuine doubt, that's the wisest course. But the Word gives us many guidelines, and there is no sense in asking if we've already been told. In fact, that's a sin, because we're refusing the guidance he's already given us.

"What are some of these guidelines?" Brother Uriah challenged the group.

"The Golden Rule?"[9] suggested Lucius.

"That's sort of included in the guideline of love, isn't it?" Hannah smiled. Whenever I act or speak, I try to be motivated by love."[10]

"The rule I try to follow," inserted Sarah, "is what Paul wrote, 'whatsoever ye do, do all to the glory of God.'"[11]

"Those are excellent," Brother Uriah agreed.

Naomi spoke up, "The verse that helps me is 'whatsoever is not of faith is sin.'"[12]

"What does that mean, Naomi?" Sister Alathea inquired.

"It means that if I'm not sure it's right—if I have any doubts at all—I don't do it."

"I haven't studied the scriptures as much as some of you," Nathan confessed. "But I feel like from the gospels I've gotten to know what the Prince is like, and I just try to follow his example."

Christine shook her head sadly. She was so far behind Nathan, let alone Sarah or Naomi, and she longed to be wise like Sister Alathea or Brother Uriah.

Godfrey was having similar thoughts, "I haven't been really trying with my letters. I guess I didn't think it was that important. But I see now I can never really grow in wisdom and knowledge without reading the scriptures.[13] I'm going to try harder."

Brother Uriah was passing out the memory verses. "This is *my* favorite definition of sin."

---

[9] Matthew 7:12.

[10] John 13:34, 35.

[11] I Corinthians 10:31.

[12] Romans 14:23.

[13] Psalm 119:9 and others.

Felicia smiled and whispered, "I know this one already. 'All we like sheep have gone astray; we have turned everyone to his own way, and the Lord hath laid on him the iniquity of us all.' "[14]

"Laid on whom?" Christine wondered.

"On Prince Jesus, when he bore our sins on the cross."

A sharp pain like a sword ripped through Christine's insides. It was the first time she had truly seen that it was *her* sins for which the Prince had died. She would have no trouble remembering this verse.

In pottery class Christine helped to load the kiln. Sister Amelia explained its mysteries. How small and fragile Christine's little bowl looked. She couldn't help praying for its safety.

Christine and Felicia had made it a custom to meet in Felicia's room after vespers to work on letters and verses. This evening Hannah and Amanda joined them. Amanda had different verses, so Christine learned those too. When Hannah and Felicia reviewed verses they had had before Christine came, she added those to her memory work also. She wondered if it would be possible to draw Sarah into this fellowship. Her first reaction was a fear that Sarah was too serious and would spoil the merry times they had together, but she recognized the selfishness of that thought.

Tuesday morning Christine reported to the pottery shop even before matins to take her turn at feeding the kiln. The morning was chilly, but Christine soon felt as though she were working inside the furnace. She didn't mind giving up morning prayers and breakfast, but it was hard not to resent missing reading. It was already time to go to clothing class when another student relieved her.

In the halls, it seemed colder than ever after the heat of the kiln, and for once she was glad to reach the steamy felt room. When Sister Tabitha came by, Christine asked her about a shawl.

"Can you knit?" Sister Tabitha inquired. When Christine had assured her she could, she led her up the many flights of stairs to the

---

[14] Isaiah 53:6.

spinning room. There Christine greeted Felicia and the others, and again longed to be part of their company. Felicia looked as though she would gladly have traded places.

Selecting a yarn from the many brightly colored skeins was a delightful dilemma. She finally chose a soft blue-violet shade.

"But when will I have time to make it?" Christine wondered.

"You'll have to figure that out yourself. Here are some needles. I'll look forward to seeing it when you finish."

Christine took a roundabout way back to the basement, stopping by her room to leave the lovely wool. She hurried, realizing she had already wasted a good portion of her work time.

It was with unaccustomed weariness she arrived at prayer class. She flopped down on the grass in the warm sun and would have dozed off if she had been given the chance. But when Felicia nudged her she sat up and paid attention.

Brother Michael always looked serious when he taught about prayer. Christine had noticed that almost any other time she saw him, he was laughing, but here in prayer class, he never laughed. Today he looked so sober that Christine would not have been surprised to learn that the outlaws were mounting an attack against the Castle.

"I wonder," he began, "if any of you realize how great a responsibility it is to be a teacher.[15] It is a task I approach with trembling, for I know I must give an account to my Lord for every word I speak or fail to speak. And today I find myself having failed to speak. I am told that one of my students is going to be leaving soon on a mission to establish a new outpost."

Christine glanced over at Naomi.

"And I have only a few days to complete all I ought to have taught her. How much..." He shook his head regretfully. "How much I still want to impart to her before she leaves the Castle. I fear she may not be fully prepared, and I will be at fault. Forgive me, Father."

Confessions out of the way, Brother Michael faced them squarely. "We were talking about burden-bearing and intercessory prayer. I don't want to abandon that subject, but there is a whole area of prayer I have not even mentioned, and we must look into that.

---

[15] James 3:1

"We have been learning how to speak to our Father, but it is equally important to learn to be quiet before the Lord and listen as he speaks to us."

Christine straightened up. She had not even thought of such a thing. Could she hear directly from the King? She listened with growing eagerness as Brother Michael spoke of the Bible men and women who had heard from the Lord in various ways.

"Our Father is just as eager to communicate with his children today. He has told us that in the last days the old men shall dream dreams and the young men shall see visions.[16] But he most often speaks to us as he did to the prophet Elijah, in a still, small voice."[17]

He went on, emphasizing the necessity of receiving guidance in prayer, and then gave the class a practical assignment.

"We have talked about bearing a burden and that it must be the burden the King gives you. I challenge each of you to ask the Lord to tell you whom or what to pray for. Expect a specific answer. Lay aside your own thoughts. Remember, his ways are not our ways.[18] Determine to pray until the answer comes."

Christine determined she would.

But Sister Chloe put them to hoeing, and Christine, who had been tired before she started, found it hard to keep up with the others.

Even though she had missed breakfast, she was too tired to eat at dinner. After a few nibbles she retired, telling herself she ought to pray, but wanting very much to sleep.

When she stepped into her room however, she saw the beautiful blue-violet wool lying on her bed. She fingered the warm softness, and decided she would at least cast on the stitches. She already had a pattern in mind. She couldn't wait to see how it would look. The chimes were a shock. Quiet time was over and she had neither prayed nor slept.

---

[16] Acts 2:16-18; Joel 2:28-29.

[17] 1 Kings 19:9-13.

[18] Isaiah 55:8, 9.

Chapter XXI

End of a Bad Day

Today Christine got her wish and was given a younger horse to ride. But much to her dismay, her pony kept breaking into a trot. She knew she was supposed to pull the reins, but she had so much trouble just holding on that she couldn't pull on the reins too. What a relief to dismount after a half hour of being shaken to pieces.

The river refreshed her greatly, but she was learning to bob now, and it seemed to drain her last reserves of energy. She would have gladly dozed in music, but Brother Jude kept them standing the whole hour.

Christine dragged to Bible class where she was surprised to see Godfrey hard at work with a pen. Looking over his shoulder, she found he was practicing writing his name.

"But you haven't even finished the alphabet," she protested.

"I finished it last night. Sister Agatha was really shocked."

Christine rather shared that feeling. When Godfrey resolved to try harder, she hadn't expected an overnight revolution.

"Tomorrow I get my Gospel of Mark."

The pang of jealousy that shot through Christine showed for only a moment in her face. She immediately controlled it, and her congratulations were only partly forced.

When she sat down though, she found it harder to control her thoughts. She had worked hard from the very first day, and now she had missed only one reading class, through no fault of her own, and he had caught up to her. Life wasn't fair.

Brother Uriah's eyes twinkled as he thumbed through the papers in his hands. "Today we are going to take up the other questions you submitted."

No! Christine screamed inwardly. You didn't finish answering my question!

Brother Uriah read, "Is chess-playing a sin?"

Everyone laughed and turned to Lucius, for he was the chess enthusiast.

"But..." Lucius was embarrassed. "I didn't write that! If I thought it was a sin I wouldn't do it."

Instead of pursuing the subject, Brother Uriah read another scrap, "Is it a sin to braid your hair?"

Suddenly Christine knew just how Lucius felt. She was the only one who wore her hair braided, and they were all looking at her and laughing.

But Brother Uriah quickly read on, "Is it wrong to drink wine? Is jewelry sinful? Is it a sin to wager? When does eating turn into gluttony? Is it a sin to think about girls?"

The last question brought the biggest laugh of all. But everyone was feeling a little uncomfortable now. Christine saw Felicia fingering the gold chain she was wearing. Nathan was looking studiously at his tight waistband.

"No doubt," Brother Uriah continued, "you would all like me to give you simple yes and no answers to these questions. Then tomorrow you could give me another list, and another the day after that."

Sister Alathea addressed Naomi, "If I tell you not to drink wine or if I say it's all right, will you be satisfied with one of those answers?"

"No," Naomi shook her head. "If Uncle told me I'd be satisfied, but from you I would expect reasons."

"Fair enough. So why didn't you ask Uncle?"

"I guess I should have," Naomi laughed.

"We could open each of these questions to debate," declared Brother Uriah, "and get some pros and cons on all of them. But would that really settle the questions?"

"No," said Sarah firmly. "Unless you can show me the answer in the King's book, I'll not change my convictions."

"I wouldn't base my beliefs on just what someone told me either," Hannah volunteered, "but if my brothers and sisters think something is wrong, I'd stop doing it until I had gotten a definite approval from Uncle."

Lucius looked dismayed. "Anything you mention somebody is going to think it's wrong."

That brought a laugh and nods of agreement.

"These questions would seem to bear you out on that, Lucius," Brother Uriah agreed. "Hannah, do you mean you'd abide by any silly rule that others made?"

"Well, not eating meat seems like a silly rule to me, but the apostle Paul said he wouldn't eat it if it were going to offend his brothers."[1]

"But don't you see," Sarah argued. "The sin would be offending your brother, not the eating of meat."

Brother Uriah asked, "Would you say that an action that might be innocent in itself can become a sin under certain circumstances, such as when it would cause a brother to be offended?"

A light went on in Christine's head. "You mean—like chess—if you play it when you have nothing better to do it's not a sin, but if you did it at the wrong time, for instance instead of going to evening prayer, then it would be a sin."

"Would you agree with that, Sarah?"

"I don't know. Wouldn't it be more proper to say that skipping prayer is a sin, not that chess became a sin?"

"I don't see how something can be a sin sometimes and not all the time," Godfrey questioned. "Isn't right always right and wrong always wrong?"

"We're running over our time," Sister Alathea broke in. "You can do some more thinking for tomorrow."

The girls huddled over the memory verse. "The heart is deceitful above all things, and desperately wicked: who can know it."[2]

Christine mused, "Verses like this used to make me feel so condemned. Now I feel like there's something here for me to learn."

The good news at pottery class was that the contents of the kiln appeared to still be intact. The nervous students praised the Lord.

---

[1] 1 Corinthians 8:8-13

[2] Jeremiah 17:9

Christine noticed that some of them looked as droopy as herself. She remembered that someone had tended the kiln through the midnight hours. Others would be up tonight. Everyone was sacrificing either sleep or something they wanted to do. For the first time that day Christine began to feel better.

The general good spirits were interrupted by the coming of a page. This was usually a serious matter. One of the young men was summoned to the courtyard. When class was ending and he still had not returned, Sister Amelia sent another student to try to find him.

"See where Daniel is. He was to have the next shift at the kiln."

Christine was finished washing up and preparing to leave, when Sister Amelia approached her.

"Daniel has been given leave to visit his family. His father is dying, and they sent for him."

"That's terrible!" Christine's tender heart was ever ready to share another's sorrow. "We must pray for him."

"Yes, I'm sure it will be on the prayer list tonight at the Chapel. But someone will have to take two turns watching the kiln. Will you do it?"

Christine was momentarily stunned.

"I know you missed breakfast, so I'll stay until you can get a bite of supper."

"Never mind," Christine replied bitterly. "I'm not very hungry."

In a few moments she was alone in the pottery shop. A wave of anger swept over her, and she felt like smashing something. She forced herself to sit down and be calm. Her body she could control, but her thoughts were exploding in every direction. The nerve of Sister Amelia!

Out of all the students why did she choose me? I'm tired and hungry and—well, yes—cross.

But it's not supper I mind missing. I wanted to go to vespers and try listening the way Brother Michael was teaching us today. And there was the time afterwards in Felicia's room. In some ways it was the best part of the whole day. Christine thought of Hannah and Amanda and the love and laughter that filled the little room each evening. She felt a warning smarting in her nose.

No, I'm not going to cry, she determined. She went to check the fires. She would not be remiss in her duty. No matter how unfairly she was treated, she would still do her best. Feeling very righteous, she carefully stoked the furnace, then wondered what to do to pass the time.

At least she could study her memory verse—if she could remember all the words. She got out the scrap of paper. "The heart is...de...deceitful above all things, and de...de..."

"Desperately wicked."

The voice behind her startled Christine, but she recognized it even before she turned.

"Uncle! How good of you to come! You always seem to know when I need you."

"Yes, but I can't always get to you. I would have been here sooner but the mental arrows you were shooting at Sister Amelia kept me away."

"Wh-a-at?" stammered Christine. "But, Uncle, you know I wouldn't be angry at you! Wasn't it really unfair of Sister Amelia to ask me to take another shift?"

"Perhaps it was. Do you think she meant to be unfair?"

"No, but she was being thoughtless and inconsiderate." Christine somehow felt on the defensive.

"And is that worse than being angry and resentful and feeling sorry for yourself?"

Christine searched for an excuse. "But I'm just new, and she's a teacher!"

"Yes, she is. Brother Michael told you today that that's not an easy thing to be. Teachers are human. They make mistakes, but we expect their students to respect them anyway."

"I obeyed, didn't I? I didn't say anything, did I?"

"Yes, Christine, your behavior has been all I could ask."

Christine looked Uncle in the face to see if he were teasing her. He looked quite sincere, a little too sincere. Yes, there was a twinkle in his eye.

"Then if I've been so good," she grinned, "why is my conscience feeling so bad?"

At that they both began to laugh. Christine laughed long and hard, not because it was so funny, but because she needed that laugh. Uncle laughed so his sides shook and the tears came.

"To answer your question," Uncle was still chuckling. "Think about medicine. Some medicines only treat the symptoms, and don't really affect the disease. Controlling the symptoms is important, and commendable as far as it goes, but it's not a cure."

"I think I see. My words and actions are like symptoms. So I controlled them, but the sin was still inside."

"Good, very good. You'll have something to share in Bible Class tomorrow." Uncle turned to go, still laughing. "I shouldn't be surprised if you have more company shortly."

Christine waved good-bye. "Thank you, thank you," she cried.

Oh, I feel so good! She hugged herself. How could I have been so full of rottenness a few minutes ago? She picked up the memory verse from where it had fallen.

"The heart is deceitful above all things..." I was so sure it was Sister Amelia who was in the wrong and that I was perfectly in the right.

"...and desperately wicked." Oh, dear, I thought I had made so much progress. What did Uncle say, shooting mental arrows? I'm just as bad as the outlaws!

But another memory verse came to Christine's mind, the first one she learned: "If we confess our sins, he is faithful and just to forgive us our sins, and to cleanse us from all unrighteousness."[3] It's true! she rejoiced. As soon as I admitted to Uncle what my conscience was telling me, everything was fine.

"Hello! Are you hungry?" came a merry voice. Felicia was at the door of the pottery shop with a plate in her hands.

"Yes, starved!" Christine responded, "But just let me check the kiln again before I eat."

---

[3] 1 John 1:9

CHAPTER XXII

HEARING GOD'S VOICE

At the first stroke of the chimes, Christine leaped from bed. She had never felt so good, so eager for a new day. She ran to her fountain, and drank all she could hold. How anxious she was to get to the Chapel. It seemed a year since she had been there. And reading class! She must catch up for yesterday. She couldn't wait until Bible class. She knew the answer now. And pottery class! Today they would unload the kiln. What a wonderful day it would be!

Still in this state of exuberance she skipped from her room and nearly lost her footing at the head of the stairs. The long, long, stone staircase suddenly sobered her. To fall down would be a serious matter. It reminded her that nearly every day since coming to the Castle, she had fallen down in some respect. It was wonderful to feel as she did this morning, but she mustn't let it make her careless.[1] Placing her hand against the wall, she concentrated on the steps.

At matins she had intended to hurry through the thanksgiving part of her prayer and get to the listening part. But there seemed so much to be thankful for. And as praise poured out of her lips, that wonderful presence welled up inside, assuring her that her Father heard and approved. At last she asked her question.

---

[1] 1 Thessalonians 2:10-12, Ephesians 4:1, 2

"Dear Father, I am willing to bear a burden for you. Tell me what or whom you want me to pray for."

Christine tried to get very quiet, but thoughts came rushing into her head. She was already praying for Amanda, and for Amanda's family. She shouldn't stop that. She was still praying about the results of her mistake last Saturday. Uncle had told her to pray about that. And she had promised she would pray for Naomi and her mission. Maybe that was her new burden? No, she felt somehow that that was not from the King, but she would keep her promise anyway.

Brother Michael had said we must not think our own thoughts, but let the King put his thoughts in our mind. It was harder than it had sounded.

Instead of the King's voice, Christine suddenly heard the chimes. She couldn't believe the hour had passed already, but everyone was getting up to leave. There was no help for it; she would have to try later.

At breakfast they excitedly questioned one another. Had anyone heard from the King? No, none of the girls had.

"Didn't you ask?" Godfrey wondered.

"Did he speak to you?" Christine asked in dismay.

"Of course, just the way Brother Michael said he would. What was the problem with you girls?"

"Well, I kind of ran out of time," Christine comforted herself.

"I didn't," Hannah confessed honestly. "I listened and listened, but I didn't hear anything."

"Lucius," Felicia asked. "Did you get an answer?"

"Nothing, but I'm going to keep trying. Didn't Brother Michael say it was something you had to learn to do?"

"Yes," Christine remembered, "but why did Godfrey hear so quickly?"

"What did the King say to you, Godfrey?" Lucius asked.

"I just asked what burden he would have me to bear, and immediately I remembered that day Felicia had spoken of her burden, and then I heard a voice—it sounded just like Uncle—saying, 'Felicia is still very burdened for her family. She needs help to bear that burden.' So I knew that I was to pray for Felicia's family."

Felicia turned grateful eyes on Godfrey. But Christine thought, she's *my* friend. I'm the one who should have that burden. Just then she looked at Lucius, and the jealousy in his face shocked her. Did he think

Godfrey was trying to steal his girlfriend? And a moment later the realization struck her, did her own face look like that?

Yes, it was jealousy she felt. Ever since Godfrey had started to catch up in reading, she had been feeling twinges of jealousy. Now he had heard from the King ahead of them all, and received a burden Christine would gladly have borne.

What was wrong with her? She had always been proud of her brother. Did she love him less since they had come to the Castle? Christine found she didn't understand her own feelings.

She looked at Hannah; would she be jealous too? After all, she was more Felicia's friend than Godfrey was. But Hannah's face was glowing like Felicia's with thankfulness that Godfrey was going to help. She might have known Hannah wouldn't be troubled by petty feelings such as Christine was experiencing. But why hadn't Hannah been the one to hear?

"How do you know that was the King talking to you?" Lucius asked testily.

"For one thing," Godfrey admitted candidly, "because I wouldn't have thought of that at all. I guess I was hoping for something grand and exciting. Besides, I didn't even know Felicia was praying for her family."

Lucius looked ashamed. "I knew she was. Maybe that's why the King didn't give it to me—because if I had wanted to share it, I could have done so before this."

Christine felt he had spoken for her as well. She just added, "I'm happy for Felicia. Brother Michael said if the King gives you the burden, he must mean to answer."

Reading class was always an exciting time to Christine. As she learned the sounds of the letters it was like making friends of them. She was even glad that Godfrey was working with her on the first pages of Mark's gospel.

Today she finished her first large felt mat. It still seemed a bit meaningless to her though, until Sister Tabitha offered, "Now, let's make you a nice warm, waterproof cloak out of this."

"Oh, wonderful!" Christine's eyes opened wide as she suddenly understood the value of her labor. "But could I make it for my brother—I mean, I'm making the shawl for me. I can make a cloak for myself later."

At prayer class Brother Michael smiled and nodded as his students related their unsuccessful attempts to hear from the King. Only Godfrey had received an immediate and direct reply.

"I should have warned you," Brother Michael admitted, "I don't always get an immediate answer. Not unless it's something to which I *need* the answer immediately."

Godfrey laughed. "If you had told us that yesterday, I probably wouldn't have heard either."

Now I see, Christine thought to herself. Godfrey didn't get an answer because he's more spiritual than I am, or at least not more spiritual than Hannah. It's because he just expected it. It's the same as when he learned to float so quickly. And it's not because he's smarter than I am, either. Almost the opposite. I try to figure things out; he just goes ahead and does them. I guess our Father likes that kind of trust, she sighed.

Brother Michael was talking, "But some of you got answers and just didn't recognize them. For instance, Christine said she knew that her promise to pray for Naomi was not the special burden the King wanted to give her. That was hearing from the King, too. It was a 'no' answer, but that's an answer nonetheless."

Christine's mouth dropped open in surprise.

"And Naomi, you complained that you couldn't stop thinking about your new mission and clear your mind to listen. I don't doubt that your mission is your burden, and if you couldn't get it off your mind, it's because you are already carrying it.

"Hannah said that instead of hearing the King's voice, scriptures just kept running through her head. Hannah, that is the most frequent way the King speaks to us. Examine the verses that came to your mind, and I'm sure you'll find they contain your answer.

"But whether you heard anything or not, don't be discouraged. Your Father loves you. He will keep trying to communicate with you. This was not an urgent matter where you had to have guidance before you could move another step. I gave you this assignment to help you get in practice so when that emergency arrives you'll be ready."

When class was dismissed the four gardeners lingered awhile on the pleasant lawn. Felicia chatted with the boys, but prayer class always left Christine thoughtful. Now as Brother Michael watched the other students strolling off, she noticed him shaking his head. He caught her gaze on him, and smiled.

"I'm worried about Justin," he confessed. "Do you notice he takes no part in the class?"

"He's awfully quiet," she agreed. "But he's still so new."

"It's not just prayer class," Lucius spoke up. "He doesn't take part in anything."

"We tried to be friendly," Godfrey added. "But he didn't respond, and then we remembered how we had frightened him the day we met him, so we decided it was no wonder if he didn't want to be friends with us."

"I've experienced the same barrier," Brother Michael said sadly. "I think I may have made a mistake in asking to be his sponsor."

Felicia asked fearfully, "Do you think he is wanting to leave?"

"That's one of the things that puzzles me," Brother Michael replied. "He hasn't even mentioned wanting to leave, and you know that's not normal."

The four friends had to laugh over their own memories.

"Well, do help me pray for him, won't you?" Brother Michael looked straight at Christine.

They all promised to pray for the newest prince.

Today Christine determined she would use her quiet time to pray. The knitting lay on the bench tempting her, so she put it in the wardrobe. She got right down to business, asking the King to forgive her for her jealous feelings, and praying for Felicia's family as she ought to have been doing without being told. She remembered to pray for Justin too, but soon she was ready to listen.

"Dear Father, please show me or tell me what I ought to pray about."

Determinedly she cleared her thoughts away and just pictured herself waiting by the King's throne, a humble supplicant, but nevertheless fully expecting an answer.

Soon another picture came into her mind. She saw again the last Sunday morning of her old life. She saw the crowds in the village streets as the ox cart lumbered through. Suddenly her attention focused on Barbara.

"Oh, no, not her!" she cried aloud. As soon as she had done so, she realized she must have received a command or why would she be protesting. But surely the King didn't want her to waste her prayers on the worst woman in the whole shire. The more she struggled against the idea the more the conviction grew that this was precisely what the King wanted. One voice inside her was saying, "I won't! She doesn't deserve to be saved." But another voice was saying, "Whatever you say, Lord. Thy will be done."

Tears of frustration and disappointment came to her eyes. Like Godfrey, she had expected a different burden. Then suddenly the thought overwhelmed her, He did speak to me! I have received an answer from the King! What did it matter if it weren't the answer she had looked for.

But then she realized the King would have to do more. She had no love for Barbara. The King would have to put it there if she were to carry this burden. So she began to pray in that vein. "Dear Father, make me love Barbara. I can't really pray for her unless you do. I'll try to intercede, but you will have to supply the love."

And this time Christine really heard the still, small voice answer, "Fear not; I will."

At the same moment she felt such pity flowing through her. Pity is not love of course, but it was a beginning. Her tears turned to tears of sorrow for this poor wreck of a woman who had no knowledge of the King who loved her so.

When quiet time ended, Christine had learned something of burden-bearing. Her tender heart was broken for a sinful woman who was fleeing from all that was good and lovely, and trying to find the love she so desperately desired in a place where love did not exist.[2]

---

[2] Jeremiah 2:13

Chapter XXIII

Recognition

At Bible class, Christine could hardly hold still for wanting to share what she had learned, but Sarah got ahead of her. "I found a passage of scripture I think we need to look at. It is exactly what we've been talking about."

"Read it to us," Sister Alathea encouraged her.

"This is Paul writing, 'All things are lawful unto me, but all things are not expedient: all things are lawful for me, but I will not be brought under the power of any.'"[1]

"That is certainly pertinent," Brother Uriah nodded. "Tell us what it means."

Sarah continued eagerly. "My question was the one about gluttony. We all know eating is not a sin. Maybe nothing is a sin in itself. Paul says 'all things are lawful.' But if something gets a hold on you, such as when food takes on an importance to you, beyond the nourishing of the body, then it becomes an idol, and you become an idolater.

"I had an idea there was more to gluttony than just whether you were overweight or not. Gluttony could be just thinking too much about food."

---

[1] 1 Corinthians 6:12

"I see now!" Nathan jumped up, knocking his chair over, "It's all right to play chess occasionally, but if I got so fascinated with the game that I couldn't stop playing then I'd be sinning."

The others laughed at Nathan's excitement. "I told you I didn't write that question," grinned Lucius.

Godfrey was still serious. "That fits in with what I learned. I kept asking myself why Brother Uriah chose that memory verse about the wicked heart, and I finally realized that that is where sin is. It's not outside us, in wine or cards or jewelry. It's inside us, when we want those things—or anything—too much."

Naomi added, "I was reading over in James, and it said that sin comes from our desires.[2] But I think the desire itself isn't wrong, it's like a temptation. It's when we yield to our desires that it becomes wrong."

"Does yielding to our desire mean acting on it," Brother Uriah wondered. "Or can it mean just thinking about it, as Sarah suggested?"

"To let our minds dwell on it is certainly yielding to it," Naomi declared.

"I guess that answers the question," Sister Alathea smiled, "of thinking about girls. I feel sure that even our Prince when he walked the earth had thoughts about some young ladies of Nazareth, but he dismissed those thoughts to concentrate on his Father's will."[3]

Christine had been looking for a chance to insert her comments, and this seemed an opportune moment. "Sin is like a disease inside us. The actions we call sins are just the symptoms."

"That's a good analogy," Brother Uriah agreed.

Christine couldn't take the credit. "Uncle gave it to me," she admitted.

Brother Uriah smiled and continued, "The name of the disease is rebellion. Remember Monday's memory verse?[4] Sin is simply going our own way. Wanting our own way is the temptation, but temptation is not sin. Even the Prince was tempted.[5] But choosing our own way is sin."

Hannah gave a deep sigh, "If being tempted isn't a sin, why do I always feel so guilty?"

---

[2] James 1:13-15; 4:1

[3] John 5:30; 6:38

[4] Isaiah 53:6

[5] Hebrews 4:14, 15

"I used to feel that way," agreed Sister Alathea. "I trembled at every temptation because I thought I was sliding into sin. Then one day the King spoke to me. He said, 'Don't look at temptations as opportunities to sin. Look at them as opportunities to triumph.'"

Eyes opened wide as this revelation dawned on each student.

"But," Felicia protested, "I still don't know if I should wear jewelry or braids or drink wine or eat meat or whatever. You make it sound as if I couldn't sin as long as I'm really seeking to do the King's will."

"I think that's correct, Felicia. If you seek the King with your whole heart, you'll find you are losing your desires for many other things. The scriptures say, 'Delight yourself in the Lord and he will give you the desires of your heart.'[6] Some people think that says he will give you what you desire, but he is wiser than that. He will give you new desires, and those desires he will grant."

"Time's up," Sister Alathea interrupted. "Here is your new verse."

The girls put their heads together. "Oh, it's a long one!" Christine exclaimed.

Felicia read, "And be not conformed to this world: but be ye transformed by the renewing of your mind, that ye may prove what is that good, and acceptable, and perfect, will of God."[7]

The last hour of the day was Christine's special time of warmth and good feeling. This evening Sarah timidly joined the group in Felicia's room. Christine was glad her invitation had been accepted, but fearful that Sarah wouldn't fit in.

She wished now she had invited Naomi as well. Naomi had a gift for smoothing awkward situations, and this was awkward. Although Sarah had come, it was clear she was not at ease. She seemed to doubt her welcome. Though it took an effort, Christine put her arm around Sarah and hugged her in a friendly way. It was much like hugging a plank, but Sarah smiled as though she appreciated it.

There was nothing forced in Hannah's welcome. Christine envied her. Amanda was a study in controlled resentment. She clearly felt an intruder had come to spoil her evening, but she was determined to be

---

[6] Psalm 37:4-6

[7] Romans 12:2

"good." Felicia was nervous. As hostess she usually took the lead, but she was overawed by Sarah's longer experience and greater knowledge.

"Well, let's begin with today's verse," she encouraged herself. "It is a rather long one as Christine said."

It turned out that Sarah had learned it long ago, but she patiently listened while the others struggled with it. At last she asked, "What do you think it means: not to be conformed to the world?"

"Don't try to be like everyone else," Hannah suggested.

"Especially not like sinners," Amanda added solemnly.

"Can we think of some specific examples?" Sarah pursued the subject.

Christine felt it should be easy to think of some, but she couldn't at first. Felicia seemed equally puzzled.

"Well, in the things we are concerned about," offered Hannah. "For instance, so many people in the world are concerned with having things or earning a living. Our Prince told us not to think of those things."[8]

"Oh, good!" Christine agreed, "or like being concerned with our own prestige and what others think of us."[9]

Amanda cut in excitedly, "Or about having fun and enjoying ourselves."[10]

"Very good, Amanda!" they all encouraged her.

"We could sum those up by saying that worldly people are mostly concerned with their own selfish interests," Sarah concluded. "What should we be concerned about then?"

"That scripture I was talking about said to seek the kingdom of God and his righteousness,"[11] Hannah answered.

"Right! So the focus of our life is quite different from that of the world. Are there other areas where we should not conform?"

Felicia almost whispered, "I thought it meant we should look different from worldly people."

"Good, Felicia," Sarah nodded. "Can people tell by looking at us that we belong to the King?"

---

[8] Matthew 6:24-34

[9] Matthew 23:5-7 and others

[10] 1 Timothy 5:6; 2 Timothy 3:4

[11] Matthew 6:33

"Before I came to the Castle," Hannah remembered, "I met some people who had a glow of happiness and love in their faces. I want to be like that."

Sarah blushed a little. "I do too. My parents have that, but I don't know if I will ever achieve it."

"I know the look you mean," said Amanda. "Sister Celeste has it, and Sister Agatha, and of course Uncle."

"Don't we all have it sometimes?" Christine wondered. "Especially in chapel when I look around, I see it in so many faces. Hannah has it a lot of the time, but I've seen it in all your faces at one time or another."

"I think Christine is probably right," Sarah smiled. "I've even seen it in the face of new parents. When love and joy and peace and the other fruits of the Spirit[12] are uppermost in our lives, our faces show it. We just have to let them grow in us."

"That's the second part of the verse!" Hannah exclaimed. "Being transformed by the renewing of our minds."

Amanda frowned, "If that part came first—I mean if we could be transformed or renewed first—we wouldn't have to worry about not conforming. We'd just be different without trying, but since the not conforming comes first we have to work at it."

Sarah threw her head back and laughed. It was the first time Christine had seen her so pleased at anything. "Where did this little head get so much wisdom?" She patted Amanda, "Can I take you back to my room to help me study?"

Amanda's frown disappeared. Sarah's praise had won her a friend.

Christine was thinking how glad she was she had invited Sarah. "This is almost as good as Bible class!"

Felicia was still frowning though. "I guess working at it was what I had in mind." She looked apologetically at Christine. "I'm the one who wrote the question about braided hair. I'm sorry, Christine. I didn't do it to embarrass you. That's what I meant about looking different. Before I came here, everyone I had ever met from the Castle seemed rather odd to me.

"Like the knights, they're so different from ordinary people. And the wandering preachers, they don't wear armor, but their dark robes

---

[12] Galatians 5:22, 23

are almost like a uniform of some kind. I thought you could always recognize people from the Castle by the way they dressed.

"Then when I got here—well, everyone seems to wear whatever they please. When you see the knights out of armor they look like any fine gentlemen. And instead of a dark robe, I've had nicer clothes than I ever had before."

"Some people do wear plain dark clothes," Christine noted thoughtfully. "But the King gave us these pretty dresses; he must expect us to wear them."

"That's what I thought," Felicia mourned, "But when someone asked about wearing jewelry, it made me wonder."

Hannah confessed, "That was my question. I read two places in the King's Book where it sounded as if you shouldn't wear it,[13] and I don't want to do anything the King doesn't want me to."

Sarah spoke in a low voice. "When my mother was a young girl here at the Castle, the King told her not to wear jewelry. He didn't say why, or that it was a sin. He just told her not to. So she never has, and I don't do it either. I guess I don't think it's wrong to do it, just that it's better not to do it."

While they were talking, Amanda had been struggling with the clasp on her bracelet. Now she had it undone. "Here," she handed it to Hannah, "now I know why you gave it to me, I don't want it either."

Hannah took the bracelet and looked at it thoughtfully. "It's lawful for me, but is it expedient? I know it doesn't have any power over me. I really don't care one way or the other."

"I'm afraid I love pretty things," Felicia said sadly. "I guess that means I should give them up."

"This is silly!" Christine leaped up with some heat. "The King wants us to be happy and enjoy life. He doesn't want us to give up everything that's good or pleasurable. As long as we don't give these things more importance than they deserve we can still use them."

"Yes, we *can*," Sarah agreed, "But is that the best choice?"

"Well, I know what I'm going to do," said Hannah. "I'm going to ask Uncle, and that will settle it."

"Me too," declared Amanda.

"I don't think I need to," Felicia hung her head. "It may be all right for you, but I think I would be sinning."

---

[13] I Timothy 2:9; 1 Peter 3:3

"Well, I don't have any jewelry, but I'm going to keep braiding my hair," Christine was positive. "I don't see how it could be a sin."

"Then what does it hurt to ask?" Amanda wondered.

"We all know it's not a sin. Remember what you said today in class?" Sarah reminded her. "The outward action isn't the sin, it's the inward attitude. Do you detect anything amiss in your attitude?"

For an instant Christine felt like telling Sarah to mind her own business, then the truth hit home. "It's pretty bad isn't it," she grinned. "All right, I'll talk to Uncle about braiding my hair."

Chapter XXIV

What is Truth?

Christine really intended to talk to Uncle right away, but the days were so busy. When she was braiding her hair in the morning she planned that she simply must see him today, but as soon as the task was done she quickly forgot.

The cloak was finished. Christine had dyed it a reddish-brown She couldn't wait to see Godfrey's reaction. From clothing class she took it with her to prayer class and presented it to him with their friends looking on. The lavish praise she received was an ample reward for the tedious hours in the felt room.

"I can't wait for some cold, wet weather to try it out!" Godfrey exclaimed.

"I'm green with envy," Lucius laughingly admitted. "I say, Christine. Couldn't you make me one?"

Before Christine could answer, the others were putting in their orders. Christine could see weeks and weeks of hard labor stretching before her—but what could be more fun than pleasing your friends? "All right," she laughed, "cloaks for everyone, but Amanda gets the first one. Hers won't take as long."

"Can mine be bright red?" Amanda looked hopeful.

"Well, if I can find some light-colored fur to use. Do you want to be Little Red Riding Hood?"

"Yes, I like that story!" Amanda stopped and frowned. She looked over at Hannah, "Is it all right to like fairy tales? I mean because they're not true, and the Prince likes things to be true."[1]

Hannah threw her hands in the air, "The questions this child comes up with!" Everyone laughed knowing how fond Hannah was of her young charge. Hannah looked appealingly at Brother Michael, "Would you answer her? Please?"

He sat down and beckoned Amanda to him. Brother Michael was so gentle; Christine often found it hard to remember that he was the weapons instructor. What a grand thing it was to be a knight of the King. Her old childhood dreams of being a knight flashed through her mind. More fairy tales! Yet here she was a princess! What could be more unbelievable than that?

"Amanda," Brother Michael began, "truth comes in many forms. When the Prince told a story about a man who went from Jerusalem down to Jericho and fell among thieves,[2] he may not have been referring to an actual incident. He probably made up the story to illustrate the lesson he wanted to teach. Or the story about the prodigal son[3] or the servants and the talents[4]—but would you say those stories weren't true?"

"If they didn't happen how can they be true?"

"Well, let me put it another way. If I said I knew a very wise little girl who understood that her Father, the King, only wanted her to think about what is true, and honest, and just, and lovely, and of a good report,[5] and then Amanda once did a foolish thing, which would be more true—my statement which describes Amanda the great majority of the time, or the incident when she was out of character?"

"They'd both be true...but I guess I see what you mean. A real happening can be less true than a general statement."

"Then can you see that the story of the Good Samaritan contains great truth even though it is fictitious?"

"But does this have anything to do with fairy tales?"

"Very much. Stories may be fictional, but whether they are true or untrue depends on how they handle reality. If the view of life they

---

[1] Psalm 51:6

[2] Luke 10:35-37

[3] Luke 15:11-32

[4] Matthew 25:14-30

[5] Philippians 4:8

express is true then the story is in a sense true—even if fantastic things happen."

"So—let me think—even though the wolf can talk, that doesn't make the story false, if the things he says and does are wolf-like."

"That's the idea," Brother Michael looked with pride at his apt pupil. "Or if the wolf is just a symbol standing for someone else, the way the father in the story of the prodigal son stands for our Father, the King."

"Then the wolf stands for the outlaws," Amanda stated firmly. "Because he talks nice to Red Riding Hood, but he's planning to eat her up."

"Excellent!" Brother Michael laughed, "and who is the wood-cutter who slays the wolf and rescues Red Riding Hood?"

"Oh, that has to be the Prince!"

"Are all fairy tales like that?" Christine asked in astonishment.

"Fairy tales have been around a long time, and represent the wisdom of the common people. They often reflect the particular culture from which they spring, but there's probably at least a germ of truth in anything that survives so many generations and so many retellings.

"Now, you, young lady," he patted Amanda, "have made us late for prayer class, and you are supposed to be at your class. You'd better run."

As the students moved to their places, Brother Michael winked at Christine, "Please make my cloak plain brown."

Christine was startled to think she could do a service for someone like Brother Michael. She found herself too tongue-tied to reply, but dropped a nervous curtsy as acknowledgment.

The day passed swiftly and Christine's question didn't come to mind until Bible class. She wondered if she might not just ask Brother Uriah, then remembered that he had already refused to give any simple answers to these questions. Today the emphasis was again on the nature of sin as rebellion. It didn't matter what the issue was, whether great or small. What mattered was whether we chose to do our own way or to obey the King. The aged couple emphasized that there were no little sins, they all involved the element of stubborn willfulness and rebellion.

The new memory verse was, "For rebellion is as the sin of witchcraft, and stubbornness is as iniquity and idolatry."[6]

---

[6] 1 Samuel 15:23

It made Christine shiver, especially when she remembered her attitude about braiding her hair. She prayed for forgiveness. "I do want to obey," she prayed. "Whatever you want me to do with my hair, I'll do."

In pottery she was trying so hard to make something good enough for Sister Celeste. She prayed over the clay, and asked the King to guide her fingers.

She had forgotten again about the braids as she hurried to supper. But there she suddenly came upon an unpleasant scene.

"But I like you to wear jewelry. You look nice in it!" Lucius's voice was low, but he was almost hissing.

Felicia's face was red either from anger or embarrassment or both. "And I don't look nice without it, I suppose."

"Of course you do! But don't you see where this line of thinking will take you? You won't be able to do anything you enjoy, just because you enjoy it."

Christine felt a twisting pain in her stomach. She knew Lucius had the same feeling inside, and Felicia was probably feeling even worse.

"Does that really matter, if I please the King?" Felicia defended herself.

"I suppose you think I should give up chess—just to prove I can."

"That's between you and the King. I don't think anything one way or the other. But it wouldn't hurt you, you know."

But they're hurting each other! Christine thought. Oh, dear Father, she prayed. Show me how to stop this!

Just then she saw Naomi approaching, and it gave Christine an idea. As though she had not observed them, she rushed right between Lucius and Felicia to exclaim loudly, "Naomi! I've been wanting to talk to you! Did you ask Uncle about wine? You said you were going to."

"Yes, I did," Naomi smiled.

Thank you, Christine prayed as her friends turned to listen to Naomi.

"What did he say?" Lucius still sounded a little belligerent.

"He wouldn't tell me the answer." Naomi watched the startled faces with amusement. "He said because I was leaving so soon I had to stop depending on speaking to him for answers. I won't be able to walk up to him with my questions when I'm at the outpost."

That staggered Christine, "How terrible! What will you do?"

"Well, the first thing he told me to do was to study the King's book, because all answers are there if I use divine wisdom to understand it correctly. But I told him that was part of my confusion, because some verses speak against wine, such as, 'Look not thou upon the wine when it is red, at the last it biteth like a serpent, and stingeth like an adder.'[7]

"And other verses favor it, for instance, 'He causeth the grass to grow for the cattle, and herb for the service of man: that he may bring forth food out of the earth; and wine that maketh glad the heart of man.'"[8]

Hannah and Amanda had come up in time to hear Naomi's last comments. "That's the very problem I'm having about jewelry," Hannah agreed. "There seem to be scriptures on both sides."

"Well, Uncle said," Naomi continued, "that the answer was there if I studied the whole book and weighed it prayerfully."

"That won't help us today," Christine moaned. "Isn't there a way to settle the argument?"

"Argument?" Hannah was surprised. "No one's arguing. I'm sure that would be much more wrong that any of the things we're discussing."

Christine looked out of the corner of her eye at Lucius and Felicia. She hadn't meant to let on that she had heard them, but they were hanging their heads.

"Christine means Lucius and me," Felicia whispered. "We were arguing."

There was a moment of awkward silence, then Naomi took each by a hand. "Well, wasn't that silly? I'm sure you won't do it any more. Come on, our supper's getting cold."

This was a bit of an exaggeration. The servitors were just setting it on the table.

Godfrey came bouncing up, "What's everybody looking so glum about?"

Only Amanda seemed able to answer, "Naomi is telling us what Uncle told her about wine."

"I was wondering about that too. Did I miss everything?"

"No," Naomi replied. "I was just about to say that besides sending me to study the King's book, he also reminded me of what

---

[7] Proverbs 23:32

[8] Psalm 104:14, 15

Brother Michael is teaching us—that we can get answers from the King in prayer.

"That's what we do when we're at an outpost," she smiled at Christine. "That's why it's so important to learn to hear from the King directly."

"Well, when you hear," Lucius sighed, "would you tell us please."

Naomi looked thoughtful. "No, I don't think I should. I think you have to do your own praying."

Lucius looked very discouraged. Hannah tried to comfort him. "Don't you see? Naomi's answer may not be your answer. Remember what Brother Uriah said. We're not making up a set of rules for everyone to follow. What matters is what the King wants *you* to do."

That night there was a Celebration. A young boy had been brought to the Castle by a knight. While dressing, Christine decided to leave her hair down, then hit another problem. She had said she had no jewelry, but what about her crown? It was of gold. But Uncle had given it to her. How was she supposed to know what to do? Nearly all the people at the Castle would be wearing their best clothes and there would be jewels in abundance. But Uncle himself would be wearing his same coarse brown robe. She must talk to him. For now she laid the crown back in the wardrobe.

At the feast another question arose. Wine was served. She had never drunk any before coming to the Castle, but she had sipped it carefully at the other Celebrations and enjoyed it very much. Now she wondered if she should. She saw Lucius playing with his glass and knew he was going through the same dilemma.

Quickly she looked around at her friends and tried to get a glimpse of some of her teachers and others. Then she thought, what difference did it make what the others were doing. She had to settle this for herself. And tomorrow she would, she resolved. For tonight—no wine.

Chapter XXV

Discerning

During morning prayer Christine kept an eye on Uncle. She would make a beeline for him as soon as the bells rang. But when she had pushed through the exiting crowd, she found Hannah and Amanda already had gained an audience. Never mind. At least she was sure Amanda would share whatever Uncle told her.

As they walked from the dining hall toward reading class, Christine pulled her aside.

"What did Uncle tell you? What did he tell Hannah?" Amanda smiled at Christine's eagerness. She seemed to be thinking of teasing her friend by withholding information, but she decided against it.

"Hannah said to Uncle, 'Please tell me if the King wants me to wear jewelry or not.'"

"Yes, and what did Uncle say?"

"He said, 'My dear daughter, your heart is perfect. You will make the right decision.'"

Christine stopped in her tracks. Yes, she thought, Hannah always did make the right decisions. But that was no help to Christine. If there was one thing she knew with certainty, it was that her own heart was still far from perfect.

"Is that all he said," she asked disappointedly.

"That's all he said to Hannah," Amanda replied tantalizingly. "Then it was my turn."

"Well, go on!" Christine urged.

"I thought I'd use Hannah's words. I said, 'Dear Uncle, please tell me if the King wants me to wear jewelry or not.'

"Then Uncle said, 'Why do you want to wear jewelry?' And I said, 'I don't. I want to please the King.'"

Christine nodded, "That was a good answer."

"So Uncle said, 'What do you think is the purpose of wearing jewelry?'

"I had never thought much about it, so it took me a little while to answer. 'I guess to make you look nice,' I said.

"And he said, 'That seems to be the idea in most people's minds, but do jewels change the way you look?'

"That seemed kind of silly when I thought about it, so I said, 'No, you look the same whether you are wearing jewels or not. It must be that you wear jewels so people will notice you.'

"Then he said, 'The King wants his children to be noticed for the fruit they bear, not the jewels they wear.'

"'Maybe,' I said, 'they want to be like others, or maybe they just get in the habit of dressing up that way.'

"And Uncle asked me if I thought those were good reasons, and of course I said no."

Christine gave a sigh. "So the King doesn't want us to wear jewelry."

But Amanda grinned, "That wasn't all. Then he asked me if I could think of any good reason to wear jewelry. I couldn't, so he told me one.

"Oh, dear!" Christine didn't want to have more complications.

"He reminded me about the prodigal son, how when he came home they put a ring on his finger.[1] He asked me if I thought that was to make him look nice.

"I said, 'No, that was to show he was restored as a son.'

"So he said, 'Then jewelry can have meaning.'

"And I said, 'Like a wedding ring!' and he looked at me that way everybody does when I say something they think is clever."

Christine laughed.

---

[1] Luke 15:22

"Then I remembered that some of the people here at the Castle wear a cross around their necks, so I asked if that was because it had meaning, and he said yes, and our crowns are like that too."

"So we can wear our crowns," Christine concluded.

"Well, we can if we're wearing them to show we are children of the King, but not if we put them on to attract attention or to look nice."

Christine sighed again. "I guess I can understand that. Our motives are what count. Is that everything Uncle said?"

"Just one more thing," Amanda blushed a little. "He said that to the King, my sparkling eyes and rosy cheeks were more beautiful than any jewels."

Christine looked at Amanda in surprise. She had changed in the short time she had been at the Castle. Christine had noticed her gaining weight, but now she saw that her wan little face had grown pink and healthy. She hugged her tight. "As always," she said, "the King is right."

Christine felt a degree of satisfaction at last. At least one question was answered. If only there weren't so many others. How was she to find the King's pleasure in every small matter? She thought disgustedly how much worry they had already wasted on a matter as inconsequential as jewelry. But then she had learned something from it. In her mind she listed "Ways to Know the King's Will." Number one was to study the scriptures. Number two, ask in prayer. Number three, have a perfect heart. And number four, thank goodness she could still get counsel from Uncle.

Knowledge of the scriptures was still such a far-off goal it seemed almost unattainable. But the thrill of learning to read was not wearing off. She learned new words everyday, and it was exciting to see an inscription she had looked at before as indecipherable suddenly leap into meaning. The day she had been able to read her adoption certificate was an unforgettable experience.[2]

Prayer, too, had gained excitement with the added dimension of listening for communication from the King. This morning as she had prayed for Justin, she had felt a voice telling her that none of them were understanding him aright. She was puzzling yet what to do with this bit of information.

---

[2] Would you like to have an adoption certificate like Christine's? You can order one from Kingdom Press. See the order blank at the back of this book.

A perfect heart? How did you get one? She couldn't imagine Hannah as ever having been different. Nor could she imagine herself attaining the sweetness, gentleness, and humility that were so evident in Hannah. But one thing she could do—she could use Hannah's wisdom second hand, as she had done that first Sunday in the crisis over Amanda and her father. There were others in the Castle worth imitating, and that's what she would have to do until she developed wisdom of her own.[3]

As for talking with Uncle, she would soon find an opportunity. And it came unexpectedly right after dinner. She was on her way to her room for quiet time and met him in the hall.

"Oh, Uncle, could I talk to you a little?"

Christine loved the smiles that came to his face when he was pleased. He turned to walk with her, "Let's go to your room. We wouldn't want to break the quiet-time rule."

Christine giggled, "The rule is to be in our rooms alone."

"I don't count," Uncle assured her.

But when they were comfortable in Christine's room, the questions seemed too silly to ask. There were much more important things. It was such a treat just being with Uncle, Christine would gladly have spent the hour with her head in his lap, not saying a word.

"You wanted to talk to me," he prompted her.

"Yes," Christine frowned. "I have a lot of questions..." Suddenly she remembered a question that didn't sound silly.

"This morning the King told me that we don't understand Justin, and I do want to help him. Could you help me to understand him?"

Uncle looked at her rather blankly. He knows that wasn't what I had intended to ask, Christine thought. Finally he said, "No."

Christine could hardly believe her ears. "You won't help me?" she exclaimed in surprise.

"You didn't ask me if I would; you asked if I could and the answer is no."

Sometimes, Christine thought, Uncle's answers are more perplexing than no answer at all. "Well, then how can I ever understand him?"

Uncle looked just the least bit annoyed. "You know," he said, "I hear similar requests everyday. They run something like 'Dear Uncle,

---

[3] Philippians 3:17

please help me understand the Scriptures.' And of course, that's part of my job—but I get these requests from people who don't ever bother to read the Scriptures, not to mention study them."

Christine pondered this. How could anyone be so foolish as to ask help understanding what they hadn't even read? Was she like that?

"You mean—I need to try to get to know Justin, and then you can help me understand him."

Uncle smiled and nodded. "You're all worrying and praying about Justin but none of you are trying to find out what he thinks."

"That's pretty silly of us, isn't it? Sorry, Uncle. I'll talk to him first chance I get."

"Now what about those other questions?"

Christine decided there was no use wondering if they were silly. Very likely she would never have any questions that were anything else. Still she felt a reluctance.

"Uncle, does the King really care very much about our appearance?"

"No," Uncle replied. "Do you?"

"Do I what?"

"Care very much about your appearance?"

"I...I..." Christine was flustered. "What do you mean?"

"You need to learn to value things as the King does. If he doesn't place a great deal of importance on appearance then you shouldn't either."

"Oh, good! So I can forget all these trivial questions?"

"That's not what I said. I didn't say the King had no interest at all in your appearance. You need to settle these questions and then stop worrying about them. But the really important thing is to consider how much time and effort you spend on things, such as appearance, and see if you are giving them more importance than they deserve."

Christine sighed. If only Uncle would give plain yes and no answers. It had been complicated enough before.

"And while you're weighing your values," he continued, "don't forget to weigh your motives. Why do you want to look nice?"

Christine hung her head, "To get compliments from people is the wrong motive, isn't it?"

"Yes, seeking to please men is always the wrong motive,[4] and anyway men are impossible to please more than momentarily. Seek to please the King, and you will succeed."

That touched a responsive chord in Christine's heart.

"I do," she cried. "I want to please the King more than anything."

"I know you do," Uncle laid a hand on her shoulder. "And when the time comes that you not only want that most, but you want it exclusively, you will have that perfect heart you were longing for."[5]

Uncle was getting up to go.

"Oh, wait!" Christine called.

Uncle turned back, as though pleased to be detained.

"There were a lot of other things," she pleaded. "I can't even remember them, but I do want to get them straightened out. I want to know if things are pleasing to the King or not, and I need help."

"Apply the principles you have learned. Is the thing too important to me? Why do I want to do it? Many times you'll realize there is no good reason for the thing, and if there's not, then just drop it—not because it's bad, but because it's not God's best. Purify your life of unimportant things and there will be more room for truly important ones."[6]

Christine shook her head doubtfully, "That seems as if it should be clear enough, but I have a feeling I'm still going to have questions."

"Don't be afraid to ask them," Uncle encouraged her. "One thing you were wondering about; I should explain that the wine we receive here in the Castle, like all the food for our feasts, comes from the Keep. It is the King's own vintage and is nothing like the wine of the world."

"Like the Castle water," Christine agreed. "It's nothing like any other water." She suddenly felt very thirsty and realized she had failed to drink upon entering her room as was her custom.

She went to the fountain, and when she had drunk deeply, it came to her that it would be perfectly all right to lay her head in Uncle's lap, and she did so and was soon fast asleep.

---

4 Luke 6:26

5 Matthew 6:22

6 2 Timothy 2:4; Hebrews 12:1

CHAPTER XXVI

JUSTIN

Right after prayer class seemed the best time to approach Justin. Christine wondered what she could say that would get him to open up and talk. She wondered why she felt so nervous. Outside the Castle she would never have opened a conversation with a stranger, but wasn't Justin her brother? Anyway she had sat in classes with him for over a week. But his quietness made it hard for her to speak to him. A voice said to her, "It doesn't have to be today. Tomorrow will do just as well." But Christine knew that was not Uncle's voice, so she gathered her determination and plunged ahead right in front of everyone.

"Justin, we are all so glad you're with us here in the Castle." It sounded forced to her own ears, and they reddened in embarrassment. She finished even more lamely, "Aren't you glad to be here?"

Justin stared at her in amazement. "Glad?" he echoed. "What do you mean by that? I'm glad to be alive, if that's what you mean. But I wish I were home. I wish I had never left home!"

The friends exchanged worried glances. That wasn't what they wanted to hear. The King was right; they didn't understand.

Brother Michael spoke in wonderment, "Then Justin, why are you here?"

Justin looked around at them in something close to anger, "You, of all people, ask me that? You caught me and dragged me here. Have you forgotten, or did I dream it all?"

Brother Michael, sensing a mystery, probed more deeply, "Justin, what happened to you here at the Castle?"

"Why I was brought before the judge, the one you call Uncle. I confessed. I saw it was no use to deny my guilt. And then your King in his great mercy spared my life. I have known of peasants being skinned alive or roasted on a spit for such crimes as I committed. And here I am condemned,[1] yet only sentenced to slavery. Do not think I am ungrateful. I shall willingly serve the King all my life. Whatever he says I will do with all my heart. My life was forfeit and I can never again call it my own."[2]

Christine protested, "Do you call this slavery? Learning to read and write and so many other wonderful things?"

"I understand that I am being trained to increase my usefulness. I am grateful for this also, for if he had made me a slave of the lowest degree doing the meanest work, I would still have considered myself fortunate to be alive. Truly your King is most generous."

Godfrey interrupted. "You keep saying our King. Isn't he yours too?"

"Free men have a king. A slave has only a master. He is my master."

Lucius was about to burst. "I never heard such rot! You have everything completely turned around!"

Brother Michael held up a hand to restrain him. "Wait, Lucius. There's something to what he's saying. Maybe we ought to look at our own relationship more carefully.

"We too were condemned criminals, worthy of death.[3] Perhaps if we reflected more on that, we would, like Justin, be grateful just to be slaves. I'm afraid we sometimes behave more like spoiled brats than rescued sinners."[4]

Felicia spoke very quietly, "I understand how he feels."

---

[1] John 3:17, 18

[2] 1 Corinthians 6:19, 20

[3] Romans 3:10-12

[4] Ephesians 2:11-12

"Dear little sister," Brother Michael lay a comforting hand on her shoulder, "She who is forgiven much, loves much."[5]

Godfrey thoughtfully recited, "'I beseech you therefore, brethren, by the mercies of God, that ye present your bodies a living sacrifice, holy, acceptable unto God, which is your reasonable service.'[6]

"I see now, because of his mercies total surrender of our lives is the only reasonable response."

"But," Christine felt they were forgetting Justin, "even though you owe your life to the King, he has forgiven you the debt. Justin, you are not sentenced to a life of slavery; you are pardoned![7] Don't you understand that the Prince paid your debt, died in your stead, purchased your pardon?"[8]

"I understood that I was somehow responsible for the awful suffering that your Prince endured. This made me twice guilty."[9]

"Yes," Brother Michael agreed, "our sins were the reason the Prince had to go to the cross. And he atoned there for every sin committed since the world began, and what is harder to conceive, for every sin that has been committed since or will be committed from now until the end of time."[10]

"Do you mean," Godfrey was amazed, "that if I sin today, that sin was borne by the Prince so long ago?"

"It had to be, or you could not be forgiven of it."

"Does the King already know the sins I will commit in the future?" wondered Lucius.

"The King knows all things, past, present, and future.[11] It is he who created Time, and he sees all of it in a glance."

"Then," Lucius reasoned, "since they're already paid for, I might as well relax and stop trying so hard."[12]

"Oh, no!" cried Hannah. "Don't you see that you are still making the decisions as to your future? When I face a temptation, I say to

---

[5] Luke 7:36-50
[6] Romans 12:1
[7] Micah 7:18
[8] 1 Peter 2:24
[9] Romans 4:24, 25
[10] 1 John 2:2
[11] Psalm 139:1-16
[12] Romans 6:1, 2

myself, 'If I do this thing it is another sin my Prince had to bear.' I decide whether or not I will add to his suffering."

"If that is so," exclaimed Godfrey in distress, "every time I sin, I am striking the Prince! How terrible! God help me! I must never sin again!"

"It is very true," Brother Michael agreed. "If we could see the true nature of sin, as the King himself sees it, we would shrink from it with such horror I doubt we would ever feel tempted at all."

"No wonder he says, 'If you love me you will keep my commandments,'"[13] Lucius nodded.

Christine herself had forgotten Justin now. She was blinking back tears as she thought with remorse of her mistakes, as she preferred to call them. Like Godfrey, she must find a way to avoid them in the future.

But Justin broke in at this point. "Do you mean I am not held accountable? Do you mean I am free?"[14]

His words were like a wave washing the ugly, guilty feelings from their souls.

"Hallelujah!" shouted Godfrey. He and Lucius leaped to embrace Justin, as though he were the salvation he had just spoken.

Brother Michael spoke slowly, "Your name is Justin, and you have reminded us all of the demands of justice. But I assure you those demands were met at Calvary, and you and we and all who choose to receive it are justified in the King's sight and judged righteous."[15]

Justin sat down quite suddenly as overcome.

Felicia began to sing with joy. The others joined in.

"When the fulness of time was come,
God sent forth his Son, his only Son,
Made of a woman, made under the law,
To redeem them that were under the law,
That we might receive the adoption of sons.

---

[13] John 14:15, 21

[14] John 8:34-36

[15] Romans 5:11-18

"And because we are sons, adopted sons,
God sent forth the Spirit of his Son
Into our hearts crying, 'Abba, Father!'

"Wherefore we are no more servants, but sons;
And if sons, then heirs of God through Christ.
Stand fast therefore, stand fast!
In the liberty wherewith Christ hath made us free!"[16]

Christine saw the joy beginning to dawn in Justin's face.

"I am not a slave? I am free to go?" he asked in awe.

Felicia dropped to her knees before him. "But don't go," she pleaded. "You are a son. Stay here with your Father and your brothers and sisters. We love you. The King loves you. The Prince loves you so much he died for you. Don't reject this love. If you leave now you will soon be a slave to sin as I used to be. Stay, please stay!"

Christine did not see how anyone could ignore that earnest plea, but Justin did not appear to have even heard.

"Uncle called me a prince, but I didn't understand." He looked at his sponsor, "*Brother* Michael?" Then at the others, "My brothers and sisters?" Then trembling he fell to his knees, and raising his hands he looked skyward. "My Father!" he cried.

Christine hugged Hannah in a fit of joy, and everyone was laughing and crying and Lucius and Godfrey were hugging Justin, and Brother Michael bounced up and down for relief and thankfulness.

They had not noticed Sister Chloe come up behind them, but when Christine started to hug her as another available neck, she suddenly remembered it was chore time. Sister Chloe did not rebuke them, but joined in the rejoicing. Soon though, they began to hurry off their separate ways. As Christine was about to follow Sister Chloe, Brother Michael touched her shoulder.

"Christine," he smiled, "thanks."

---

[16] Galatians 4:4-7 & 5:1

Chapter XXVII

And if we die...

Saturday found Christine shivering in the bustling courtyard in the gray half-light of not-quite-morning. She wished for the new shawl, but it still lay in her room, less than a third finished.

Hannah and Felicia huddled with her. Sarah was helping with the packing. Naomi was so busy she scarcely seemed to notice any of them. Christine's eyes and nose were running, but she wasn't sure herself whether it was the lonely, forsaken feeling or just the cold that brought the tears. Hannah was trying hard to smile, but her teeth were chattering, so it was more of a grimace.

"I wish I knew enough to help like Sarah," Felicia was saying for the fourth time.

Christine thought they would all rather have been busy, if only to keep warm. But cinches were being tightened. Sarah was tying a knot on a pack. Some of the group had already mounted. It looked as if the moment of parting was very close.

"No, no, no," Christine was muttering under her breath. She had not become in the least reconciled to her friend's departure.

"None of you woke me!" a reproachful voice declared at her elbow. Amanda had appeared rubbing sleep from her eyes. Then Naomi was approaching. The courtyard was dotted with small groups of well-wishers.

The eagerness of Naomi's face contrasted sharply with the looks of dismay on her friends'.

"I'd give anything to be going with you," Sarah sighed. "I don't think I'll ever be approved."

"Do take care," Felicia sniffed, embracing her. "You've been just like a mother. We'll miss you terribly."

Hannah took her turn to hug the adventurer, "When the going gets tough, remember we'll be praying for you."

"I'll be counting on it," Naomi nodded.

Amanda threw her arms around Naomi's waist and in child-like innocence wondered, "Will we ever see you again?"

At that, Christine burst into sobs. Amanda had spoken the thoughts of her own heart. She had planned to say something about sending them word if an opportunity presented, but she couldn't even speak. Naomi put comforting arms around her.

"You shall most assuredly see me again, if not in this life then in the next."

Those words did have a reassuring effect, but Christine couldn't stop crying. Then suddenly the courtyard was very still. She had to choke back the sobs.

Uncle was standing on the steps of the Great Hall, and he had signalled for prayer. Christine felt her blood stir as Uncle's voice filled the courtyard—not a prayer for safety, but a prayer for boldness, not a word about their safe return, but petitions for their success, and lastly a fervent prayer for unity and love within the group.

The prayer ended with a cheer from those assembled, and Naomi tore herself away to spring into the saddle. The gates of the courtyard were pushed wide open, and the cavalcade had soon passed through. Naomi turned once to wave, but it was clear that her heart was no longer with them.

As she watched the little band down the hill and across the bridge, Christine could feel a little of the thrill, and for the moment she understood Sarah's sentiments, but when they were lost to sight, the desolation returned.

From high above the chimes rang, calling them to matins. Christine went, but her feet dragged, and most of the hour was spent arguing with the King that he ought to keep his children safe at home.

A holiday atmosphere filled the Castle as breakfast was hurriedly attended to. She heard references to "Apple Day" and was pleased to learn that today their activities would take them no further than the Castle orchard. Indeed the orchard was a hubbub of activity. A rich, winey aroma filled the swiftly warming air. Younger men were scaling ladders, and the bounty of crisp ripe fruit was descending into baskets.

Christine squeezed up to a huge tub where women were washing and sorting the apples, talking and laughing as they worked. When she had culled a full bucket for immediate use, Amanda appeared as if called and carried it off. Christine picked up a tray of the best apples and took them to the cellar. Returning, she found work at a table where women were coring and chopping apples to fill a great copper kettle.

Many apples disappeared into the mouths of the workers, but there seemed to be more than could ever be eaten.

Christine's turn came to stir the kettle. How could she ever have thought it a cold morning? Her spirits warmed too. The good feelings and gaiety flowing around her were irresistible. Yet even as she joined in the laughter, she felt a sense of mourning within. Naomi should be here with them.

When finally relieved at the kettle, Christine was enormously thirsty. She went to the river and drank long and deep. She thought she had never been so happy, yet part of her still cried for Naomi.

She saw Lucius with some other young men toting heavy barrels of cider toward the cellar.

"Where's Godfrey?" she called.

"By the press," Lucius gasped as if he had no breath to spare.

Christine found the press. A team of horses turned the huge screw, but they were resting just now as Godfrey scraped the pomace from the press. Christine recognized one of them as the stolid old mare whose back she had climbed so many times, and she gave her an apple. Now the press was ready to be filled again by the continual stream of apples from the baskets of small boys who were gathering the windfalls. As soon as the screw commenced to turn again, Godfrey drew off two cups for Christine and himself.

Cider fresh from the press had always been one of Christine's favorite treats. This was the best she had ever tasted. Godfrey's eyes sparkled at her over his cup. But when he spoke, it was not the cider he praised.

"Isn't it wonderful, Sis? I mean everything, everyone. Isn't our Father good?"

Yes, it was better than anything she had ever dreamed. It seemed to get better all the time.

Lucius approached them, and held out his hand for a cup.

"You've already had two," Godfrey protested.

"Right," Lucius panted, "the more I carry in my stomach, the less I have to carry on my shoulder."

Christine laughed, and Lucius made a face at her which made her laugh the harder.

But in spite of his protests, Lucius rolled a barrel under the tap to fill as he drank his cider, and he was soon on his way again.

Christine decided she should get back to work too, but just then she saw Uncle coming toward the press. He had one handle of a basket and was helping a little fellow who could hardly manage the other side.

Christine smiled as she thought that Uncle could more easily have carried the basket by himself, but that was not Uncle's way. When they had tipped its contents into the vat, Uncle reached out and mussed the boy's hair a bit.

"Now, next time don't fill it so full," he cautioned.

"I won't, Uncle," the rosy-cheeked youngster promised, and ran off for another load.

Just then a passing mongrel noticed Uncle and came over to rub against his legs. Uncle reached down and scratched a ragged ear.

Christine watched the dog and thought, that's exactly what I would like to do. And Uncle, knowing her thought, walked over and put his arm around her and drew her close.

Walking along in that fashion, Christine felt so good and comfortable, but the other thought was still there, so she asked, "Uncle, will Naomi come back safely?"

"Whether or not she will come back I cannot say, but I promise you she will be safe whatever happens to her."

That answer wasn't what Christine wanted. He meant that even if she died she was still safe.[1] But it was no use asking further, so she asked instead, "Dear Uncle, how can I be so happy and still feel sad?"

Uncle gave a long sigh. "My child, that is the nature of the bittersweet life you mortals live. Even at its best, this fallen world is not home, and you are not meant to feel at home here. Perfect happiness

---

[1] Hebrews 11:13-16

only exists over there." He waved his hand at the great wall separating them from the other part of the Castle.

Christine had not realized they were walking that direction. She was surprised to find herself much closer to it than she had ever been. Its immensity awed her. Enormous blocks of alabaster were fitted so tightly, they seemed almost a monolith. The top reached upward until it was lost in the clouds. She was seized with a longing for the life beyond that wall. "Is it...?" she hesitated. "Is it lawful to touch it?"

Uncle nodded, and let her move forward. When her fingertips touched it, she shrank back. It was so cold. She had not expected that in this hot sunshine. But then she pressed her hands, her face, her body against it. It felt like a cool hand on a fevered brow. She would have let it swallow her up if stone would have yielded.

She felt Uncle gently tugging her away. "Not yet, my child. It is not time for you to pass over that wall."

Christine reluctantly let herself be drawn back. There was perfect rest there, and peace, and how many things had she sensed there for which her soul longed?

"What is it? What did I feel there? It's only a blank wall, but it seemed better than anything in the world."

Uncle smiled, "It is death, child. And you see that it is not the enemy you were taught to think. But for those who have not entered the Castle by the Door, and cleansed themselves in the Blood, and been adopted as sons and daughters of the King, it is the most terrible enemy of all.

"In the Castle all things are changed, and so that which you most feared, now becomes your greatest hope."[2]

---

[2] Philippians 1:21

Chapter XXVIII

Assignment

Days flew by. Celebrations were frequent. Christine found work a pleasure. She spent a week as a milkmaid, and renewed her friendship with Lily.

The next Saturday they went walnut picking. Sister Tabitha was as anxious for the hulls as Sister Hephzibah was for the nutmeats. Christine used some of them to dye Brother Michael's cloak.

She finished a simple but lovely bowl in time for the wedding. It was the most wonderful wedding she had ever attended. She had a hard time deciding what was the best part. Flowers, as well as the wedding feast, had been sent over from the Keep. Sister Celeste was as beautiful as a sunbeam. Christine was not the only one who thought Felicia sang like an angel.

It wasn't until she lay in bed that night that she realized the best thing was the love. It had shone in Sir Alexander's face, beholding his bride as though a miracle had come into his life. Though Sister Celeste kept her eyes modestly downcast, love and joy radiated from her entire being. But that was only the beginning. From every person in the Hall, love had flowed toward the young couple in a sea of prayer and good wishes. Still greater Love flowed down from the dais where Uncle stood, observing the ceremony, and Love's presence filled the air like the fragrance of the flowers.

Christine dreamed of the day when she would have a wedding like that. Whom would she marry? What a thrilling thought that the King probably already had someone picked out! Of course he wouldn't be a great knight like Sir Alexander, but he would be a royal prince, and the King would choose someone who would love and cherish her. She could afford to be patient, now that she had a glimpse of what was in store for her.

At the end of two more weeks, Sister Agatha had an exciting announcement. Felicia was able to graduate from reading class. Christine was almost as happy as her friend. That night they thumbed together through the pages of the new Bible. Christine was nearly through the Gospel of Mark, and was looking forward to John. But as she thought happily of her own graduation, a discomfiting thought came to her. She loved reading class. What could she possibly do that she would enjoy as much?

"What will you be doing now?" she asked Felicia, suddenly less brightly.

"Oh, didn't I tell you?" Felicia obviously had no regrets for reading class. "I'll be learning to play the harp!"

Christine could understand her friend's excitement. She pictured Felicia singing and accompanying herself on the huge golden harp that stood in the music room. Hannah was taking flute lessons of course. They would be able to play together, but Christine found it hard to put herself in the picture. Oh, she liked music, but she didn't want to spend hours practicing an instrument, and she suspected that no amount of practice would make her really good.

"I suppose that's the next thing," Christine speculated without enthusiasm. "Boys become pages and girls take up instruments."

"Oh, no, there are many other assignments," Felicia hated to dash her friend's hopes, "but maybe you could ask Uncle and he'd let you learn an instrument."

"That's all right," Christine grinned. "I remember you said it was better to let him choose."

Monday morning after breakfast, they were about to part. Felicia was so eager to start on the harp, Christine thought it would almost be worth missing reading to watch her first lesson.

Uncle had come up without their noticing. He put a loving arm around each of them. "Felicia, I want to tell you that the King is very pleased with your first effort at sponsoring. Christine has made excellent progress under your guidance."

No joy in the Castle was to be compared with Uncle's praise. Felicia was so happy she thought she would melt. Christine basked in the warm glow also. "Excellent progress"—how wonderful that sounded!

"So," he continued, "after your harp lesson instead of spinning, you may report to the reception hall to await a new sponsorship assignment."

Felicia squealed with joy, but Christine asked in dismay. "You mean Felicia's not my sponsor anymore?"

"My dear, we believe you are able to continue now without a sponsor. You are to be congratulated."

"Thank you," Christine replied somewhat uncertainly. "I do appreciate your confidence. But shan't I get to see Felicia anymore?"

"Silly!" Felicia slipped her arms around Christine and kissed her. "You will always be my very best friend. Do you think anyone could take your place?"

Thus assured, Christine realized how much she depended on Felicia's love. "I do hope," she returned the hug, "we will always be together. May we please, Uncle?"

"I can't answer that. But love is stronger than time and space. You can be together in spirit if not in body.

"Now, get on to your harp lesson," he sent Felicia scooting. "I want to talk to Christine."

Burning curiosity swept over Christine. What would Uncle say? Surely nothing bad after he had just praised her! Oh, please, nothing bad, she prayed silently. I've been trying so hard.

When they had walked a few steps, Uncle turned to her. "Christine, are you afraid to leave the Castle?"

"No!" she blurted at once, then retracted a little. "I mean, I'm not afraid of the outlaws anymore, but I guess I'm a little afraid of myself. I don't want to make any more mistakes."

"My dear child, the only people who don't make mistakes are the dead ones."

Christine sighed. "Well, I'd rather be dead than be responsible for keeping someone away from the Castle."

Uncle nodded gravely, "We appreciate that attitude in you, Christine. Your consistent prayers for your village are heard and honored. That is why I am offering you this assignment. It would normally go to one more fully trained."

Oh, dear, thought Christine, but aloud she said, "What assignment?"

"In our shire here, there is a young woman who has been thinking much about the Castle. Her situation is getting desperate. When she heard that you had come, she almost decided to make the break, but then she heard that you had been killed, so she hesitated. Now she is nearly ready to try even if it costs her life. I need to send someone to fetch her. Will you go?"

"Yes, please let me go," Christine volunteered eagerly, but a moment later she had second thoughts. "Is it certain she will come?"

"That will be up to you."

"Oh, dear! Send someone else then. I don't want to be the blame if she doesn't come."

"You will have to learn to accept responsibility if you are ever going to serve the King. I can send someone else, but you are my first choice. If someone else goes and fails, do you think you are absolved? She might have come if you had gone."

Christine felt trapped, "I'll do whatever you say, but I'm afraid it's a mistake."

"Do you mean I am making a mistake?"

Christine's head shot up. Had she implied that? "Oh, no! I know you don't ever make mistakes."

"Then how could obeying me be a mistake?"

"I don't know what I was thinking. If you want me to go, then of course I'm the right one to go." Even as she said it, it still sounded wrong to her. I'm not trusting, she thought. I must obey, but I must have faith too. Suddenly she remembered the way she had learned to float. If the King says it, then it must be right.

"The woman's name is Margaret. I think you know of her."

Christine was stunned. "Margaret who lives by the mill? That's so far. And her husband is a drunkard. What will he say if I try to take his wife away?"

"I didn't say it was going to be easy."

"Don't they have a baby? I'll have to bring it too, won't I?"

"I'm not sending you alone. You may take a companion of your own choosing."

That was encouraging. Christine thought only a moment. "Uncle, please, I want you to go with me."

Uncle smiled. "I will go with you, but you will not see me. Listen for me, and you will know I am there. I meant you can take one of your friends."

Christine thought first of Felicia, but she wasn't sure that was the right choice. Felicia was wonderful at times, but at other times her inexperience showed. Maybe she should take Hannah. Hannah always seemed to know the right answer. Or she could take Godfrey. She would feel safer with him or Lucius along. She remembered how Sarah had longed to go with Naomi. She would be thrilled at this opportunity. Even Amanda was apt to feel hurt if she knew she had been passed over. Why was everything so difficult?

Or was it? "Uncle, please choose for me. You know best."[1]

Uncle nodded sympathetically. "Take Felicia. You work well together. Make your preparations today and start tomorrow morning. I'll meet you in the courtyard at daybreak."

The two girls were almost frantic with excitement. They solicited prayers and advice from everyone they met. As Christine had foreseen, their friends all wished they could go along, but only Sarah seemed really sad about not being chosen. She was not resentful, however, and suggested they ask for horses for the trip. Christine thought that a good idea until Felicia pointed out that Margaret would not know how to ride.

Felicia wanted to take her new Bible, but Christine thought they would be carrying too much even without it. She had expected Brother Michael to instruct them in how to deal with outlaws they might meet, or at least how to intercede before their journey, but he simply urged them to take plenty of food.

That reminded Christine of the need for water bottles. Whatever happened she didn't want to run short of water. She was grateful that her new shawl was ready, but Felicia needed one. Sister Tabitha supplied her with a lightweight cloak, and sent along a large shawl for the young mother and baby.

"What will you do if you meet outlaws?" Godfrey worried. He offered to loan them his sword, but the girls protested they did not know how to use it. Lucius thought they should at least carry daggers for protection, but they declined that also.

---

[1] Proverbs 3:5, 6

"If there were danger of that kind, I'm sure Uncle would have let one of you boys come, or even sent a knight to guard us. He knows we're inexperienced; he wouldn't send us into a dangerous situation undefended."

Hannah agreed with that, but feared danger from the drunken husband. "You must avoid him someway. Don't risk a confrontation with him."

Christine's first thought was how cowardly that sounded, but she remembered her meeting with Amanda's mother and decided that, as usual, Hannah was right.

Sister Alathea suggested some of their memory verses that might be useful when they talked to their prospect. Brother Uriah warned them to be positive. "If she has been bullied by a sotted husband she may have difficulty making decisions for herself. From what you say, she has already wavered back and forth considerably. You may have to help her."

"Once you start back with her," Sarah admonished, "don't stop for anything. Get her here as fast as you can."

"Yes," Nathan agreed, "We'll all be waiting on pins and needles."

The excitement continued to build. By vespers Christine thought everyone in the Castle must know about their little adventure. Total strangers stopped to speak a word of encouragement. In Felicia's room they carefully packed bags for the next day, then spent the remaining time in prayer.

Hurrying back to her room just before curfew, Christine was surprised to meet Justin who seemed to have been waiting for her. Even since the day he had come to understand his position in the Kingdom, Justin had said very little. He was a naturally quiet person, Christine had decided. Apparently he had not wanted to speak before the others, and had waited to see her alone.

His face glowed though with his newfound joy, as he approached Christine. "Tell her," he said softly, "that the Prince loves her."

"I will, Justin," Christine assured him. "I'll be sure to tell her that."

Chapter XXIX

Venturing Out

The sky was lightening a little in the East when the girls reached the courtyard, but it could hardly be called daybreak. The yawning porter opened the gate for them, but they had to wait a cold half hour before Uncle showed up.

"What took you so long?" Felicia laughed between chattering teeth.

"I said daybreak, and here I am," Uncle replied cheerfully. "I'm glad you had the sense to wait."

"Never fear!" Christine asserted. "We're not going any place without you!"[1]

Uncle did not detain them longer, but knelt with them on the pavement and prayed for a successful conclusion to their journey. Then they were on their way. The exercise warmed them at once.

Christine felt strange approaching the little village where she had lived her whole life. Here at the bridge the outlaws had pursued them that last day. She remembered the terror they had evoked, and though it had seemed so far away and long ago when she was in the Castle, now it seemed like yesterday. She found herself looking in all directions, not fearfully, but the action reminded her of those old fears.

---

[1] Exodus 33:14-16

Do I still have them? she wondered to herself. And she firmly answered, no!

Felicia was staring at the mists rising from the river. Christine wondered what her thoughts were, then decided to talk to dispel the gloom. She had never told Felicia the story of that Sunday they had come to the Castle, so she began it now.

Soon they reached the first houses of the village. Dogs barked as they approached, and other sounds came to their ears. Someone was chopping wood. An odor of frying pork had drifted into the street, and the more subtle aroma of oatmeal. The girls suddenly remembered breakfast. Candles glowed in some windows, a sign of the shortening days, but the street was quite light now, and a few people were moving about. As they passed the bakery they heard voices, the baker yelling at his apprentices. The anger in the voice surprised them. They were no longer accustomed to the sound. Their hearts hurt for the poor lads thus addressed, not remembering how calloused those lads had long since become.

A louder noise grabbed their attention. They were in front of the tavern and evidently the night's revels were still in progress. Suddenly a figure was propelled through the door and into the girls' arms. Though almost knocked down, their noses sent them reeling even farther from the newcomer. Then a series of oaths sent their hands to their ears.

Christine saw with horror that the poor wretch was a woman, or had once been. As she staggered to regain her balance, Christine recognized her.

"Barbara!" she cried in surprise. All her feelings of disgust had suddenly changed to pity. Here was the object of her prayers, sent into her path no doubt by God's own hand. The love she had been building over the past weeks of prayer poured into her heart, and her arms opened to the reprobate as though to a long-lost sister.

The woman blinked at her stupidly, "Whoeryou?" she slurred.

Christine did not know how to answer. She must not repeat her former mistake. Would Barbara even remember her? They had never been actually acquainted. She decided to just make a new start. "My name is Christine. I've just come from the Castle."

"Oh, yeah," Barbara did not seem very interested. But she looked at them now, noting their fine clothing. "Well, beg yer pardon, didn't mean to go mussin' ya er whatever."

In consternation Christine saw that Barbara was doing her best to turn around and re-enter the grog shop.

"Here, let me help you." She grabbed one of Barbara's arms and attempted to steer her to a bench near the door. Felicia reacted quickly and grabbed the other arm.

"Le'go. Dunwanna sit down." She sat nevertheless.

The girls plopped down too, one on each side of her, but now Christine did not know what to say. It seemed unlikely that she could impress anything into this rum-soaked brain.

Felicia did not hesitate however, but plunged ahead. "My name is Felicia. I'm glad to meet you, Barbara."

"Pleeztermeetcha," she muttered in a monotone and now seemed about to fall asleep. Her head drooped to her chest and her eyes closed. The girls kept hold of her to keep her from falling off the bench.

Christine looked across the tangled mass of hair at Felicia, and framed the words with her lips, "What can we do?"

"Barbara! Barbara!" Felicia got no response, so she whispered. "If we could find a cart we could put her in it and take her back to the Castle."

Like an erupting volcano the woman burst to her feet, knocking the bench and girls over backward. Her face suddenly livid with hate, she cursed them and spat on them. Then turning away she ran down the street as though her feet had never been unsteady or her head blurred with alcohol.

Christine looked after her in disappointment. Then the tears came.

Felicia was stunned, "Well, what in the world possessed her?" She struggled to her feet. The new cloak was covered with dust, and her bag had split open.

"I'm sorry," Christine wailed. "I always get you into something like this."

"Oh, hush! You didn't get me into anything. I wanted to help her too. Do you know her?"

Just then the tavern door opened again. A large red-faced brute stood in the doorway. His bleary eyes and sagging jaw showed him far gone in his cups. "Whereshego?" he asked the air.

He flung out his arms as a blind man might, and to Christine's horror caught hold of Felicia's cloak. "C'mere. Teachya ter run off!" he mumbled, dragging her toward him.

Christine thought of the sword and dagger she had turned down and suddenly wished she had them. She snatched a thick stick from a stack of firewood, and swung at the man with all her strength. He went down like a tenpin, and lay there mumbling.

She grabbed Felicia's hand and they fled down the street. Only when they reached the last house did they stop to look back. The man still lay stretched out where he had fallen.

"Did you kill him?" Felicia asked wide-eyed.

"No, I wish I had!"

"Christine!" Felicia was shocked.

"That," Christine stopped for a deep breath, "was Margaret's husband."

The girls stared at one another. Finally Felicia said sheepishly, "I lost my bundle."

Christine shook her head sadly. "We haven't been gone an hour and we've had enough trouble to last me a year."

"You're not thinking of giving up!" Felicia exclaimed.

"I'm not thinking at all," Christine admitted. "Let's sit down some place."

Christine shared out some bread and meat although neither of them felt hungry. "Come on," she urged. "I'll bet this is what Brother Michael would tell us to do."

When they had eaten and taken a long drink, they were amazed how much better they felt. Looking back up the street again, they saw the man was gone.

"I'm going to get my things," Felicia declared stoutly.

"We're going," Christine corrected her.

More people were moving around now. A few looked at the girls, but most of the passers-by paid them no attention. Felicia put the shawl around her shoulders and used the cloak to wrap her broken bundle. That done, they were glad to hurry away from the village.

Christine explained now about who Barbara was, and how she had been praying for her. She didn't see any use of saying how discouraged she felt.

"Now that I've met her, I can help you pray. You know, she is carrying a burden like mine, but she hasn't seen it yet. When she sees it, you can be sure she'll want to be rid of it."

"Felicia," Christine shook her head in wonder, "aren't you sorry you came?"

"Sorry! Of course not! We're really serving the Prince now. I've been longing for this. You're not sorry you brought me I hope?"

"Not if you're not. But I promise I won't let myself get sidetracked again. I'll try to stay out of trouble."

"But Christine, you didn't arrange that. I think Uncle wanted us to see Margaret's husband so we'd know what she's been going through."

Christine walked on silently, thinking that over. After all there was no real harm done. Had she forgotten Uncle's promise to be with them? Had *he* arranged that? What had he said? "Listen, and you'll know I'm there."

Christine stilled her heart to listen. One of her memory verses came to her, "In every thing give thanks; for this is the will of God in Christ Jesus concerning you."[2]

Presently they came to a fork in the road. Christine explained that the left fork would lead across the river again and eventually to her old home. The right fork continued downstream and led to the mill. This was their route today.

Felicia suddenly thought of something, "Where does Abigail live? Don't you remember we promised we would go see her if we ever were able?"

"I had forgotten, but I would surely have remembered when we got to their farm. They're right on this road."

The sun climbed higher, and the girls were glad to take off their shawls. They stopped to drink several times, and it was already difficult to remember the anxieties of the morning. When they approached Eldred's cottage they saw him working in the garden. Christine flew up the path. It seemed so good to see the old couple again.

Eldred saw them coming and called, "Abigail, they're here."

Felicia had to be introduced to Eldred.

"Well, well," he patted her shoulder, "this is a pleasure. I've certainly heard a lot about you. Come in, girls. Abigail's been waiting dinner on you."

Christine had never been inside the cottage before, yet she felt like a daughter returning to her parents' home. Certainly no daughter could have received a warmer welcome. At the table places were already set for them, and they sat right down to a delicious meal from the old

---

[2] 1 Thessalonians 5:18

couple's garden. Christine made some friendly table chatter about fall gardens; it was so homey to discuss everyday subjects again. It made her realize how completely taken up with the King's business she had become.

It was Abigail who brought them back to the reason for their journey. "I haven't seen Margaret for about three weeks. She used to pass by on the way to the village and I always tried to have her stop for tea, but she doesn't often go to the village anymore. I don't think she has anything to buy or trade with."

The girls looked at one another puzzled. "How did you know we were on our way to see Margaret?"

"Why bless you, don't you think Uncle keeps us informed? He told us Sunday you were coming today."

Christine had to laugh, "Well, he didn't tell me until yesterday! And then he spoke as if I had a choice."

"Of course you had a choice, dear. Uncle never forces anyone. But don't you think he knew what you would choose?"

Felicia began then to tell of what had happened at the village.

Eldred shook his head sadly. "It seems only yesterday that Margaret was a happy bride, and Avery so intent on making a go of the holding."

"The first year Avery made remarkably good crops, and he was offered a good price for his surplus." Abigail related.

Eldred picked up the story. "It proved too much of a temptation for him. He sold his entire production, not even keeping out his tithe, or winter food, or seed for the next year.

Abigail continued, "The baby was born in the very dead of winter, and if neighbors and the church hadn't helped, it wouldn't have had a stitch to wear."

"But," Felicia protested, "what became of all the money?"

"We don't really know. I don't think Avery really knew himself. Few young people are able to handle large sums. But he started spending his time at the tavern, and the money vanished."

"Poor Margaret!" Felicia mourned.

"We've been praying for her all this time, and for Avery too."

Felicia giggled. "Christine wanted to kill him!"

Abigail shook her head, "Child, you don't know what spirit you are of."[3]

But Eldred chuckled, "I've had the feeling myself."

"I guess your prayers were what saved him," Christine acknowledged. "Godfrey—you remember my brother—tried to get me to bring his sword, and I didn't want it. If I had had it, I would have used it."

Eldred clicked his tongue. "You still haven't learned to check your impulses. Don't you remember the trouble they can cause?"

"Yes, Brother Eldred," Christine hung her head. "I do remember. I have been praying about that mistake as you told me to, and that's why Uncle is giving me this chance to undo a little of the damage."

Abigail put her arm around Christine and shook her finger at Eldred. "Shame on you! How would you like someone to go around reminding you of past mistakes?"

Felicia thought it time to change the subject. "We've really enjoyed our visit. Dinner was just lovely, but I think we'd better get going. I don't know how we'll ever get back by nightfall."

"Oh, you couldn't. You're to spend the night here and start again early tomorrow." Abigail seemed to have it all planned. "Avery is no doubt on his way home now. He passes by about this time each day. You don't want to try to talk to Margaret while he's there. He'll sleep until dusk, then head back for the village. I don't know why he goes home at all."

The prospect of a prolonged visit delighted the girls. They felt an urgency to be at their task, but remembered Hannah's advice. There seemed nothing to do until morning. Then they could take Sarah's advice about coming straight back. This was obviously the right way, yet Christine fidgeted.

"He's coming now," Eldred called from the garden where he was again at work. The girls ran to the window and watched a lonely figure trudging slowly nearer. He looked so forlorn, it was easy to pity him now.

"Oh," Felicia moaned, "He's carrying a burden too." They watched old Eldred cross the road and walk alongside the man. He seemed the younger of the two. They could not hear his words, but saw that he spoke earnestly. The man shook his head and walked on.

---

[3] Luke 9:54, 55

Felicia volunteered to help Abigail with the housework, so Christine went out to work in the garden. The neat, productive beds were a pleasure to tend. Eldred worked on his knees, neither hurrying nor stopping. Christine noticed that his lips moved as he worked.

"What are you telling the chard, Brother Eldred?"

The old man laughed. "Ah, child, my thoughts weren't on the chard. This is one of my favorite times to pray. My hands are so used to the work they need no direction, so my mind can fellowship with the King. My neighbors see me tending my garden and pity me at my drudgery. Little do they suspect I am in the spirit and communing with the Prince himself."

Coming to his feet with an effort, he offered, "I'm thirsty. Can I bring you a drink?"

"We brought water with us. Wouldn't you like some Castle water?"

"My dear girl, do you think we could live without it? Our well draws from the Castle's underground streams. You will find it just as good and fresher than your bottles."

Christine learned many things that afternoon, and in the evening the two girls sat by the fire as Abigail and Eldred told stories of the many years they had spent in the King's service.

"You've had such an exciting life," Christine spoke admiringly.

"Serving the King is the most exciting life in the world. Nothing else begins to equal it. You'll find it true. You are so blessed to have come to the Castle in your youth."

Abigail unrolled pallets for them near the hearth, and Christine slept as though in her own room at the Castle. In the night she dreamed that the little cottage had somehow changed into a magnificent palace, and though she woke on the same stone pavement with the thatch a short distance above her head, she felt that her dream was really true.

Chapter XXX

The King's Work

By the flickering firelight she saw Abigail and Eldred kneeling in prayer, their hands clasped together. Ashamed, she realized they had deprived the old couple of their beds. It was about the hour of rising at the Castle. Christine quickly got up and joined them in prayer. Though she took care not to disturb her, Felicia awoke a few minutes later and joined them also.

When light came, Felicia again volunteered to help Abigail, so Christine followed Eldred to the byre and did the milking while he cleaned stalls.

After breakfast they gathered their things. Felicia had mended her bag. Christine didn't feel right. Abigail had been talking to Margaret for months. She and Eldred had prayed long and hard. This night they had prayed the night through.

"Abigail, won't you go with us? You know Margaret and we don't. You should be the one to talk to her."

"Are you arguing with Uncle, child? No, I've tried and tried, but now it's your turn. May the King prosper your way. We'll be watching and praying until you return."

"But it doesn't seem fair."

"That one sows and another reaps?[1] Don't look for fairness in this world. But the sower can rejoice with the reaper." Abigail kissed them both and pushed them out the door.

Walking swiftly through the morning mists, they soon saw the mill looming ahead.

"It's the next lane on our right," Christine cautioned. They slowed their steps and soon came to an overgrown gateyard. Christine thought the place deserted; none of the cheerful sounds of a working farm met her ears. Were there no chickens? No cows? No dogs?

Then she heard a sound she knew—the creaking of a well winch.

Following the sound, the girls found a thin young woman hauling at a well bucket.

"Margaret?" Christine had not seen her since her wedding, and the careworn face did not match the one she remembered.

The woman looked at them nervously. Their clothes set them apart from the ordinary.

"Yes, I'm Margaret," she dropped a graceful curtsy, but her eyes darted about fearfully.

"Don't be afraid of us," Christine implored. "We're just girls. Not long ago we were just like you." Doubt came into the woman's face.

"Yes, we were just peasant girls before we went to the Castle. My name was Mara, daughter of George, and I lived on the road south of the bridge."

The woman's mouth dropped open. She looked more closely into Christine's face. "I...I didn't recognize you!"

Margaret was confused. She seemed to think she should do something but didn't know what.

Felicia helped her. "May we come in? We'd like to talk to you."

"Oh, yes, yes, come in. Forgive me. I should have asked you."

The interior of the cottage was still quite dark, and the girls were surprised to find it dank and cold.

"You don't have..." Christine was about to say, "a fire," and decided that would embarrass her. "...to make a fuss over us," she finished. It was not a good choice either. There was obviously no means for "making a fuss." Even the stool she offered Christine had a cracked leg.

---

[1] John 4:35-38

But Margaret tried valiantly. “I was drawing water to make some tea. Just let me get the bucket, and I’ll soon get a fire going...” She trailed off as she went back for the bucket.

Felicia and Christine looked at each other sadly. “I had no idea anyone in our shire was this poor,”[2] Christine apologized.

“Let’s help her get the fire started,” Felicia suggested. The girls quickly heaped the tinder and kindling, but there was not the tiniest coal among the ashes of the fireplace.

“How will she start it?” Christine wondered.

“She’s been gone a long time, just to go to the well,” Felicia worried. “You don’t think she’s run away from us?”

“No, I’m sure the baby’s there in the cradle.” The girls tiptoed over and looked at the sleeping child. Just then Margaret returned breathless, the heavy bucket dangling from one hand and a small pan clutched in the other.

“Oh, thank you,” she gasped seeing the fire laid. “I always get coals from the mill. It’s silly to keep a fire burning when the weather hasn’t turned really cold yet.”

“Yes,” Christine agreed, “a terrible waste of wood.”

From the rafters hung a good supply of wild herbs, and soon both girls were sipping good hot tea from wooden bowls.

“This is delicious,” Felicia told her sincerely. “Clover is one of my favorites.”

And, thought Christine, it’s supposed to increase breast milk. She gushed appreciatively over the tea also, but she was thinking, are we just going to pretend we don’t see this is all she has for breakfast? In a moment her mind was made up. She dug into her sack and laid meat, bread, fruit, and cheese on the table.

Margaret’s eyes went wide, and she had to grab at her skirt to keep her hands under control.

“Margaret, the King sent us to visit you, and of course he sent you a little gift.”

“The King had you bring all of this to me?”

Christine just nodded, the King or Brother Michael or both or whatever; she was sure it was not an accident.

---

[2] Proverbs 23:21

Once she started eating, the girls actually had to restrain her. They were afraid she would harm herself. At last Christine gathered it up saying, "Let's save the rest until dinner now."

"Tell the King how very grateful I am. I didn't suppose he knew I existed."

"Why don't you tell him yourself?" Felicia suggested.

"What do you mean?" Margaret was surprised.

Christine saw that it was getting sunny outside. She decided to come right to the point. "Margaret, the King knows you are unhappy. He sent us to bring you to the Castle."

For a few moments Margaret did not answer. Finally she confessed, "It's true. I am so miserable I sometimes wish I were dead." And at that admission the tears began to flow.

"Then come with us," Felicia urged, "now!"

Margaret glanced around as though taking stock. There was surely nothing to regret leaving, Christine thought.

"My baby?"

"He goes with us, of course."

"What about my husband?"

"What he does is up to him. The King would welcome him if he came."

"Will you stay until this afternoon? Will you talk to him when he comes home?"

"No!" Christine flatly refused. "If we wait for your husband, he will not come, and he will not let you come."

"But I can't just leave him. He needs me. Just yesterday he came home with a great gash and lump on his forehead."

Felicia looked at Christine, and Christine looked at the rafters.

"I know," Margaret apologized, "you think he's no good. But he's just had bad luck. He's really a fine man when he's not drinking."

Christine was amazed, "You still love him?"

"He's my husband. You girls aren't married; you can't understand."

Christine felt anger rising up in her. That drunken beast! she thought. If I tell her what we saw, I wonder how she'll feel then. But there was a persistent tug at the corner of her mind. At last she admitted it was Uncle trying to get her attention. He warned her sternly: She loves him. She'll defend him. Attack him, and you'll lose her.

While Christine fought this out in her mind, Felicia took up the conversation.

"But Margaret, you can't continue like this. You're not really doing yourself or him any good. And you have your son to think of too."

Margaret nodded tearfully. "Look at this," she walked to the cradle.

The girls followed and watched her carefully unfold the blankets. The little boy's legs were curving outward. It was an advanced case of rickets.

"I've been trying to keep him from standing up. Can you imagine a mother not wanting her child to stand? He'll be two in January. He wants to walk, but his bones can't bear his weight. What am I going to do?"

Christine put her arms around the sobbing young mother and tried to comfort her.

Felicia continued urging. "There was a time in my life when I didn't know what to do. I was in despair and ready to die. But at the Castle my whole life was changed. The King took me in and made me his child."

Suddenly Justin's words came to Christine. "Margaret, the Prince loves you. He loves you even more than you love your son or your husband. And he loves them too. You can trust him. If you will give yourself to him, he'll take care of you and the baby, and he'll do all he can for Avery too."

Margaret cast that appraising glance around again. "I guess I have nothing to lose. Things can't be any worse than they are."

Christine and Felicia exchanged hopeful glances.

"You're right. Avery would never let me go. What will he do when he finds I'm gone?"

"Maybe he'll come too," Christine suggested though she didn't really believe it.

"Do you really think so?" Margaret's face lit up with a spark of hope.

It was hard for Christine to answer truthfully. At last she said, "There's certainly a greater chance with you there, than if you stay here."

"Let's go at once." Margaret seemed worried that she would lose her nerve, and the girls were more than willing.

When she lifted the baby though, he began to cry. She had to sit down and nurse him. The supply of milk was soon gone, and he continued to whimper with hunger.

Felicia took out the large shawl. "This is another gift from the King. And when we get to the Castle there'll be plenty of everything, and your son will soon be strong and well."[3]

Margaret seemed to have no packing to do. She put out the fire, from habitual economy, and they started. At the mill she went in to leave word for her husband. "Tell him," she said triumphantly, "I've gone to the Castle."

The miller's wife shook her head. "I've wondered you didn't leave long ago. Whatever the Castle's like, you'll be better off than you are here."

"The King sent these nice girls to take me there," Margaret said proudly.

The older woman shook her head doubtfully, then kissing her neighbor good-bye, made her promise, "Can you send me word, you will now, won't you?"

"You'd be welcome at the Castle, you know," Christine warmed to the good-hearted woman. "You should come, if only just to visit Margaret."

"Well," the idea was quite new. "I might at that. I'd dearly love to know how the tyke gets on."

"You won't know him," Felicia promised. "He'll he running around straight and strong."

---

[3] Romans 8:32

Chapter XXXI

Journey Home

It was a good beginning. The day was already starting to warm up. Felicia was so happy she had to sing. But Christine was worrying. She didn't think Margaret was strong enough to carry the baby, and she was afraid if they were delayed they might meet Avery on his way home.

"Please let me take him," she urged Margaret. Margaret surrendered the child readily enough, but he wasn't used to strangers and began to cry. Christine wasn't used to babies either, and the more she tried to quiet him, the louder he wailed.

"Here," said Felicia, "let me try." But he was upset now, and they soon had to give him back to his mother.

They were moving too slowly to suit Christine. As the sun rose higher, she began to look apprehensively down the road. By now Avery had surely started for home. What would they do?

"I'm afraid I need a rest," Margaret was apologetic. They stopped in the shade of a tree, and Felicia took out some food. The baby accepted a crust to suck on. Christine felt near panic. She went behind the tree and fell on her knees.

"Dear Father, you must help me. I need your wisdom. Don't let me lose Margaret." She was tempted to tell the King how to arrange it. It would be very convenient if Avery had an accident. But she resisted that thought. "You know how to keep us safe. I put all my trust in you."

This is one of those times, she thought, that Brother Michael was speaking of, when we need an answer immediately. Yet no answer seemed forthcoming.

"Nevertheless, I trust you," Christine concluded her prayer.

The little boy had fallen asleep. Christine picked him up ever so gingerly, and they were able to proceed at a better pace. Eldred's cottage came in view, and the good folk were standing at the gate waiting.

Abigail embraced Margaret and assured her she was doing the right thing. She lovingly exhorted her to be strong and steadfast. But Eldred pulled Christine aside.

"You're running late, If you continue on, you'll run straight into Avery."

"I know; what can I do?"

"You'd better wait here until he gets past, then continue on."

"If we do that we won't have much of a start on him. He may come right after us, and we can't travel as fast as he can."

"Then what will you do?"

"I don't know, but I think we should keep going." Christine was keenly aware now of Uncle's nearness. It was he who was urging her on.

Just then the little boy roused, and finding himself on Christine's shoulder he began to scream. Margaret had to take him again.

"He's too heavy for you," Eldred protested. "I have an idea." In a moment Eldred was back with a wheelbarrow. The child was delighted with this novel conveyance and willingly let Christine push him along. They waved good-bye to Abigail.

"We'll be praying," she called.

Faster and faster, Christine hurried her party along. Felicia looked at her questioningly, and at last the problem occurred to Margaret too. "Won't Avery be coming home on this road?" she inquired.

For a moment Christine did not know how to answer her, but then just ahead she saw the fork that led to her old home. She remembered how she and Godfrey had taken the footpath the day they had gone to the Castle. "Yes, he'll be on this road, but we'll be on the other one."

It was longer, but they would not only avoid meeting Margaret's husband, they would not be so easily found if he pursued them. Christine cut across a plowed field to reach the other road. The baby laughed as the wheelbarrow took the bumps. Before long they reached the bridge and crossing it, started down the little footpath. Christine felt safe at last and ordered a halt for lunch. But first she fervently prayed and thanked the King for guiding her this way.

The afternoon's walk turned into a leisurely pleasure jaunt. All three took turns pushing the wheelbarrow. On the little uphill parts, they turned it backward and two of them took the handles and pulled. Christine was interested to see that the bridge had been repaired. She looked for the bundle she had dropped on that other day, but there was no sign of it.

The sun was setting as they stopped again for a rest and meal just before leaving the little path. It was so close now, but Christine wanted them well prepared for what they might meet in that last mile. She knew very well that Avery might now be ahead of them. In fact she was depending on his having reached the Castle and turned back frustrated. It was nearing the hour when he returned to the tavern, and she hoped habit would take him there.

Coming out of the trees they saw the Castle on its hill. The thrill in her breast told Christine that this was truly home. Felicia too gave a cry of joy as she gazed rapturously at the turreted walls. It was Margaret who saw the outlaws.

A small band was coming toward them as though heading for the village. Margaret was alarmed. She wanted to hide, but Christine told her there was nothing to fear.

"Fix your eyes on the Castle up ahead, and keep walking toward it. Don't pay any attention to them. They'll try to frighten you, but if you don't let them do it, there is nothing else they can do."

Felicia and Christine put Margaret between them and walked steadily up the road. The outlaws parted as if to let them pass, but they were forced to walk through the midst of them. One of them sidled up to Christine.

"Well, well," he said. "If it isn't little Mara, daughter of George."

"You're right," she smiled. "It isn't."

Another had approached Felicia and made an obscene gesture. She ignored him completely. They had nearly left the outlaws behind when one called out. "Hey, that's Avery's wife. What's she doing here?"

Margaret gasped and glanced back over her shoulder. It was all the encouragement the outlaws needed. They crowded around the girls with threats and curses. One of them reached toward the baby. Christine was quicker. She snatched the child from the wheelbarrow and pressed him into Margaret's arms. Then she joined hands with Felicia to form a protective barrier around mother and son. But they had come to a standstill. The outlaws hemmed them in on every side. They couldn't move. Christine marvelled that she felt no fear, only disdain for the ruffians.

"It's all right," Felicia was telling Margaret. "They can't hurt you. The King sent us to bring you back, and he won't let them prevent us."

Then quite suddenly the outlaws broke and ran. Christine looked toward the Castle to see three riders bearing down on them at a full gallop. The two outside ones rode badly enough, she thought, but the center one looked as though he had never been astride a horse before.

She waved an arm in greeting, as the riders slowed. Yes, it was Godfrey and Lucius as she expected, but who was the third rider? Margaret gave a scream of joy and ran toward them. The center rider fell rather than dismounted, but he leaped up to clasp Margaret in his arms.

Christine stared dumbfounded. Felicia began to hop up and down for joy. "It's Avery!" she shouted. "It's Avery!" The little boy was howling wildly at having been left, so Christine wheeled him to his parents. She couldn't believe it. Looking at their faces now, she remembered their wedding day.

Godfrey put an arm around her. "You all right, Sis?"

"Where did he come from?" Christine wanted to know.

"Oh, he got here about two hours ago. We told him his wife wasn't here, but he wouldn't believe us and insisted on coming in to look for her. He had an argument with Uncle and a fist fight with Brother Michael, and after he had been knocked senseless, Lucius and I held him under a fountain. When he came to, he was ready to listen, and anyway he's just been washed in the blood, and Uncle gave him permission to go with us to meet you."

Christine needed to sit down. She plopped into the wheelbarrow for lack of any other place. Lucius laughingly grabbed the handles and wheeled her up the hill. The big gate was open, and Hannah, Amanda, and Sarah were waiting there for them. They hugged Christine and Felicia.

"You did it!" Hannah rejoiced with them. "I knew you would do it."

But Avery took his wife's hand, and led her to the small door in the wall.

The Celebration that night was the best Christine had attended. Not only because she had the joy of having brought in the new prince and princess, but it was the first time she had seen a husband and wife come together. Not only two lives, but a marriage was mended. The baby, sitting on his father's lap, was the innocent beneficiary of the transaction. It was so beautiful Christine couldn't stop crying. This was the way it should be, she thought.

She was slightly disappointed that Felicia wasn't allowed to sponsor Margaret, but married women were assigned to married women. So a married couple took Prince Maynard and Princess Letitia under their wing.

Chapter XXXII

Happy Winter Days

Winter was beginning in earnest. One day wood was delivered to their rooms, and when they gathered in Felicia's room that night, a cheery fire crackled.

Swimming had been suspended since Sister Celeste's wedding, and now Brother Michael's class was moved indoors. The days were so short that reading class had to be moved to a later hour so the day began now with music.

Christine's efforts to teach Amanda to read had gone so well that Sister Agatha asked her to take Justin as a pupil also. Christine agreed at once, but it was not the pleasure Amanda had been. Justin seemed to make very little progress, and Christine at last realized he was a little slow mentally.

Finally the day came when Christine had finished the gospel of John and was ready for graduation. As with Mark, she had duplicated the book of John as she read it, and now she showed both finished books to Sister Agatha. Sister Agatha was astounded. She said she had never had a pupil do this before, nor had she ever seen a first effort of such quality. Christine glowed in her teacher's praise.

By great effort and determination, Godfrey had managed to keep up and was ready at the same time. Christine was very proud of him. Sister Agatha showed that she was proud of them both. Christine had been looking forward to this moment for months. She would have a

New Testament of her very own. But she had dreaded it too. Although she had come to enjoy all her classes, even riding, reading was still her favorite.

In Sunday morning service Uncle announced Godfrey's appointment as a page. Christine was thrilled for him. But that afternoon when she saw Uncle approaching her, she almost wanted to run away.

I can't learn an instrument, she thought. I just can't. But I must be obedient. If that's what the King wants me to do, he'll have to give me grace.

Uncle's face was beaming as usual. "Well, my dear, I have a dilemma."

Christine had never known Uncle to be uncertain.

"Sister Tabitha would like me to assign you to her. She is very pleased with your work."

Relief spread through Christine. The felt room was not her favorite place, but at least she was competent there. Anything would be better than music.

"But Sister Amelia has been appealing to me to have you spend mornings in the pottery shop. She says you have artistic talent, and could become a really good potter."

Christine's heart swelled. If Sister Amelia said that, it must be true. She didn't praise people without a reason. Christine enjoyed the clay, and felt she would not be unhappy if that were her lot in life.

But Uncle continued. "However, Sister Agatha never has enough copyists..."

Christine leaped on Uncle in an ecstasy of joy. "You! You were teasing me. You knew I wanted to work with books. And I'd rather work for Sister Agatha than anyone in the Castle. And you've let me worry this whole time, when you were planning something wonderful!"

Uncle straightened his robe where Christine had rumpled it. "I'm sure I didn't tell you to worry." But he was smiling happily, delighted to bestow a blessing on one of his children.

Monday morning after music, Christine reported to Sister Agatha instead of going to the felt room. She was glad she had finished her own cloak, all but the sewing, and all her friends had been supplied. Now she would sew or knit in her spare time, but no more felt.

Sister Agatha greeted her with a long embrace, and when she released her, there were tears in her eyes. "I'm so glad to still have you. You've become very dear to me."

"You can't be more glad than I am," Christine had a link with the older woman she couldn't altogether explain, except as she had once told Felicia, some people were easier to love than others.

Sister Agatha gave her instructions in ruling a page then gave her a stint of pages to do. They weren't the fancy ones. She would have to work up to those. But it was a portion of scripture that was new to Christine, and she became very excited as she read.

> "Behold, what manner of love the Father hath bestowed upon us that we should be called the sons of God: therefore the world knoweth us not, because it knew him not. Beloved, now are we the sons of God, and it doth not yet appear what we shall be: but we know that, when he shall appear, we shall be like him; for we shall see him as he is. And every man that hath this hope in him purifieth himself, even as he is pure."[1]

She called Sister Agatha back because she had to ask, "Who wrote this? Is it in my New Testament? How can I find it?"

"This is from the first epistle[2] of John. It's near the back of your Bible. One of the next things you need to do is memorize the books of the Bible, so you can find them."

"Is it the same John who wrote the gospel I just read? Which did he write first? If it's a letter, whom is it to?"

Sister Agatha laughed. "If I answer all your questions I don't think you'll get any copying done. But these are good questions. Either ask me later or ask one of the other teachers. Maybe I can find a book you can read that will tell you some of these things. Learning all this is part of studying the King's book. But you can't learn it all today."

"But it's so wonderful! I'm going to memorize these verses. Do you remember the day in class you told me what my name meant? Remember you sang one of these verses that day?"

"I remember, and I've been watching it coming true in your life."

---

1 1 John 3:1-3

2 An epistle is a letter.

"Oh, but these are about when the Prince returns. That's when we will change."

"When we see him? Yes, that refers to his return, but it's also for now. Haven't you seen the Prince?"

"Well, when we first came, Uncle showed us the Prince."

"And that was when the transformation began in your lives, but have you caught no glimpse of him since?"

Christine puzzled for a moment. "When I read the gospels it's almost as good as really being there. I guess you could say I see him in them."

"And in preaching and teaching, in songs and in the lives of others—don't you sometimes see him in those things?"

"Yes," Christine was bubbling over, "and when I pray, especially when I worship him. And in nature too, I'm learning to see him everywhere!"

"And all the time you're changing, becoming more like him."

"Oh, thank you, Prince! Thank you!"

Now there were two hours of copying followed by an hour of teaching reading. Christine had five pupils of her own. Her other classes remained about the same. Prayer class had been moved to music's slot in mid-afternoon. She still spent two hours a day in the pottery shop, and she found great satisfaction in a growing skill there.

In the evenings they still met in Felicia's room. Sarah had brought a new dimension to these evenings as she shared her extensive knowledge of the King's book and provoked thought and occasional irritation as well. Christine usually took her knitting. She was making mittens for all her friends to match the cloaks she had made earlier. Hannah and Amanda were usually embroidering, and Christine took an interest in this, especially since she was now always looking for new decorative effects for her manuscripts and pottery. She embroidered little designs on the backs of the mittens, and undertook to make a small tapestry of one of the pictures in her New Testament.

It was from the book of Matthew and showed Jesus with the lilies of the field and the fowls of the air.[3] Godfrey pointed the passage out to her shortly after they received their New Testaments and she had liked it at once. It was easy of course, here in the Castle, not to worry about your physical needs, but Christine knew it would be much harder when they were sent out into the world. She thought the tapestry might help her remember.

Some days the weather was too bad for riding class and she enjoyed the extra half hour in her room. Winter had a way of closing you in. Godfrey was delighted to be assigned to wait at the small door of the reception room for two hours each day, but this time of year few strangers found their way to the Castle. Celebrations became rare.

Christine knew from experience that peasants were huddling in their cottages, just waiting. The best thing about winter was the certainty that it would pass.

Advent season brought some visitors. Sarah's parents arrived early in the month for a visit, and Christine found them curiously unlike Sarah. They were easy to get close to, and Christine was sorry to see the visit end. They wanted to be back at their outpost in time for the Feast of the Nativity. When they were about to depart, they took Christine aside.

Sarah's mother hugged her, "We want to thank you for the way you're helping Sarah. You've been a good friend to her."

"I haven't done anything," Christine protested, not from modesty, but from guilt because she still had difficulty feeling any warmth toward Sarah.

"You've done much more than you realize. Sarah asked us to bring you this gift." Sarah's father held out a large, heavy box.

Christine didn't feel she ought to accept it, but they insisted, and when she had opened it, she was so overcome, she couldn't thank them enough. Christine now had her own Old Testament.

At vespers she found herself asking forgiveness. She had thought Sarah was cold and insensitive, yet she had not overlooked Christine's service, and she had chosen the one gift that Christine would appreciate more than any other.

On Santa Lucia day there was a wedding, and although Christine did not know the couple, she rejoiced in the beautiful occasion.

---

[3] Matthew 6:24-34

Felicia was allowed a short visit to her family home. Her friends all met for prayer before she left. She desperately wanted to bring back some member or members of her family. Christine decided to fast the whole time Felicia was gone even though the Castle was full of holiday treats. It was a great disappointment when Felicia came back alone.

Just two days before Nativity, Christine and Felicia were summoned by a page to a small room off the Castle courtyard. What a pleasant surprise! Letitia and Maynard were already there visiting with the miller and his wife. Eldred and Abigail had come too, and it was quite a merry party. Just as Felicia had promised, the little boy was now able to run about on straight sturdy legs.

The days were short and the journey long. The guests had to spend the night, and next morning when they would have departed, they allowed themselves to be persuaded to stay another day. With the evidence of Maynard and Letitia's changed lives, and the best persuasion that Eldred and Abigail could offer, and an interview with Uncle, and the prayers of the whole Castle going up for them, the miller and his wife at last left the courtyard gate only so they could re-enter at the small door.

What a grand Celebration that Christmas Eve!

The chimes Christmas morning found everyone already awake and headed for a special service in the Great Hall instead of matins in the Chapel. The choir sang the story of Christ's birth from the Gospel of Luke. Christine sat with Godfrey and Lucius. Felicia even had a solo part:

"Behold the handmaid of the Lord; be it unto me according to thy word."[4]

Christine wiped her eyes throughout the service. She had always loved Christmas, but it had never meant so much as this year. It staggered her to realize that the Prince himself, the Creator of the Universe, the one whose name was Wonderful, Counsellor, the Mighty God, the Everlasting Father, the Prince of Peace,[5] had become a tiny human infant, the most helpless of all living things.

---

[4] Luke 1:38

[5] Isaiah 9:6

The how of it was beyond all understanding, the greatest miracle known to man. The why was even more incomprehensible. It was easy to picture God coming to earth in the words of the Revelation, mounted on a white horse, eyes as a flame of fire, many crowns upon his head, a sharp sword proceeding out of his mouth.[6] But for God to come as a baby, totally dependent on poor Jewish villagers, unable to even speak, destined to endure all the trials and temptations of growing up in a fallen world—why had he submitted himself to such humiliation? Why had the Father permitted it?[7]

Christine knew the answer: for the sake of sinful men. But such love was more than she could imagine. So while her mind wondered, her heart accepted, and the tears flowed.

After breakfast the cycle of plays began. Christine was in the very first. The potters were doing Creation, and she was cast as a lioness. The part made her laugh to think she had come so far from timid, fearful Mara. She had to get out of costume quickly because the agricultural students were doing Noah and the Ark, and the lioness was needed again.

The colorful tapestry of the Scriptures unrolled—or maybe unraveled—with considerably more humor than dignity. Christine's costume saw service again with Daniel in the Lion's Den. The scribes did the Raising of Lazarus[8] and Christine played Martha. Godfrey and the other blacksmithing students finished the program with the Last Judgment, and the flames at least were real. It was a bit more sobering than they had intended. Christine remembered the verse about the Lake of Fire,[9] and wondered how she had lived so long under the threat of it.

---

[6] Revelation 19:11-15

[7] 1 John 4:9-10

[8] John 11:1-46

[9] Revelation 21:8

Chapter XXXIII

Christmas Surprise

Dinner was later than usual, but such a feast more than made up for it. No supper was scheduled, and no one missed it.

After dinner, Christine began distributing her gifts. She had made graceful ceramic vases for Sister Agatha, Sister Tabitha, and Sister Alathea. For everyone else there were mittens. She had even knitted a pair for Brother Philip.

Giving presents was such fun. Everyone seemed very pleased with the gifts she had made them, and then there were the gifts to be received in return. Lucius had made wrought iron candle holders. Hannah presented felt slippers to everyone. Sarah had woven jute bags, but Christine didn't expect one. She already had an incomparable gift from Sarah, but Sarah had a bag for her too.

Christine had worried needlessly about Felicia. She was afraid the gift-giving might be embarrassing for her again. But Felicia had planned ahead this time. She had collected dried flowers, leaves, and seed pods during late fall and now surprised each of her friends with a lovely spray.

Nathan had carved beautiful angels from cedar wood. "They're guardian angels," he explained. "Hang them in your closets to guard your woolens from moths."

Godfrey got oohs and ahhs over the miniature swords he had made as letter-openers. Justin had pomanders made from apples and cloves. But suddenly Christine missed someone.

"Where's Amanda?" she asked Hannah.

Hannah shook her head. "She's in her room. She won't come out."

"What's the matter?"

"Can't you guess?"

Christine could guess. Amanda had requested permission to visit her family and been refused. Christine hadn't honestly felt sorry. "I'm sure Uncle knows best," she had glibly told Amanda. But the child had been retreating a little more each day since. Now Christine felt her anger rising. How ungrateful! She received a hundred-fold more love here than she ever had at her house. Christine felt like shaking her!

On the heels of those thoughts came conviction and guilt. Only this morning she had been marveling at the Prince's love for sinful humanity, and now she was angry at Amanda for having the same kind of love. Suppose, she thought, my parents were out there. I would probably behave worse than Amanda.

Leaving the group, she stole up to Amanda's room. But on the way she stopped to pray. "Dear Father, don't let me say the wrong things and make it worse, but Amanda should be happy, especially at your Son's birthday celebration. Help me to help her."

She knocked and waited. After a moment Amanda opened the door. With a great effort she managed a smile to greet Christine, but it vanished in an instant.

"Merry Christmas, Amanda, I have a gift for you and had to come all the way up here to deliver it."

It was a disappointment to see the uninterested way Amanda received the bright red mittens. "Thank you," was all she said. Again selfish thoughts came to Christine. She had worked hard on the mittens anticipating the joy in Amanda's face when she gave them to her. She felt cheated.

Listlessly Amanda went to her wardrobe and picked something out. "This is for you," she offered without enthusiasm.

Christine received the little strip of felt, painstakingly embroidered with flowers and bearing the words, "We love him because he first loved us."[1] A wave of shame engulfed her. Amanda too, had worked and anticipated, but now her pain was too great to ignore.

"It's beautiful, Amanda. I needed a bookmark. I'll treasure it always." Christine tried to put all her feelings into the words.

Amanda smiled a little, "I'm glad you like it." But again the smile was only a momentary flash.

Christine didn't know what else to do. She sat down and took the child in her lap and rocked her as though she were a baby. Amanda made no sound, but she buried her head against Christine and presently Christine felt a little dampness there. Now her anger turned elsewhere. That selfish bunch downstairs! Laughing and enjoying themselves while Amanda's heart is breaking!

Ah, yes, Christine, where were you a few minutes ago? And then it was Amanda who was wrong not to be where you were. Everyone else must behave just as you do or bear judgment.[2]

Christine knew that voice. She had learned now to talk with Uncle when he wasn't visible. Be patient with me, she pleaded. I don't want to be that way. But, dear Uncle, can't you help Amanda?

"Amanda, I have a secret!" Christine had been saving this surprise for the right moment, and now seemed to be it. "I have a secret I haven't told to anyone. But now I'm ready to tell everybody. It's a really good secret!"

She had succeeded in getting Amanda's attention. "What is it? Tell me."

"No, you have to come downstairs. I want to tell everyone at once." Christine really did think it was a wonderful secret, but she hoped Amanda would agree. She didn't want to build her up and then disappoint her.

Amanda looked at her sadly, "You are just trying to make me happy. Thank you for trying. I'm sorry—I don't want to spoil Christmas for my friends. If I came downstairs I'd just be a damper on everyone."

"You know Felicia understands how you feel. She's praying for her family too, and think what a let-down it was to go home and see them and still not be able to bring them back."

---

[1] 1 John 4:19

[2] Matthew 7:1-5

"Yes, I know, but I wish I could have gone." She heaved a sigh, "Maybe I'm wrong, but at least I could find out how they are."

Christine saw a little deeper, "Amanda, the very first morning I was at the Castle, the first lesson I had to learn was to turn my cow over to the King."

"Lily?"

"Yes, I'm afraid I loved her almost as much as a person. But I had to just put her in the King's hands and leave her there. Ever since then I've been learning more about trusting the King. I guess it's just about the most important lesson we learn here. At least, that's what you need to do right now. The King knows what's happening with your family. He wants them to come to the Castle more than you do. Can't you trust Him?"

"I do trust him. It's just the waiting is hard. Hoping every week that this Sunday Daddy will be here, and then never seeing him. If I could only get some word."

"That reminds me of my secret. Won't you come share it with us? Please?"

"All right. I need to give out my other bookmarks." Amanda forced a smile. "I'll try not to think about my trouble."

Amanda gathered up her bookmarks and let Christine lead her down to the others. Christine patted her pocket. The surprise was still there, a long cheery letter from Naomi. In it she instructed Christine to share it with their friends, and Christine had thought it would be a fitting close to a beautiful holiday.

Gift exchanging was still going on. Christine had a few more gifts to distribute, and as she sought out her teachers, she and Amanda gathered their little circle of friends back into one place. Amanda was making a real effort to be enthusiastic over her presents, but the more she tried, the closer she came to tears. Warm hugs and good wishes from understanding hearts were more precious than gifts.

At last the little knot of friends found a quiet corner, and Christine mounted a block to be better heard.

"Ahem, now please listen, everyone. I have a very special Christmas surprise for you."

As though on cue, a hubbub erupted in the hallway, and all eyes turned from Christine to see what the approaching "surprise" could be. Christine, a little irritated at the interruption, turned too. Could she believe her eyes?

Amanda screamed and went racing toward the ragged, dirty figure who was coming down the hall.

The whole Castle seemed to have been drawn to the spot, and shouts of praise were rising from the crowd.

Christine ran too, but the crowd was so thick she couldn't get close. At her shoulder she heard Hannah's voice, "Thank you, oh, thank you!"

Two pages demanded access, and the crowd reluctantly let them through. Christine at last got a glimpse of the center.

Prince Hugh was there. Amanda was folded in his arms. Uncle was at his side. The crowd closed in again, and Christine made her way to the edge, wanting to sit down. Godfrey came up and gave her a big hug.

"What a great surprise! How did you ever keep it a secret? I don't know how you managed it, but you've certainly made Amanda the happiest little girl in the Castle."

Christine shook her head. She didn't mean to take credit, but Godfrey was gone again. She leaned her forehead in a corner of the wall, "Yes, dear Prince. What a wonderful, wonderful Christmas present. Thank you with all my heart."

She was still sitting there a good while later when the excitement had died down and the crowd dispersed. Amanda was coming toward her, leading her daddy by the hand.

"Oh, thank you, Christine!" she exclaimed. "This was a truly wonderful secret!"

Christine started to protest, but she saw in Amanda's face that something was very wrong. She looked at Prince Hugh. The pages had dressed him in robes once more, and washed his face and hands. She thought again how awkward he looked. But he had a peace in his face this time she had not seen there before, and yet with the peace, a great sadness.

"Oh, Prince Hugh, I do hope you will stay with us this time."

"Yes," he nodded. "I've come to stay. I have found out the hard way that obedience is best."

Christine looked questioningly at Amanda. The child sniffed and replied, "Baby Seth is dead."

"Oh, no!" Christine took Amanda in her arms to comfort her.

Hugh nodded emphatically. "I'm afraid it's true. He grew sicker and sicker. Late last night he went into convulsions and died. There was nothing I could do. All I could think was that I had disobeyed the King, and now I had no one to call on in my hour of distress. When it was over, I saw that two paths lay before me. I could blame the King and blaspheme and continue in my stubbornness and see what more could go wrong, or I could repent and return to the Castle and commit my way to him. I decided to put my trust in the King."

"That's just what Christine was telling me to do. I'm so glad you came back, Daddy. Not because I missed you, though I did, but because I want you to have the Prince for your very best friend. And you can trust Seth to him, just as Christine trusted Lily."

"Lily?"

"Never mind." Christine had to ask, "What about your wife and your other sons, Amos and Mark?"

The old look of distress came into Hugh's face for a moment. "They're outside, just like the other time. She won't come in, and she won't allow the boys to."

"I'm going out to see them," Amanda declared firmly, then added hopefully, "if Uncle will let me."

"It won't do any good," Hugh sighed.

Christine wanted to second that, but instead she said, "Let's go ask him."

When Uncle had heard the request he looked very solemnly at Amanda. "If I told you that you would be hurt, it wouldn't make any difference, would it?"

"No, sir," Amanda's gaze did not waver. "I'd still want to go."

"Then so be it," Uncle sighed.

Christine wanted to ask if she could go along, but she had learned better. But Uncle, knowing her desire, advised her, "You and Hannah may watch from the wall. You had better hurry. It's nearly dark. Young lady," he turned back to Amanda. "This is to be a very brief visit. You understand that?"

"Only a minute or two," Amanda assured him. "Thank you, dear Uncle," and she hugged him tightly about the waist.

Uncle and Amanda started toward the Castle reception hall. Christine ran to find Hannah. Hugh hesitated a little then followed Christine.

When they arrived panting on the wall, there was just enough daylight left to see the three figures huddled below. The weather was damp and chill. The light snow they had had earlier had turned to a drizzle. Almost at once the door opened, letting out a bright stream of radiance. Christine remembered it had been about dark when that door had opened for Godfrey and her. She and Hannah joined hands and began to pray. A bright little figure stepped from the door and rushed to the others. They did not hear Amanda's greeting, but the shrill voice of the mother rose to them.

"You demon!" she shrieked. "It's your fault my baby is dead. You couldn't be there when I needed you. You had to go play the fine lady. Now your selfishness has killed your own brother! I hope you're satisfied."

Christine's insides curdled in anguish at that well-remembered voice. Hannah's hands which she held began to shake. "Poor Amanda!" Hannah mourned.

If the child replied, the watchers could not hear it, but she seemed to stretch her arms to her mother. Suddenly one of the woman's hands leaped out and seized Amanda by the hair. In the other hand she had a walking staff, and she began to beat the child in a frenzy of pent-up anger.

For the first time, Amanda's voice rose to the turrets, "Amos! Mark!" she cried. "Run! Run in the little door! Run!"

The two boys hesitated only a moment, then took to their heels. They were illuminated a brief instant by the open door then passed inside it. Hugh turned from the wall where they were standing and ran down the steps.

Christine felt helpless. It was a long, circuitous route from where they stood to the scene that was only forty feet below them.

Amanda's mother continued to beat and curse her, so that it was a wonder she did not run out of breath.

"Now you're coming home where you belong. You've destroyed our home with your stubborn disobedience. I've nothing left to live for, but by God, I'm your mother, and I'll do my duty to you if it kills me."

Christine could not believe what was happening just out of her reach. They were moving further from the door. Amanda was being dragged away. "Stop! Stop!" she shouted, but no one seemed to hear. She glanced at Hannah. The girl had dropped to her knees and was moaning in prayer.

The two were moving faster. Amanda was growing weaker. Soon they would be out of sight in the dusk. But then the sky was illumined by a swiftly moving light. Awestruck, Christine saw that it was a shining knight from the other part of the Castle. He flashed down in front of the striving pair like a stroke of lightning. Incredibly the woman did not seem to see him. She tried to continue, not perceiving the immovable obstacle against which she struggled.

Again Amanda's voice carried to Christine's ears, "Look, Mother, look!"

But the woman could no more hear than she could see. The great glittering horseman reached down and pulled Amanda from her mother's grasp.[3]

"So," the woman cried, collapsing to the ground, "you are stronger than your poor old mother. And do you have any pity or mercy for her trembling old limbs? Don't go! Don't leave me alone here to die!"

Amanda had moved no more than a step away, and she seemed to be pleading with her mother.

"Ungrateful beast! To turn on your own mother after all I have sacrificed for you. And you have no conscience, no remorse. You can cast me aside and feel no guilt. Ah, but the King, the righteous judge, will judge between us today. He will punish you for your wickedness. He knows I have never harmed you nor any living soul, but have suffered silently under your cruelty and that of your father."

Christine felt the Castle shake under her feet, and a voice boomed out of the darkness as though the stones themselves had spoken: "Beware, blasphemer!"

The shining knight raised his sword as if he were about to strike the whining wretch, but Amanda leaped between them. "No, no! Give her another chance. She doesn't know what she's saying. It's only her way. Forgive her!"[4]

The shimmering sword was lowered. "For your sake, little maid," the knight spoke, "and more so for our Prince's sake who so dearly loves each one of you poor, miserable creatures."

Then a voice issued from the door, "You have stayed too long, Amanda. Come at once."

"Coming, Uncle!" Amanda called. Christine saw her stoop to kiss her mother and then come running back to the Castle.

---

[3] Psalm 34:7

[4] 1 John 5:16

The door closed, and Christine was looking into total darkness. The shining knight had vanished. "Did you see him?" she asked Hannah excitedly.

"See whom?" Hannah raised her head from praying. "Is Amanda safe?"

"Yes, she's back in the Castle."

"Oh, thank God, thank God!"

"Amen!" Christine agreed. Amanda's safety was the most important thing, but she would never forget what she had seen. Truly the power and glory of the King were more splendid than her mind could grasp.

The Celebration that night for the two young princes, John and Noel, was almost anti-climatic to Christine. She was as exhausted as a soldier after a battle. Hannah cleaned up Amanda and carefully groomed her, but some bruises still showed. To the two girls who had watched from the wall, Amanda's good spirits were almost unbelievable.

She explained, "My prayers for Daddy and the boys were answered. Someday my prayers for Mama will be answered too."

It was the next day before Christine got a chance to read Naomi's letter to her friends.

Chapter XXXIV

Hannah's Story

Right after the new year, Sister Agatha decided to introduce Christine to the Castle Library. It was a world of enchantment to the young book-lover. Until now she had seen only Bibles and scripture portions. She had never dreamed that a whole world of books existed.

The librarian, Sister Sophia, picked out a small, fairly easy one for her. Christine carried to her room *The Lives of the Saints* and read it through in a night.

She was back the next day begging for more. Soon she discovered that reading was a pleasure she must severely limit, for if she had been given the choice, she would seldom have done anything but read and copy.

The Castle still offered her a cornucopia of delights. The morning chimes rang while it was quite dark, but the fireplace in her room welcomed her with its glowing bed of coals. She had never spent a winter so cozy and warm. The corridors were chilly, but she had warm woolen clothes to wear, and she was surprised to find silk a very warm fabric.

The hour of morning prayer now seemed too short. There was so much to talk to the King about. Christine had found a freedom in music class. She knew her voice was not as melodious as some of the others, but she felt that the King was pleased by it, and she sang out loudly, even if occasionally off-key. Teaching reading gave her great satisfaction whether her pupils were slow or quick, but she was apt to be impatient when she felt they weren't trying.

Whether they held a needle, a pen, or a shimmering mound of clay, her hands found much opportunity to produce what was beautiful and useful. This was no small element in her happiness.

Bible class and prayer class grew ever more beloved, and she even looked forward to that half-hour ride through snowy woods on a willing mount. Her friends grew nearer and dearer. There had been a change in Sarah, very gradual, almost unnoticeable, but she was not so stiff, not so sure, easier to know. The day Sarah was approved as a sponsor was nearly as exciting to Christine as her own approval which came a week later.

Not every Saturday was a workday, and on some cold winter days she went sledding or skating with the other young people. One evening they celebrated Hannah's "birthday," the anniversary of her coming to the Castle.

"You came in weather like this?" Christine shivered at the thought. Also she had been spending an hour in the middle of every day in the reception hall now, and she knew how rare were those magical moments when Uncle appeared with a newcomer to select a sponsor.

Hannah just laughed, "It was worse than this! I came in the middle of a blizzard."

Christine grew suddenly curious. She had never heard Hannah's story. "How could you reach the Castle in a blizzard? Tell us about it."

With everyone looking at her expectantly, Hannah grew a little shy, but with downcast eyes she began. "My parents were members of an outlaw band, and I was born there." This brought gasps of surprise.

"But when I was too young to remember, I was sent to live with my grandmother. She was a funny old woman. She told me stories all the time. Some of them were fairy tales like Amanda's. Some of them were stories from the King's book, though I didn't know it then. We lived alone in a great forest and seldom saw other people. I think the stories were more real to me than the life I led. Or maybe I thought our life was part of the stories. When I played in the woods, I don't think a dragon or a giant or anything else would have surprised me.

"We lived very simply, tending a garden, a cow, and a few chickens. Grandmother's sewing brought in a little, and she taught me to sew. I was quite happy. But then my grandmother became ill. I tried to take care of her, but I didn't know what to do. Before she died, she drew me a map that she said would lead me to my parents."

"But you didn't know who your parents were?" Sarah wondered.

"No, I had no idea where I was going. Finding my way was a terrible ordeal. I had never been far from our cottage and seldom spoken to strangers. The map was a mystery to me, and I had to get people to help me understand it. I slept wherever I happened to be and ate what I could find or what strangers gave me.

"If only you had met someone from the Castle!" Godfrey exclaimed.

"I did. I met a wandering preacher who told me many things. I listened with joy, because he confirmed so many of the stories I had heard from my grandmother, but when he invited me to come to the Castle, I refused. I had become excited with the idea of seeing my parents, and I was nearing the end of my journey. I asked his prayers, but I went on my way.

"How old were you?" Amanda wanted to know.

"I was just a little bigger than you."

Amanda slipped a loving arm around her sponsor, and Hannah continued. "When I walked into that nest of outlaws I had no idea that anything was amiss. I was so inexperienced that I had no notion of how others lived or acted. My parents welcomed me warmly, as did the others, yet I did not feel the joy I had anticipated. I felt somehow disappointed, but I couldn't tell why. At first I tried very hard to fit in. I was very obedient, but instead of that making me one of the group, it seemed to set me apart. It's hard to explain except that as the days passed I was more and more certain that I didn't belong there. Equally plain was that the others sensed it. I was excluded from everything. If they were talking when I came near, they began to whisper. I didn't know what to do. I had come prepared to love my parents, but most of the time they disgusted me. I blamed myself, and tried harder to be what they expected, but it wasn't in me."

"Couldn't you see they were doing wrong?" Christine inquired.

"Not right at first, but gradually that became a suspicion, and when at last I fully realized that I had come among outlaws, and that my parents were nothing more nor less than outlaws themselves, I determined to leave and seek my own way elsewhere."

"Hurrah!" shouted Amanda.

"Foolishly though, I confronted my parents, and told them that I now understood their ways and as they were not my ways I planned to depart. They forbade me, and when I remained firm in my intention, they imprisoned me."

Hannah's listeners drew in their breaths.

"They kept me in an underground cell and only let me out to work. And though it was only kitchen work or other such common tasks, I hated the thought that I was contributing to their lives."

"But you couldn't help it," Lucius sympathized.

"No, I had no choice that I could see. But my thoughts began to dwell on the preacher I had met. I regretted now that I had not accepted his invitation, and it did not look as if I would have another opportunity. As the time passed my treatment grew worse, for I was subjected to insults and abuse by the outlaws who abhorred me as much as I did them."

"How did you ever escape?" Felicia asked with tears in her eyes.

"I didn't. I don't believe anyone who is under their power can escape by his own efforts. In fact, I was losing more than my freedom, for I began to hate. I hated them all so passionately I could scarcely stand to look at them. At times ugly words arose in my throat, and it was more fear of their anger than my own conscience that kept them from being spoken. I even began to think of violence. When I handled a knife in the kitchen, I thought how gladly I would use it on my tormentors."

The others looked at one another. This was not the Hannah they knew.

"You see they were winning. I was becoming one of them. I praise the King that even in the midst of this, my conscience did not go to sleep. I saw my danger, and helpless as I was to prevent these thoughts, I knew they were wrong. Often at night I would cry myself to sleep, not in self-pity for my condition, but in self-loathing for the thoughts I had entertained during the day. In a clumsy way, I even prayed."

"How long were you this way?" Sarah's eyes were moist too.

"Years. I speak of them briefly, and now they seem like a brief period, but they dragged on endlessly when I was going through them. I saw the seasons come and go, and no relief appeared. Still I had not given up hope. My childish fairy tales told so many stories of mistreated children who were rescued at last, that I tried to believe I was one of them. If I could only keep a sweet spirit I knew help would come. But I often despaired because I knew my spirit was not sweet, and I feared I was the mean stepsister destined for destruction.

"But the King had not forgotten me. Perhaps it was the prayers of the preacher I had met. Whatever, about a year ago the outlaw band of which I was a prisoner, attacked a group of travelers who had become stranded in a snowstorm. They didn't realize until too late that the travelers were from the Castle. There were several knights in the party, who not only repulsed the attack, but pursued the outlaws to their den. I was gathering chips for the fire when I heard the shouts and din of a battle. I did not think twice, but ran towards the sounds, screaming for help as I went."

Hannah shrugged, "There, that's the whole story. The good missionaries welcomed me and brought me here to the Castle. And I've invited you all to my birthday party and then made you unhappy with my sad tale. Please forgive me."

In the days that followed, Christine often thought of Hannah's story. She compared her with Felicia, who had also come out of great suffering, and she began to wonder if that was a prerequisite to spirituality. She was copying the book of Romans, and found some things there hard to understand. Paul kept talking about being dead, but he was applying it to the people to whom he was writing.[1] This was death in a different sense than Christine knew anything about. He seemed to be saying that the sons and daughters of the King were already dead.

After thinking a great deal about it, she began to see how you could say that about Felicia. She had been as good as dead when she was under her burden. Hannah too had been in a situation that could be described as death. Even Justin had used that phrase, "as good as dead." This life at the Castle was truly a second life for them.

But Christine had never known despair. She and Godfrey had found a new life, but they had never really died to end the old life. Was it possible that this lack would hamper them for the rest of their days? She wondered if this was Sarah's problem. Was she failing to grow because life had been too easy for her? Christine could see the possibility, and she prayed that the King would make up in her life whatever was lacking. If dying is needful, she prayed, is it too late for

---

[1] Romans, chapter. 6

me? She considered the matter of suffering, and it appalled her. She did not want an experience like Felicia's or Hannah's, but she was willing to face that, rather than miss the King's very best. This became a matter of urgency in Christine's prayers.

She had gleaned another truth from Hannah's story. Many a time she had asked the King to open Barbara's heart, to make her desire the way of righteousness. Now she realized that Barbara could not change her own mind. She was more a captive of the outlaws than Hannah had ever been. So Christine began to pray that the King would rescue her, would send a warrior from the Castle to fight for Barbara's freedom.

Chapter XXXV

Discovery

As the winter lengthened Christine saw a restlessness in some of the residents of the Castle. For three weeks the sun didn't shine. The weather was cold and damp. Christine knew all the symptoms. She had gone through them every winter of her life. Nathan complained he was bored and spent more time playing chess with Lucius. Even Felicia seemed to take less interest in her studies. She said she was tired of memorizing. She had stuffed so many verses in her head she didn't believe there was room for one more. Christine found the hours in the reception hall especially dull. She read or sewed, when she really wanted to nap. But still the usual winter apathy didn't take hold of her as in previous years.

She wondered what was wrong with the others. In the little one-room cottage when they had known nothing of reading or of the exciting life of the Castle, when candles were too precious to be wasted, and the long evenings had been passed with no better entertainment than the crackling fire, it was perfectly natural to get in the doldrums. But here there was no reason for it. Christine spent more time in the library as her friends drew in on themselves. She could never get enough of books, but sometimes her eyes warned her she had read enough for the time. Then she pursued her new interest.

Ever since Sister Agatha had shown her to the Library, Christine had been marveling that this enchanting place had existed in the Castle without her knowledge. And this set her to wondering further what other unexplored realms might be waiting to be discovered. So her chief exercise these winter days was the game she called "Exploring the Castle." She had set about making a map of the Castle, and it was a complex task. She had to step off distances, and make very certain of directions. She had already discovered many new places, the Armory, the Carpenter's Shop, the Sheep Fold.

In every one she had learned exciting new lessons. The day she discovered the Armory there was no one else there, and she spent a leisurely hour inspecting the weapons. Then she grew bolder and took up a sword and shield. On the sword was inscribed "TRUTH" and on the shield, "FAITH."[1] She began to swing the sword with vigor, acting out her old fantasies. For several minutes she was an avenging angel, destroying outlaws right and left. Then she began to be uncomfortably aware of the weight of these implements. Christine was strong, but the shield had to be held up, not merely carried, and the sword, which would have been easy to support in an upright position, was quite unwieldy when held horizontally to threaten her imaginary enemies. She kept on for a short time, but soon realized again that she was not a knight. No wonder Godfrey and Lucius spent two hours of every day training with these weapons. Battles might last all day, and Christine could not even imagine the strength required of a knight.

In the Carpentry Shop she had found a number of people at work, including Nathan. The surprise was finding a great stained glass window there, as large and beautiful as any in the Chapel. It showed Joseph teaching the young Jesus the skills of their trade,[2] and Christine thought carpentry must be the most noble of pursuits with such an example.

The Sheep Fold was full the day she found it. An old shepherd who sat whittling explained that the snow was too thick for the sheep to get any grass. But she sat for more than two hours as he talked about sheep, their docility, their flocking instincts, their incredible stupidity. Christine remembered that the King had called his children, sheep,[3] and she found it very enlightening.

---

[1] Ephesians 6:10-17

[2] Mark 6:3; Matthew 13:55

[3] Psalm 100:3 and others

Almost every day she spent some time on her map and the excitement of filling in the blank spaces was surpassed only by the discoveries themselves. She was only working on the ground floor, and there was so much, she doubted if she would ever get to the second level. Besides this, at every new corridor and room she found designs worked in stone or tapestry or wood or even silver and gold. And these she copied into her notebook to be used in the borders of her manuscripts.

One cold, sunny day, she had been copying a stained glass window in the Chapel, and she realized that she didn't know what was outside the windows. Braving the chill, she opened a richly carved door and found herself in the Castle graveyard. High walls hemmed her in, and with the sun it was not as unpleasant as she had expected. She decided to take some time to inspect the tombstones. To her delight she found them a treasury of new ornamental designs. She went quickly from one to the other, determining to come back in her cloak to make copies. The names were all strange to her of course. She reflected that though there had been two marriages and several births since she came to the Castle, she had yet to attend her first funeral. That would have to happen eventually. Don't let it be anyone I know, she prayed.

Suddenly she stopped in her tracks. The tombstone read, "Tristram, son of George, of the King's own shire."

It gave her the oddest sensation. For a fleeting moment she thought, my brother is dead and I didn't know it. Then she knew that wasn't right. She looked at the date. It was a well-remembered date indeed, the Sunday last summer when they had come to the Castle. Christine leaped to the next stone, and read "Mara, daughter of George, of the King's own shire."

"It's true then," she said aloud. "I did die."

"Yes, it's true." Uncle had come up silently and was standing behind her. "I wish everyone could recognize the truth of it."

"But what does it mean? I don't feel dead."

"To all that is outside the Castle you are dead: to sin, to guilt, to offense, to harm. When a person dies he is freed. He is free of the law, free of debt, free of bondage. When he lived he may have been a slave, or a sentenced criminal serving his term, or entangled in partnerships and alliances to his own grief. But death frees him from all of that.[4]

---

[4] 1 Corinthians 7:39 (Death ends all contracts.)

"When he lived he was in fear—of threats, bodily injury, loss of possessions or loved ones, sickness, and of death itself. When you have died there is nothing more to fear. A living man is at the mercy of others. They may insult, dishonor, and abuse him, and finally kill him, but that is the end of what they can do. When he is dead they cannot touch him."

"I never thought of death like that. But if I am dead to sin, why do I still have wrong thoughts?"

"Thoughts are temptations, not sins. Remember what you learned. It is not wrong to be tempted, only to be overcome by temptation. But don't think of temptations as chances to be overcome, but as chances to overcome."

"But I feel angry or jealous. Sometimes I think I have more of those feelings now than I did before I came to the Castle."

"That was because you didn't know you are dead. Now you know. Dead people never feel anger or jealousy because no one can do anything to offend them. Dead people have no feelings, so they never have their feelings hurt."

Thrills shot through Christine with the beginning of revelation. "I think I understand. I am free of all necessity. I don't have to do anything!"

Uncle clapped her on the shoulder. "Exactly! Now you are really able to choose, because you are dead to both the pressures and demands of flesh and the world."

"Before I couldn't do or be what I wanted to. I was only able to react to outside forces. If people were kind I loved them, and if they were mean I hated them; but now I can love the mean ones. They can't make me angry or afraid or anything else! Thanks to the Prince I'm free! Hallelujah!"

Christine had such a feeling of elation, it was like the first time she realized she was a princess. This was just as good. She whirled around and hugged the tombstone.

"I've got to bring Godfrey here. Does he know he's dead? Everybody's been rather grumpy lately. I'll bet it's because they don't know they're dead!"

"Hurrah!" she shouted. "I'm dead!"[5] And she went running off in search of her friends.

---

[5] Colossians 3:3

A real change came into Christine's life, almost as great as when she had exchanged the life of a peasant for that of a princess. If anger or resentment started to rear their ugly heads, she just laughed and said, "You can't bother me. I'm dead!"

The disappointment was that she had trouble explaining this to her friends. Lucius said, "You're loony is what you are."

Sarah said, "I know that's what it says, but I guess I can't quite believe it. It just doesn't seem to work for me, and it's no good pretending."

"I'm not pretending," Christine told her. "I know I'm dead."

"Well, I'm glad for you," Sarah agreed, "but I'm afraid my old man is still very lively."[6]

Nathan was cautious, "You mean you don't feel even a little bit irritated when things go wrong? I think I'll just watch you and see."

Christine laughed, "If I weren't dead, I'd be perfectly furious at all of you right now."

But Hannah just nodded and said, "Yes, you've found the secret."[7]

"I can't understand what you're telling me," Felicia mourned. "But I want to believe you. I need something like that."

The only victory for Christine was Godfrey. When she explained it to him as well as she could, he shook his head doubtfully. But when she showed it to him in the King's book, and took him to see his own tombstone, he exclaimed, "You're right!" and did a cartwheel on his grave.

Then Lucius said they were both loony. But nobody in the Castle was happier.

They shared their new discovery in Bible Class, and Brother Uriah and Sister Alathea confirmed it, so Lucius apologized. But none of the others could catch hold of it. Felicia and Sarah even prayed that they might see it, but to no avail.

Finally Sarah humbly confessed, "I used to think I knew more than anyone else, but you've passed me up. I still have so much to learn."

Christine didn't know what to say. She just put her arms around Sarah and said, "I love you." The wonderful thing was that it was true.

---

6 Romans 6:6

7 See *The Christian's Secret of a Happy Life* by Hannah Whitall Smith

Chapter XXXVI

An Offering

It was a Saturday afternoon and they had spent the day ice skating. When they returned to the Castle, Christine felt worn out. She decided to have her evening prayers at once and go to bed early. There wasn't a soul in the Chapel. Christine couldn't remember ever finding it completely empty before. A voice inside her said, "See, you are the only one in the Castle who wants to pray." Christine laughed. She recognized that voice and answered, "Silly Pride, you'd like me to believe that wouldn't you?"

As she knelt there, Christine thought back. When she had first come to the Castle she had done some very foolish things, but she had learned to bring her actions into line. Controlling the symptoms, Uncle called it. How much harder to bring her thought life under control, but praise the King, she was winning that battle too. A perfect heart, she prayed, help me to have a perfect heart.

Christine heard that voice again, "Ask the King to send you someone to sponsor. You want to be a sponsor. You've been waiting for weeks now."

"No, Impatience, I'm on to you too. I'll wait until the King's time."

"But Christine, now that you can be whatever you want to be, what do you want?"

That was a different voice, the voice Christine loved best. She turned around. Uncle was there.

"Dear Uncle, thank you for coming. You always make my prayer time so much easier."

"Christine, when you first came to the Castle I asked you what you desired most. You have come a long way since then, so I'm asking you again. What do you desire above all else?"

Christine knew the answer this time. She had made up her mind long ago. "I want to be like the Prince," she declared firmly.

Uncle looked very solemn. She knew her request sounded arrogant, but she had assurance that this was the King's will for her.

"You ask a hard thing. Seeing you have such a high ambition, what token do you give of your sincerity?"

Christine thought wildly, what do I have? What could possibly be worthy? Suddenly she extended her right hand. She could think of nothing more precious. "If it would please the King, as token, I offer my right hand." Her hand trembled in rebellion, but she held it forth.

Again Uncle eyed her solemnly and long. "You are sure?" he asked. And from the sheath at his belt, he drew out a long sword.

It shone so gloriously Christine was dazzled. She had seen many diamonds since coming to the Castle, and she believed the blade of that sword was not of metal at all, but was a single diamond. In the dim light of the Chapel it seemed to have its own radiance, scattering rainbows of light in every direction. Just the sight of that sword is worth the price of my hand, she thought. But her hand seemed to have a mind of its own. She couldn't hold it still, so she reached out and grasped a railing. That sword is so sharp, I shan't feel a thing, she told herself. Aloud she said, "I'm sure."

"The King accepts your offering." Uncle raised the sword, and Christine turned her head away and concentrated on holding to the rail.

Instead of the expected blow, Christine felt Uncle's hand on her shoulder, "My child, the King has no use for a severed hand."

"Then what can I offer?" Christine cried in dismay.

Uncle was smiling now, "The hand is accepted, but keep it attached where it can labor for the King. Do you think we want to lose a good copyist?"

Mixed feelings swept back and forth in Christine's mind. She was relieved to keep her hand, but not sure that the King was as well-pleased as if she had lost it. But she had been willing. Uncle had seen that.

"Make no mistake," he cautioned, "I didn't reject your offering. It's not your hand now. It's the King's."

"I see," Christine understood. "Thank you, dear Uncle. I'll treat it with proper respect. And my request?"

"You'll see it come to pass."

Christine walked to her room glorying in that promise. She carried her right hand carefully in her left. What a privilege to have the King's hand attached to her arm! She would never forget that he had let her keep it so that she could use it for him. She longed to do great and mighty deeds with that hand, but for now she would copy his book.

Going to her fountain, she drank and then carefully washed the King's hand. She was glad to minister to him in even this small way. When she had washed and dried it, she suddenly wondered with frustration, how could she wash her left hand? Well, it would simply have to shift for itself. She couldn't use the King's hand to wait on herself. Undressing was a bit of a challenge, but she said to herself, if Uncle had cut it off, I would have had to manage.

Lying down, she put the precious hand on her pillow and contentedly fell asleep. In the morning it was the first thought in her mind when she awoke. She looked at the hand as wonderingly as if it had turned to gold. She kissed it, and thought that none of her friends would understand, but what did that matter? She hurried to the fire and warmed the King's hand. Her own hand added fuel and fanned it into a blaze. Dressing was again awkward, but I'll get used to it, she consoled herself. She unbraided her hair and brushed it out.

Suddenly she had a problem. It was impossible to braid her hair with one hand. Perhaps if she pulled it around to the front and held it with her teeth...

No, the strands kept getting tangled together. After several attempts she gave up. She would have to wear it down today.

Christine remembered the controversy last fall. After much thought and prayer, she had concluded that since she wasn't braiding her hair for adornment, but because it was the quickest, easiest way to take care of it, that she could go on doing it. Well, it certainly wasn't quick and easy now. What should she do?

Hurrying to the Chapel, she was pleased that she could use the King's hand to praise him. At breakfast it was another story. She laid his hand in her lap and fed herself with her left.

"Is something wrong with your hand?" Godfrey inquired. Christine had expected this, and she would have liked to ignore him, but eventually she would have to explain. She waited until she had everyone's attention so she wouldn't have to tell it twice, then she gave them the whole story.

"You were awfully brave," Amanda spoke admiringly.

"Oh, Uncle wouldn't have cut it off," Godfrey assured her. "He was just testing her. Remember the story of Abraham offering Isaac?[1] The King never wants to hurt us."

"Well, Abraham didn't know that," Felicia protested, "and neither did Christine."

So when they had all agreed that it was very brave, there didn't seem to be anything else to say. Christine knew that they were thinking it was also very stupid.

If Lucius thought being dead was loony, what would he say about this? She challenged him, "Lucius, don't you have anything to say?"

Lucius had learned a lesson. After a moment's thought, he said, "Was the sword really made of diamond? I would like to have seen that."

The others quickly agreed to this also. Christine could feel how uncomfortable she was making everyone. She dropped the food from her left hand, and excused herself.

At Sunday service it was easier. She could almost forget her handicap and rejoice. But something else was happening. Her hair, which had seldom been released from its braid for more than an hour or so at a time, was beginning to—what could she call it?—expand. Full of static, it was rising into the air. Out of the corners of her eyes she saw more and more coming into view. She tried pushing it down with her left hand, but touching it only confirmed what she was seeing. Her beautiful, long, thick hair was sticking straight out in all directions. She wanted to run and hide.

She would just sign the duty roster and go straight upstairs. But as she hurried there, she caught a look at her shadow and almost screamed in horror.

---

[1] Genesis, chapter 22

She looked around and saw Godfrey staring at her with a strange expression. Felicia frowned at her sympathetically and whispered, "Do you want me to braid your hair?" It seemed to her that everyone was looking at her. She caught worried, puzzled glances, and then people turned away.

I look hideous, Christine thought. Worst of all, she saw Brother Michael looking at her with that same strange expression she had seen on Godfrey's face. She couldn't stand it any longer and fled to her room.

What a relief to be back in the privacy of her room. She ran to the fountain and drank thirstily. Then she looked at her reflection. It was even worse than she anticipated. She tried to think what she looked like, but truthfully she had never seen anything to compare with it. "Oh, dear Prince," she wept, "why is this happening to me? I only wanted to please you."

Christine tried to think what she had done wrong that had brought this about. She couldn't find an answer. Grabbing her brush she began to work furiously. She had to keep reminding her right hand not to help. But her hair was a mass of tangles, and the more she brushed, the more it crackled with static. In desperation she dipped her head into the fountain. The hair lay down at last.

Water soaked her gown, chilling her, but she felt calmer. Now she patiently brushed out the tangles, and finally her hair lay straight and smooth down her back.

Christine looked at the King's hand, and it was hard not to accuse: *You* are the cause of all this. She denied the thought, but it was there. Other accusations soon came to join it. I've ruined my life. Only a fool would give up their right hand. It's not as if the King had asked for it. Who ever heard of anyone else doing such a weird thing?

"Be still!" she ordered those clamoring voices. She drank again, and tried to pray. "Dear Prince Jesus, I love you so. I only wanted to be like you, and I know that's not wrong. Why is it turning out so badly?"

Uncle's voice ran soothingly through her mind, Isn't it rather soon to judge how the matter has turned out? One problem and you're ready to give up?

Christine felt the trouble draining away. It was only her appearance after all, and Uncle had warned her not to be too concerned about that. Everything would be all right. Give it a chance.

Christine went to her wardrobe, and took out her tapestry. Yes, she thought looking at it, if she would only seek the Kingdom everything would come out right in the end.[2]

Could she work the stitches with her left hand, she wondered? For two hours she stitched awkwardly. The stitches somehow didn't match the others. Then—it was happening again. As her hair dried it began to rise up. No, no, no, she sobbed.

She put on her cloak and pulled up the hood to cover her hair. That made her feel as if she were going somewhere, and she remembered she still hadn't signed up for her chore; she must do that. She sneaked around like a thief not wanting to see anyone. The only opening left on the duty roster was after "Empty and clean chamber pots." Christine signed her name.

Her friends would be gathered somewhere, enjoying themselves. Would they miss her? Yes, but her absence would cause them less discomfort than her presence. Christine slipped into the Chapel and hidden in her cloak spent the evening in prayer.

It was with a heavy heart she went to bed, and awoke in even greater heaviness. She wet her hair to go to morning prayer, and it was still damp at breakfast.

Her friends exchanged wondering looks, and Felicia asked timidly, "I went to your room last night, but you didn't answer the door."

"I was in the Chapel."

"Oh," Felicia did not pursue the conversation.

No one seemed disposed to talk at all, and Christine knew it was because of her, her wet hair and useless right hand. She felt miserable and quickly left the table.

---

2 Matthew 6:33

Chapter XXXVII

Total Consecration

Music class was better, and Christine comforted herself that most of her day was spent in work for the King. She anticipated her copying even more than usual, she could forget her loss, and use the King's hand freely.

As soon as she climbed to her stool and leaned over her desk, however, her hair fell onto her work. With her left hand she gathered it behind her back, but it wouldn't stay there. Every time she bent to work, it was back in her way. She tried holding it, but that was too awkward. It affected her penmanship. She twisted it into a kind of knot and shoved it down the neck of her gown, but it shook loose in no time. Christine was aware that Sister Agatha was observing her, and it added to her discomfort. Other people wear their hair down, she thought. It's just a matter of learning to cope. She thought darkly of cutting it off. Then a happy thought occurred to her. If she had something to tie it back with... Could she tie a bow with one hand? No, but maybe a knot? It would be nearly as difficult as braiding.

Accusing voices rose within her. The sweet freedom you were enjoying is gone. You have come under bondage. You've made a foolish error. Be sensible. You'd better tell Uncle you need your hand back.

"No! I won't!" Christine vowed softly. I'll learn to manage. A tear fell on the parchment smearing the ink.

Christine grabbed her blotter and looked around. Sister Agatha was standing at her shoulder. "Christine, can't you tell me your trouble?"

A sympathetic ear was a great temptation, but Christine didn't want to recite her tale again. "Please," she begged, "do you have something I could use to fasten my hair back?"

Sister Agatha frowned a little, "I'm sure we can find something. Why don't you come up to my room with me?"

As Christine followed her up flight after flight of stairs, she understood why she had never seen Sister Agatha out on Saturday workdays. The older woman got all the exercise she needed inside the Castle. Christine had thought the scriptorium was on the highest or nearly highest level of the Castle. She thought of her map, and despaired of ever charting all this. Practice with the map had helped her learn to keep her directions though. She knew the scriptorium was on the north side of the Castle, and she thought they had moved around to the east side.

At last they started up the winding steps of a tower. Around and around and still upward they climbed. The tower grew narrower as they went, so Christine thought it couldn't be much further, but looking up, it seemed to rise a great distance yet. She had to ask Sister Agatha to let her rest.

At the very top they entered a little room. It resembled the other bedrooms of the Castle in some ways, there was a fountain and a fireplace, but Christine chiefly noticed the differences. Instead of a wardrobe, Sister Agatha's dark robes hung on a row of pegs in the wall. In its place near the window was a writing desk, and on it copy work was in progress. Directly in front of the window was a prayer bench. The bench and stool were covered in a rich Moroccan leather of darkest red. The draperies of the bed were velvet of the same dark red, but caught back with ropes of gold.

What drew Christine's attention were the rows of shelves. Sister Agatha had her own library! And mixed between the books were curios of remarkable sorts. Christine was sure each one had a story behind it. How she would like to examine them and get Sister Agatha to tell her about them.

Sister Agatha had gone directly to the fountain when they entered the room, and now Christine followed her example. When she rose, Sister Agatha gave her a hairbrush. "Here, smooth it out a bit first."

Christine took the brush unwillingly. Sister Agatha would see that she was using her left hand, and she would have to explain. I might as well get it over with, she thought. Telling Sister Agatha was somehow easier than telling her friends. The old teacher nodded encouragement as she talked. When she saw the difficulty Christine was having brushing her hair, she took back the brush, and began to brush it for her. It was more snarled and tangled than Christine could ever remember, and though Sister Agatha was gentle, there were some sharp pulls before her hair once more lay in shining ripples.

Now Sister Agatha went to the pegs and lifted down a veil such as she herself wore.

"Can I put it on with one hand?" Christine worried.

"I think so, the cloth is crepe and rather sticks to itself." She showed Christine how to bend down and drape the cloth over one side of her head. "If we put it on the right side first, then you can just pull it around. There, make it snug. It will stay by itself until you can slip this pin in it."

Christine flopped her head back and the veil stayed in place. What a relief! She went and looked at herself in the fountain. "All my hair is hidden!"

Sister Agatha smiled, "Does that matter?"

The last vestige of Christine's vanity died at that moment. "No, it doesn't." Suddenly a question occurred to her. "Sister Agatha, that's not why *you* wear a veil, is it? I mean you didn't give *your* hand away?"

"No," she laughed. "That's not why. I wear a veil because in the King's Book it says women should cover their heads when they pray."[1]

Christine was shocked. "Why no one has told me that! Hardly anyone in the Castle wears a veil."

"Christine, I think you're learning that each of us has to follow the Lord without worrying what others do, or even what they might think of us."

Christine tried to remember which women wore something on their heads and which did not. She found that she had never really paid attention. "Do the other women know about the command?"

"Those who read their Bibles must."

---

[1] 1 Corinthians 11:4-16

Christine looked again at her reflection. She felt confused. She knew that obeying the King ought to be a joy. "Sister Agatha, was it foolish of me to give the King my hand?"

Sister Agatha sat down and took the hand in her lap. She began thoughtfully. "What you did was really a sort of Old Testament concept. Under the law of Moses individuals used to consecrate or devote certain things. Often it was for a specific time. For instance, a farmer might consecrate a certain field, and then all the production from that field would be given to the Lord. The vessels of the Temple were consecrated. It was strictly forbidden to use them in ordinary ways.[2] Read about Belshazzar and you'll see what happened to someone who did.[3] If an animal was consecrated it would usually be sacrificed, though for an unclean animal it might be either redeemed or killed."[4]

"But in the New Testament?" Christine asked.

"As Christians we don't practice that kind of consecration. We have a different viewpoint."

"Should I ask for my hand back?"

"Christine, your mistake wasn't in dedicating your hand." Sister Agatha seemed to be pondering how to make it clear. "You can't use this hand to brush *your* hair—but couldn't you use it to brush the King's hair?"

Christine was puzzled. "How could I do that?"

"Well, if you gave your hair to the King, then it would be the King's hair, just as this is the King's hand."

"Splendid!" Christine cried seeing a solution to her problem. "But...would the King want my hair? I mean, it's not good for anything."

"Did you think your hand was good for anything? Do you really think the King needs anything we have to offer?"

"Then I'll give him my hair. Oh, thank you, Sister Agatha."

"But Christine, I said we don't look at it that way anymore. We don't consecrate one of our possessions or members."

"What do we do?" Christine wondered.

"Well, think of the tithe for example. Those outside the Castle are still under the law. They owe a tenth of their income to the King and

---

[2] Numbers 18:3

[3] Daniel, chapter 5

[4] Exodus 13:12, 13

then the other ninety percent is theirs. If they so choose they can give more, and we call that an offering. But we in the Castle don't pay tithes. When we work at a task, *one hundred percent* of the fruit of our labor is the King's. If we use some of it on ourselves that is appropriate because we are the King's. Really when you came to the Castle you gave not only your hand, but your whole body, soul, and spirit to the King. If you brought any possessions they were no longer yours, but the King's. The New Testament concept of consecration is not to consecrate this or that but that we ourselves are consecrated."

"Justin once said he was a slave. It is kind of like that, isn't it?"

"Not at all. I remember when I first started wearing a veil, the spirit of self-will rose up in me and said, 'This is legalism. You've come under bondage.' And I struggled with that for sometime, until one night the King spoke to me in a dream and showed me the difference between bondage and submission. Everything in the Castle is voluntary. I had chosen to wear the veil, desiring to please my King. That is not bondage.

"When a vassal swears allegiance to his lord, he does so out of self-interest. When a bride vows to obey her husband, it is her choice to do so. They are not slaves, not under compulsion, but they are in submission."

Christine sat and thought a long while, "Yes, I am free. I know it again. Thank you, Sister Agatha. You've helped me so much. And I love your room. Can I visit you here again sometime?"

"Anytime. You are always welcome. I saw you looking at my souvenirs. When my husband was alive we served in an outpost by the sea for many years. Those are things I collected then. But you haven't seen the best part of my room yet."

"No?" Christine glanced around wondering what was hidden.

"Go open the window."

Christine moved quickly to the wooden shutters. She didn't have to wonder if she could use her right hand now. She was doing the King's work with both hands, with her whole being. She spread the shutters and looked out. Luminous clouds shifted before her eyes.

"We're at the top of the wall!" she cried breathlessly. "These are the clouds I saw at the top of the wall."

"We are actually a little above the top of the wall," Sister Agatha smiled. "I spend many hours at that window. It is as bright at night as in the day. Occasionally the clouds thin a little and I get a glimpse of the other side."

"Oh, how did you ever get such a wonderful room?" Christine marvelled.

"It is a reward. The King is pleased with faithful service and rewards his children accordingly. Now my heart is more over there than over here. Sometimes I seem to hear voices calling me from that other side. Sometimes I see wonderful things. It is a good place to pray."

Christine agreed. She knelt on the little bench and lifted her eyes to the window. "Dear Father, I so much thank you for the privilege of belonging to you. I want to serve you long and faithfully. I consecrate my whole life and being to your service. Send me where you will. Let me be useful in your kingdom. Help me to forsake my own selfish ways and follow after your holiness, whatever it costs. I love only you."

Christine saw something moving in the clouds. It was more blue-white while the clouds were creamy-white. It was a dove, and he was flying towards her. As he neared the open window she saw that he was almost three times the size of an ordinary dove, but what was more remarkable was that his body was transparent. It struck her that the bird was made of crystal. Though the outlines were glistening white, the body of the dove was clear as Castle water, and refracted light threw rainbows all around him.

But he moved like an ordinary bird, fluttering, the head pulling back, the wings braking in the air. She stretched her arms toward him and he landed in her hands. The resemblance to crystal had made her somehow expect something hard, but he was soft, softer even than a real bird, softer than anything could be. She stroked his breast with her finger as she had often done to tame chickens. He was so vibrant, so much more alive than normal life.

Christine could not get enough of this extraordinary softness. She laid her cheek on the bird and cuddled him against her breast. Suddenly he was gone. But Christine felt where he had gone. He was inside her now. She could still feel the movement and the exquisitely downy caress of his feathers. She turned to Sister Agatha wondering if she had seen.

Sister Agatha nodded. "The Holy Spirit has many forms. Uncle is only one of them."

"Why did he come to me in this beautiful way?"

"You prayed to serve the King. This is the anointing that will enable you to truly serve. Without it, all service is vain labor. Do not keep it imprisoned in your breast. Go and be used."[5]

End of Book One

[5] Acts 1:8

Appendix A —The Feudal System

Our story is set in western Europe around the tenth or eleventh century. The feudal system as it was operating there began at the top with a king who ruled over a kingdom. The king did not personally control the entire kingdom, however. It was divided into fiefs, and each fief was ruled over by a vassal. So that the king had one fief under his direct control and the other parts of his kingdom were ruled by dukes who swore allegiance to the king. Each dukedom was in turn divided into fiefs which were held by lesser nobles, such as earls, and these swore fealty to the duke. These fiefs might be divided again, being ruled by barons. The term lord could be applied to any noble, and was particularly used as a less formal, even affectionate, term.

Sons of the nobility went through a system of training which led to knighthood. This often began as young as seven years of age. The child was sent to the court of another noble to serve as a page. In his teens the boy became a squire, that is, an apprentice to a knight. After serving his knight faithfully and honorably and passing certain tests including religious ones, he was made a knight. As part of this he would swear numerous oaths including fidelity to his lord and adherence to the code of chivalry. Most knights were retainers of some lord, living at his expense and fighting his battles. If a knight obtained land, he was then a baron. Or if he were the oldest son he would succeed to his father's lands and titles.

Around the castle of a nobleman were farms and a village. This was his manor. All the land belonged to the lord, and the serfs, or peasants, were given holdings to operate much as modern tenant farmers. The serf was required to remain on the holding and give a share of his production to the lord. He was also required to help farm the lord's private lands. All fish and game were the property of the lord and could not be hunted by the peasant.

The village might be as simple as a church, a mill and a blacksmith shop, or it might include a large number of artisans. Though the lord might place taxes on the villagers, they generally had less obligation than the peasants. Like the peasants, they relied on the lord's protection from marauding bandits and pillaging Vikings. Even below the serf in the social system was the slave. He had no holding, no rights. He was merely property and could be bought and sold.

The feudal system gave almost absolute power to each lord, and was in application as good or bad as the particular lord. Lords were supposed to be paternal toward their subjects and some were. Reasonable lords demanded a fifth of their tenants' production, but there was nothing to stop them from demanding more. The lord arranged the marriages of the serfs, and some lords demanded the right to lie with the bride on the wedding night. Crimes were judged and punished by the lord, and the punishments were cruelly harsh at best, and barbarous and sadistic at worst.

The church was very important to lord and subject alike. It received a tithe of the produce of the land. This was paid in kind, cash being scarce. The priest was generally about as poor as his congregation, but some churchmen became rich landholders and powerful lords, creating a sort of rival nobility. Only in the church did literacy exist.

Women, whether noble or peasant, were valued chiefly for their ability to bear a son, a task they performed at great risk to their own lives. The first son was eagerly awaited and greatly valued as he would carry on the father's position. Additional sons were of even less value than women, except as insurance against the first son's untimely death, for life was a chancy thing. Religious orders was the only alternative career open to these second and third sons, as it was the only alternative to marriage for women.

Appendix B — MEANING OF PROPER NAMES

Abigail -- *Heb.*, father of joy.

Agatha -- *Greek*, good woman.

Alathea -- *Greek,* truth.

Alexander -- *Greek*, defender of men.

Amanda -- *Latin*, loved.

Amelia -- *Germanic*, labor.

Avery -- *Old Eng.*, boar and favor.

Barbara -- *Greek*, barbarian.

Caleb -- *Heb.*, bold.

Celeste -- *Latin*, heavenly.

Chloe -- *Greek*, green shoot.

Christine -- *Old English*, diminutive of Christ.

Eldred -- *Old English*, old and counsel.

Felicia -- *Latin*, happy.

George -- *Greek*, farmer.

Godfrey -- *Germanic*, God's peace.

Hannah -- *Heb.*, grace.

Hephzibah -- *Heb.*, my delight is in her.

Hugh -- *Germanic*, heart and mind.

Ida -- *Germanic*, labor.

John -- *Heb.*, Jehovah has been gracious.

Jude -- *Heb.*, Praise.

Kenneth -- *Celtic*, handsome.

Letitia -- *Latin*, gladness, joy.

Lucius -- *Latin*, light.

Mara -- *Heb.*, bitter.

Margaret -- *Latin*, *Greek*, pearl.

Maynard -- *Germanic*, strength and hardy.

Michael -- *Heb.,* Who is like the Lord? also see Jude 9 and Rev. 12: 7.

Mildred -- *Old English*, moderate power.

Naomi -- *Heb.*, pleasant.

Nathan -- *Heb.*, gift.

Noel -- *Old French from Latin*,
birth, nativity.

Penelope -- *Greek*, a weaver.

Philip -- *Greek,* lover of horses.

Sarah -- *Heb.*, princess.

Sophia -- *Greek,* wisdom.

Tabitha -- *Aramaic,* gazelle;
see also Acts 9: 36-40.

Tristram -- *Celtic*, tumult.

Uriah -- *Heb.*, Jehovah is light.

Appendix C — GLOSSARY OF TERMS

adze -- a tool used for smoothing timbers.

banns -- an announcement of intention to marry.

byre -- a shed for cows.

chamber pot -- a portable receptacle used in a bedchamber as a toilet.

copyist -- one who copies manuscripts.

croft -- a small field near a house farmed by a tenant.

dais --a raised platform, as in a lecture hall, for speakers or honored guests.

fief -- a landed estate held under feudal tenure.

keep -- the principle tower of a medieval castle, where the lord and his family live.

kiln -- an oven for firing pottery or burning bricks.

liege lord -- a feudal sovereign or superior.

matins -- morning prayers.

pomace -- the solid part of fruit, especially apples, left after the juice is extracted by crushing.

scribe -- one who writes or copies manuscripts.

scriptorium -- the writing room of a monastery.

shire -- a political division equivalent to a county.

vassal -- one who held land by feudal tenure, a liegeman.

vespers -- evening prayers.

windfall -- something, as ripening fruit, brought down by the wind.

winnow -- to separate the wheat from the chaff, usually by fanning or tossing it up in a breeze.

Kingdom Press

"Helping Christians grow"
1869 Top Road
Mounain Grove, MO 65711
Phone (417) 926-3340

Name ____

Address ____

City, State, Zip _____________________________________

Phone ________________________

❐ I would like to order ____additional copies
of *Learning—Life in the Castle* @ $11.95 each $ __ __

Missouri residents add .56 per book sales tax ________

Total amount enclosed $ ________

❐ Put my name on your mailing list to receive notification of future publications including Book Two.

❐ I am a pastor. Please inform me of special quanity discounts and other exclusive offers.

❐ I would like a personalized Adoption Certificate suitable for framing. Circle one— Male Female

Name to appear on Certificate

Date I became a child of God

Use additional sheet for more names. Send $4.50 for each certificate.

Make checks payable to **Kingdom Press**.